SPELLSHIP

MAGITECH CHRONICLES BOOK 3

CHRIS FOX

CHRIS FOX WRITES LLC.

For Reader Rick.
Keep making me laugh, and I'll keep writing.

PREVIOUSLY ON TECH MAGE

Whenever I start the second or later book in a series, I have a dilemma. Do I go back and re-read the first book(s), or just dive right into the latest release?

I include these previously on sections as a solution for those who want to dive right in. You'll get a quick recap of events from the first two books, each broken into its own chapter, so they're easily skippable.

If you want to know more about the setting, there's a whole bunch of lore, artwork, and other goodies at magitechchronicles.com (including a mailing list). There are also character sheets at the end of this book! And yes, I am working on a roleplaying game too.

Okay, let's get to it.

In an announcer's voice: *Last time on* **The Magitech Chronicles...**

The story begins with Major Voria, who is arriving at a floating palace over the world of Shaya.

Shaya refers to a goddess who got kacked (that's totally a word). Her body is, apparently, a giant hippie tree that crashed on a barren moon. Because Shaya's all magicky, her body created a breathable atmosphere around that part of the moon.

Voria meets with the Tender, a superhumanly beautiful woman. She's the Guardian of Shaya, a demigod mystically empowered by Shaya to watch over her people.

The Tender told Voria she'd deciphered an augury showing Voria's involvement in a war with the draconic Krox, foreshadowing some awesome dragon on starship combat. Then we switch to another PoV.

Aran wakes up in restraints with a number of other prisoners / slaves.

His captors are a pretty girl-next-door type named Nara, and a muhahaha style villain named Yorrak. Yorrak tells the slaves that they're about to make a run on the body of a dead god, called a Catalyst.

This particular Catalyst, a giant floating head full of very angry tech demons, is called the Skull of Xal. The slaves clash with the demons, who tear most of them apart. Aran makes friends with a man named Kaz, and the two fight their way past the demons. They have a choice: Die, or dive into the scary purple god-light where Nara and the slavers disappear. They choose to brave the light, and enter the mind of a god.

Aran sees Xal's memories, and for a brief instant understands the secrets of the universe. He learns Xal was killed by a gathering of gods, convinced by Krox that Xal had betrayed them.

All this god-politics stuff becomes important later, but at

this point all we really care about is the fact that Aran comes out of the Catalyst with *void* magic.

We also learn that magic items can catalyze, too, and Aran's spellblade awakens after touching the mind of Xal. It hasn't yet reached snarky-sidekick-level intelligence, but you guys know that's coming. Although, in this case, the sword is more murderous than snarky.

Kaz survives, too, and also gains *void* magic. When they come out of the Catalyst, Kaz attacks Yorrak, and Aran helps him. Yorrak responds with a morph spell that turns Kazon into a hedgehog. =O

Aran finishes off Yorrak while Nara and her friends join the mutiny. Together, they overcome Yorrak's guards, but Nara immediately takes over and makes Aran a prisoner. We're shocked (we're not shocked).

The joke is on Nara, though, because Voria conveniently arrives with the Confederate Battleship *Wyrm Hunter*. Nara pilots Yorrak's spellship, but Voria easily catches her and disables her vessel.

Nara begs Aran to help fight, and claims that if the Confederates capture them, they'll mind-wipe them and conscript them into the Marines. Aran agrees to help, because plot.

Voria sends a boarding party of tech mages, under the command of Captain Thalas (aka Dick Sock), who kicks the crap out of Aran. Aran does manage to disarm him first, ensuring that Dick Sock has ample reason to hate him for the rest of the book.

Nara also attempts to betray Aran, and claims he was one of the slavers and she was one of the slaves. Captain Dick Sock is not impressed, and takes both her and Aran prisoner.

It turns out Nara was right. Voria mind-wipes her,

destroying her mind and replacing her with an innocent woman with no memories. This raises some very troubling moral questions about slavery, in case you ever need a quick excuse to tell your English professor that *Tech Mage* is totally valid for your book report. Make sure you use the word "themes" when you try to sell it.

Voria spares Aran, though she doesn't explain why. The reader already knows it's because Aran was in the augury the Tender showed her. Aran isn't sure how to feel about this, and of course doesn't trust Nara even though her newly wiped self seems sweet.

Anyway, the wonder twins are introduced to their squad of tech mages: Specialist Bord (the comic relief), Corporal Kezia (a short, pretty drifter who talks like the characters in the movie Snatch, Irish Travelers), and my personal favorite...Sergeant Crewes. Crewes is a badass who brooks no nonsense, and has most of the best dialogue in the book. Love that guy.

Anyway, Aran and Nara get a Team-America-style training montage (Montage!), where they learn how to use spellrifles, spellarmor, and other basic magic.

Voria takes Aran to a place called Drifter Rock so they can load up on potions, especially healing potions. Thanks to the convenient augury, she knows he will be instrumental in their battle against the Krox, and she uses this as an opportunity to get to know him.

Voria trades her super-powerful, ancient eldimagus (living magic item) staff for every potion the drifters have. This includes a potion the drifters claim can bring someone back from the dead, which was my attempt at sneakily foreshadowing the fact that someone was going to get resurrected. That particular cheat is rampant in *Dungeons &*

Dragons, which inspired much of the setting for the *Magitech Chronicles*.

Enter Nebiat, the antagonist (dun dun dun). Nebiat is an ancient Wyrm who likes to spend her time in human form. She uses binding magic to mentally enslave the governor of a planet called Marid, and we're all *gasp*, because that's the planet from the augury.

The Krox invade with a full dragonflight and a bunch of troop transports. They wipe out the defenders, who come from a planet called Ternus. Rhymes with burn us, as in "Shit, these dragons are burning the crap out of us."

At this point, the politics in the book aren't very clear. Ternus is a human world with no magic, and they have the largest technological fleet in the sector. But they suck at defending against magic, and for that they need Shaya. Both Shaya and Ternus are part of the Confederacy, though Shaya is clearly in charge while Ternus is the annoying younger sibling.

To complicate things further, there is a third group called the Inuran Consortium. The Inurans buy technology from Ternus, and take magic from Shaya, then use both to make spellrifles, spellarmor, and spellships.

Voria needs those weapons and armor if she's to have any prayer of taking down the Krox. Fortunately, the head of the Consortium is looking for Kazon, the guy who got turned into a hedgehog earlier in the book. Kazon turns out to be the son of the Inuran Matriarch, and controls a shit-ton of voting stock she'll lose if he dies.

The *Wyrm Hunter* arrives in-system and we finally get some dragon-on-starship combat. The *Hunter* kills the mighty Wyrm Kheftut (Nebiat's brother), then links up with the Ternus defenders who survived the battle with the Krox.

For those who asked: yes, both Kheftut and Nebiat

sound Egyptian, and that is a theme for the Krox (woohoo, another one for your book report). And yes, there are subtle links to my Deathless setting, which also links heavily to Egypt.

Voria comes up with a plan, and manages to take back the orbital station the Krox conquered. This plan is a success only because Aran and Nara do an end run and drive the binder off the station, so they're the heroes of the day.

Unfortunately, there's a complication. Captain Dick Sock orders the Confederate Marines to suicide against the Krox position to weaken the binder. Aran, Nara, and Crewes mutiny to stop this. They save the Marines, but Dick Sock wants them dead—especially Aran.

Things come to a head when Voria finally meets with the Inurans. She trades back Kazon (who turns out to be her brother, *gasp*), but Kazon insists they also free Aran, since Aran saved his life at the Skull of Xal.

Dick Sock demands Aran be put to death for assaulting a superior asshole, and has the law on his side. Technically, Voria has to execute Aran. Or course, technically, she's been stripped of command, and Thalas should be in charge.

Shit.

Voria is already in deep. She's been officially stripped of command, but refuses to step down. If she does, she knows her people—and the people on the world below—will die.

So Voria charges Dick Sock with treason, and executes him on the spot. This solves her immediate dilemma, but also creates a whole bunch of problems that she's going to run into in this book.

Crewes steps up and asks Voria to promote Aran to Lieutenant, because Crewes doesn't feel qualified to lead and thinks Aran can. Voria's hesitant, but agrees because of the augury.

The Confederates head down to the planet, and, because Nebiat has bound the governor, it's a trap. =O Hundreds of Marines and thousands of citizens are killed in a surprise Krox raid.

Aran manages to kill two different binders, but pays a high price: Bord is killed. It's terribly sad. I mean, you felt bad, right? Bord was kind of an ass, but he was amusing. He at least deserves a moment of silence, you savages.

The Krox retreat back into the swamp, leaving the Confederates to recover. Voria suspects the governor, but doesn't have proof yet. She heads to the local archives and meets with the head archivist (powerful mage / librarian).

She learns what Nebiat is after in the swamp: some sort of potent *water* Catalyst that appeared during the godswar, when a god's body crashed to this world and formed the crater the city was built in. Voria realizes she needs to get out there, but before they can leave there are a few things she needs to take care of.

She talks to Aran about how terrible it is to lose a man under your command, then she's all *Psych!* She uses the potion they got from the drifters to bring Bord back from the dead.

Cheating, maybe, but I don't like killing characters when I can avoid it. As Rick would say, "We can only do this a few more times, Morty." That means I can't keep doing fake-outs. Someone has to get the axe, or you'll think people have plot armor. Will someone die in this book? Now you'll wonder...*muhahahaha*.

Anyway, Voria confronts the governor, proves he is bound, and has him removed from power. She calls for volunteers, then the Confederates and their new colonial militia allies head into the swamp to find Nebiat.

There's lots of *pew pew RAWR I'm a dragon*, and Aran kills the binder who got away on the station. They find Nebiat's super-secret ritual at the heart of the swamp, and they begin their epic brawl.

It's clear from the start that the Confederates are outmatched. How were Aran and Voria going to beat a much more powerful army of dragons? Many readers began suspiciously waiting for the *deus ex machina*. I mean, I had to have one. There was no other way for them to win.

Things got worse when the Marines finally arrived at the battle with the newly minted militia. They were wiped out to a man, and their bodies were animated and sent to attack Voria and Captain Davidson.

Throughout the book, I kept mentioning the Potion of Shaya's Grace that Aran received as a gift from Kazon (along with his new Proteus Mark XI Spellarmor). Aran pops the potion, which makes him faster and stronger, and gives him the ability to see several seconds into the future.

Aran grabs Nara and the two of them fly up to the summit of the mountain where Nebiat has placed the ritual. On the way up, Aran makes the (not so) casual observation that the mountain looks like it's a real face.

He brawls with a bunch of enforcers while Nara tries to stop the ritual. We've seen her latent true mage abilities manifest several times, so we aren't surprised when she steps into the circle and begins manipulating the spell.

This is the part where I hoped all my little hints paid off. The mountain was actually the ancient Wyrm Drakkon. Drakkon is crazy-powerful, and super-old. If Nebiat enslaves him, the Confederates are screwed, and that's exactly what her ritual is designed to do.

Voria hoped destroying some of the urns holding the magical energy would stop the ritual, but they were only able to blow up the *spirit* urn. *Spirit* magic is used in...*drumroll*...binding. (If you want more details about the magic system, I've got a ton of it at magitechchronicles.com, including a video.)

Nara realizes the spell can be completed if she removes the binding portion. The rest of the spell is designed to wake a creature from mystical slumber.

She completes the spell, and the mountain stands up. Drakkon crushes the Krox forces, and Nebiat goes full GTFO. She flees the planet, and doesn't stop running until she reaches her father's system.

Voria, Davidson, Aran, Nara, Crewes, Kezia, and Bord all Catalyze in a blast of magical energy from the *water* Catalyst.

This provides a glimpse into Marid's mind. Aran experiences the god's death, which happens some time after Xal. Her last act is to create a living spell, one designed to stop Krox even though Marid herself died. That spell is very important in the book you're about to read.

Drakkon (finally) explains the Big Mystery (™) to Aran. Nebiat wanted to enslave Drakkon, because he's the Guardian of Marid. Controlling him would give her an army of drakes with which to assault the Confederacy, and Ternus would fall within months.

Drakkon was vulnerable, because in his grief over his mother's death he went into something dragons call "the endless sleep." Before seeking solace, Drakkon used a potent spell to move the world where Marid died. He put it in a far-away system, where other gods would struggle to find it.

Then Drakkon positioned his body over the wound that

had slain Marid. He covered the heart wound, muting the magical signature and preventing primals from all over the sector from being drawn to that world.

Now that he's awake, he's pledged to raise the drakes on Marid, and when the time is right he will bring them into the war against Krox. So, in the end, Voria accomplished her mission. She stopped Nebiat, but sacrificed almost her entire unit to do it.

Aran and Nara lived, but both are missing their past. Aran desperately wants to reclaim his, while Nara is still hiding from hers.

Crewes, Davidson, Kezia, and Bord survived, but everyone else died. The survivors are tired, and they are out of resources...but they are alive.

Now, Major Voria must atone for her actions.

Nara must learn to be a true mage.

Aran must learn who he really is...

On to Void Wyrm!

PREVIOUSLY ON VOID WYRM

V *oid Wyrm* kicked off with Voria returning home to find herself on trial. We're introduced to the tribunal, which consists of Admiral Nimitz from Ternus, Skare from the Inuran Consortium, and Ducius from Shaya.

Ducius turns out to be Thalas (Dick Sock)'s father, and is more than a little pissed that his son died. He's determined to see Voria executed, and lobbies hard for that. Skare, who looks a bit like Rick from *Rick and Morty*, remains impartial. Nimitz wants Voria prosecuted, because of the catastrophic losses to the marines on Marid.

Mid-trial the Tender and Voria's famous war mage father, Dirk, show up to offer testimony. Aurelia (the Tender) reveals that it was her augury that caused Voria to act as she did, and begs leniency. There's some posturing, a vote, and Voria is stripped of command and demoted to the rank of captain.

She's understandably discouraged, but Aurelia and her father offer hope. Aurelia has another augury, this one pointing to a world in the Umbral Depths. They can get her a broken down piece of crap ship, if she can find a crew. Voria realizes that a loophole will allow everyone to take four weeks of leave after their campaign on Marid.

While all this has been going on, Aran has been enrolled in a war mage Kamiza (martial arts dojo), under the tutelage of Ree, an insufferable Shayan noble who addresses Aran as Mongrel. She's racist against drifters, and she's mean to Nara. Yeah, we don't like her.

The master of the Kamiza, Erika, is one of the most famous war mages in the sector. She's also working for Nebiat, and has been bound for decades. She dangles Aran's past in front of him, offering to tell him about the Outriders. But first, he needs to prove himself through training.

He gets a montage (montage!), and improves his physical conditioning and combat abilities. Then, we switch over to Nara.

Nara has been enrolled at the Temple of Enlightenment, the Shayan university devoted to magic. She's greeted by a strange flaming girl who introduces herself as Frit. Frit is the emo goth kid from every CW show, except that she's an Ifrit, with void flame. She becomes Nara's only friend and ally at the temple, against her new Master...a dick by the name of Eros.

Eros is the archmage who runs the Temple, and one of the foremost mages in the sector. He refers to Nara as Pirate Girl, and generally treats her like garbage. But he does teach her how to duel, and how to hard cast spells. The very first thing he does is disintegrate her spellpistol so she'll have to rely on her own casting.

After Nara's montage, Aran gets word that one of the stipulations in Voria's trial concerned him. Instead of being awarded a whole bunch of medals, he's being given no special commendation. Instead, all his medals are going to

Thalas posthumously. They're honoring the racist guy who expended marines like bullets, and Aran is less than thrilled.

He rushes off to Voria, and she, of course, ropes him into this new quest to go into the Umbral Depths. This time they're after a world there that Aurelia discovered, and she believes there is a tool of incalculable power there (spoilers, there is). She asks Aran to convinces Crewes, Bord, and Kezia to join them, while she heads off to convince Nara.

Aran starts with Crewes, and we get our first look at Crewes's home life. He's staying with his mom, who's not at all impressed by him, and likes to drink warm beer (who does that?). He's more than happy to go with Aran just to get out of there, particularly because it turns out the prosecutor in Voria's trial was his own brother.

Aran has less luck with Bord and Kezia. Kez is unwilling to leave her family without more to go on, and it's clear that Bord has it bad for Kezia, so he stays too. Aran and Crewes return alone to Voria's new ship...the *Big Texas*.

The *Big Texas* is a broken down Ternus cruiser that the *Serenity* would look down her nose at, and it comes complete with its own mechanic. Pickus is a technological wiz, but knows absolutely nothing about magic.

They leave Shaya, but on their way to the planet's umbral shadow they're attacked by a massive *air* Wyrm. It turns out to be Khalahk, a Wyrm from Virkonna. He's there because Nebiat told him about Aran, who Khal blames for killing his grandson Rolf (see *The Heart of Nefarius* for details).

Khal far outclasses the *Texas*, but Aran launches a daring plan and they manage to slip away into the darkness while something large, dark, and tentacled wrestles with the Wyrm.

The *Texas* is a huge mess badly in need of repairs, and Pickus proves his ingenuity. He keeps the vessel limping along long enough for them to find the planet from Aurelia's augury. It is shrouded in darkness, but as they approach, magma balls streak up from the surface and slam into the *Texas*.

The already damaged vessel breaks into two pieces, with Nara and Aran being flung one way, while Pickus, Crewes, and Voria are flung another. When they land they are assaulted by arachnidrakes, which are just what they sound like…disgusting spider dragons. Eww.

Nara summons a giant illusion of Drakkon, which scares them off long enough for our heroes to sneak away. They find a little cave and batten down while they try to figure out where they are and what they're supposed to do.

Aurelia's augury is guiding them toward a large mountain, which they can see in the distance. Unfortunately, in order for them to fly the several kilometers to get there they need to brave the arachnidrakes again. That's suicidal without some sort of distraction. Crewes volunteers, but before he can do so they hear a commotion in the distance.

Khalahk has arrived, and is tearing apart arachnidrakes and the remains of the *Texas*, clearly searching for them. They use him as a distraction and make a break for the mountain.

Yay, they make it! They're greeted by a more civilized looking arachnidrake who claims to be a custodian. They are, unsurprisingly, expected by the goddess it works for. He gives them quarters to rest in, so they may prepare for an audience with the Keeper of Secrets, Neith.

Voria is brought first. Before arriving she spends a little time in the library, which purports to hold all knowledge, all the way back to the beginning of time. Voria investigates

Nebiat, and learns that she's loose on Shaya. Not only is Erika bound, but she helps Nebiat bind Voria's father, Dirk. Her plan is to not only murder the Tender, but cause a civil war between the drifters and the Shayans.

Voria is understandably pissed, and also emotionally scarred, since she saw her father naked. She goes to her audience with Neith, who is *drumroll* a really big arachnidrake. Shocking, I know. Neith explains to Voria that she has manipulated events to lead to this moment, that Khalahk attacking was necessary to them being able to reach this place.

He explains about the First Spellship, which Voria will need to find if she's ever to beat Krox. To this end, Neith gives her the ability to perceive possibilities like a god. He also gives her a potent Eldimagus with its own personality... which likes poop jokes. Ikadra the staff is the key to the First Spellship, and also acts as a spell matrix for the *Talon*, the vessel Neith provides them to get home. But I'm getting ahead of myself.

Aran also has an audience with Neith, and finally learns about his past. Neith shows him formative scenes from Aran's upbringing on Virkonna, and drops the shocking revelation that Aran's entire life has been sabotaged to make him unremarkable. This hid him from Neith's enemies, and allowed him to reach this moment.

Aran was an unremarkable Outrider, but now Neith needs him to be an unstoppable killing machine. Neith grants Aran upgraded *fire* magic, which allows him to be both faster and stronger. He also enhances Aran's armor with the same ability, and catalyzes Aran's as yet unnamed sword with *fire* magic, making it even stronger.

Nara has a similar audience, and is given vastly increased cognitive ability. She's offered her past, but declines, saying she doesn't really want to be that woman any more. The past is best left right where it is.

Pickus and Crewes also get cool *fire* magic powers, and the crew rockets back to Virkonna. Khalahk ambushes them again, of course, but this time they're armed with a state of the art spellship, and thanks largely to Aran's ingenuity they whoop his scaly ass.

They arrive back at Shaya and immediately divide forces. Voria takes Ikadra to see if she can reach Aurelia before Nebiat begins her attack. Everyone else goes with Aran to stop Voria's father from igniting a civil war by crushing one of the largest drifter cities with one of Shaya's own limbs.

Aran, Nara, and Crewes join forces with snotty Ree and her war mages. They battle their own master, Erika, who cuts down most of the war mages and flees to join Dirk. Aran presses the attack, and they catch up to Dirk, Erika, and Eros. They've all been bound, and are working together on a potent ritual.

Erika and Dirk engage Aran and his ragtag band, while Nara tries to stop Eros from finishing his ritual. She realizes that, if completed, it will summon the heart of a star into the tree, causing a massive explosion. The 2nd burl will be blown off the tree, and onto the community below.

Nara quickly modifies the spell to convert heat into light, reducing the power of the explosion. Aran has an epic fight with Dirk. He and Crewes barely take him down, but Aran pulls it out at the last second. Almost as if the author planned it that way, somehow.

The explosion happens and they're sent spinning out into the air miles above the ground. Pickus uses his new *fire* magic to pilot the *Talon* to them, and they use it to blast the second burl into chunks of wood. Those chunks land safely outside the city, and not only does this save the drifters, but they're able to loot the hyper valuable shayawood, and bring a massive amount of wealth into their impoverished community.

Dirk dies, but Erika and Eros are both saved.

Meanwhile Voria and Ikadra show up at the Tender's palace and witness a massive magical battle between Aurelia and Nebiat. The palace is shredded as Voria uses Ikadra to add her own powerful spells.

Aurelia has clearly been poisoned, and badly needs the help. Together they drive Nebiat off, but Aurelia is killed in the process. Nebiat has won. She morphs into a bird and leads the Shayan spellfighters on a chase before escaping back into the city below.

Eros is selected by Aurelia as the new Tender, once the bindings have successfully been removed. Nara and Aran both go back to studying in their respective schools, and Voria's rank and reputation are reinstated.

The final chapter of the book was from Frit's point of view. She seemed like a minor character, but in this scene she longs to be free. While she is pining, a tiny dragon lands outside her window, and introduces herself as Nebiat. She has plans for Frit. Very important plans muhahahahha.

Three months have passed. Aran and his company have been called upon countless times to hunt down binders. They are doing everything in their power to eradicate the Krox influence on their world, but it isn't enough.

... Welcome to Spellship

KAHOTEP

Kaho tensed as he strode out onto the veranda. Such a quaint human term. The idea that they would have so many separate words to describe their homes touched the root of why they would lose this war. They were decadent, and distracted.

His tail flicked behind him as he stepped next to the waist-high railing and rested a scaled hand on the dark golden wood. Sloping planks blocked the sun, muting the shiny black of his scales. He flexed his wings, his grip tightening on the railing.

Beside him, his brother raised a spellrifle to his shoulder. Kaho suppressed a sigh. In a way, he wished he could share Tobek's single-minded ferocity, his belief that every problem could merely be destroyed.

"Calm yourself, elder brother," Kaho rumbled.

Tobek turned a slitted eye in his direction, then slowly lowered his rifle. The floorboards creaked under the bulk of his heavy, draconic body and his equally heavy spellarmor. The midnight metal had been enchanted with disquieting, screaming faces, and every time Tobek killed another foe the armor added another.

"We should murder them all." Tobek stared up at the floating palace above, fully repaired since their mother had slain Aurelia there. "You and I could bring down this untrained Tender."

"Keep your bravado," Kaho replied calmly. He studied the mightiest tree in the sector, staring down the many-kilometer drop from Shaya's lofty heights. It ended in the area they referred to as the dims—the area their mother had claimed would be obliterated so they could begin the next part of the plan. "Mother was wounded. Badly. Had she not used every bit of her magic to escape, you and I would be half orphans now. We should depart this world, now, not launch a suicidal assault."

"You whine like a toothless." Tobek turned a mocking eye on him, its golden iris growing as the pupil narrowed. "Our work is nearly complete. This time tomorrow, we'll be on our way to Virkon."

"Perhaps," Kaho muttered. His tail swished as he stared down at the branch below them. Eight tiny golden spellfighters sat arrayed outside one of the most famous Kamizas on the planet—the same Kamiza that boasted the hero who'd prevented the destruction of the dims.

Intense, powerful magic crackled inside the manor house behind them. Kaho squeezed his bulk through the narrow doorway, which had been made for Shayans, into the villa's spacious dining area. They'd converted it into a makeshift command center, and pairs of younger enforcers guarded both exits.

Most of the activity centered around a tall, broad-shouldered Shayan: Caretaker Grahl, one of the strongest faction leaders remaining on this world. Not quite as well known as

Ducius, but also not as heavily scrutinized. Kaho had no idea when their mother had bound the man, but judging from his enthusiastic pointing and short, impatient shouts, he was fully committed to the resurrection of Krox.

The magic that Kaho had felt finally manifested physically, a small crack veining through the empty part of the room they'd designated for Fissures. It widened to a precise three meters, and a pair of enormous clawed hands seized the edge.

Nebiat's scaled head pushed through, but she began her transformation into human form and had completed it by the time she landed with a hollow thump on the wooden floor. The Fissure snapped shut in her wake, and she spent a moment plucking lint from the shoulder of her dark dress.

Kaho found her appearance as unsettling as their location. Unlike most Wyrms, Nebiat managed to perfectly mimic human hair, right down to the little patches directly above each eye. She even smelled human. That kind of mastery took centuries, and was a subtle reminder of just how much more powerful his mother was.

"Welcome, Mother," Tobek murmured. He moved quickly to her side, dropping to one knee beside her. His tail lay submissively on the ground, and his wings pressed flat against his back.

Nebiat raised a gloved hand and stroked Tobek's chin. "Rise, child. You, at least, know how to show your Mother proper deference. Unlike your petulant brother."

"Petulant?" Kaho snapped. He moved several meters closer, but refused to bow. "You've been gone for three days, off Krox knows where. The new Tender's initiative has become a game to these people. Every last war mage on the planet is hunting for binders. Half the people they kill have never even met a Krox, but they are zealous, not incompetent. Sooner or later, that kind of zeal will lead them here. Some are decadent, but not all. They have powerful true mages among them. Eros—"

Nebiat gave a soft, musical laugh. "You remind me so much of your uncle, Kheftut." Her eyes narrowed dangerously. "Take care not to meet the same fate."

"That's precisely the issue," Kaho shot back. He refused to be intimidated, even by her. He thrust a scaled hand at the veranda. "Every day their kill squads get closer. They could streak through that window at any time."

As if to punctuate his words, he heard the distant whine of spelldrives rumbling to life. Kaho lowered his arm with another sigh as he waited patiently for his mother to react. The time for squabbling was over.

"Before I head to Ternus, I have business to attend to below," Nebiat explained. She stalked to the veranda, and Tobek followed. After a moment Kaho did, too. His mother stared over the side, down at the eight spellfighters. Tiny figures swarmed around them, disappearing inside. "I do not have time to deal with this."

"Leave it to me, Mother," Tobek rumbled proudly. "I will destroy them."

"I've no doubt you could, but it will not be you commanding." Nebiat reached up and rested a hand on Tobek's arm. "Do as your brother commands. Finish your work here, then head for Virkon."

"You're placing Kahotep in charge?" Tobek roared. He stabbed an accusing finger at Kaho. "He's a coward. When the war mages come, he will run. All this will be lost."

"Kaho," Nebiat said sweetly, ignoring Tobek's protest. "Sacrifice our pawns here. Kill as many of their mages as you can, then escape through a Fissure. I want you on Virkon within seven days."

"That leaves us almost no time, even if we departed now," Kaho protested. "And what about the rest of the work?"

"Never mind the rest of the work. I have another servant in mind for your task." Nebiat smoothed her dress, then raised a hand and began sketching multicolored sigils. *Dream* and *air*, both aspects Kaho had yet to master. The illusion rippled outward, and his mother disappeared. He could still hear her heavy heartbeat.

"Mother." Kaho forced the irritation from his tone. "Even if we escape here, and if we make it to Virkon, Aetherius will not listen. He will not even meet with us. He will be insulted that you have sent...hatchlings." Kaho hated that term. He hated that it applied to him, and would for at least another decade. He was neither old enough nor powerful enough to be considered a full Wyrm.

"Reach the planet and send me a missive," Nebiat's disembodied voice said. "I will help you deal with Aetherius when the time comes. Now you'd best tend to your defenses, if you wish to survive the next few minutes."

The scream of spellfighters had grown closer.

"Tobek," Kaho snapped. "Get our tech mages into position. I will inform Caretaker Grahl of our predicament."

"You're certain this is it?" Aran whispered. He crouched behind the redwood's thick trunk, peering at the manor about fifty meters away. The high, keening wind covered any sound the company's approach might have made.

He still thought of them that way, though they were little more than a squad now.

"This is the place," Nara whispered back. She dropped down next to him, planting her back against the tree.

Unlike him, Nara was encased in her Mark V spellarmor. So were Crewes, Bord, and Kezia, though they waited in a small stand of trees near where they'd parked the ship. Frit stood a few meters away, crouched down next to a root. The ground near her feet had already begun to smolder. She avoided eye contact with Aran. With everyone really.

The strange mage wasn't too social, and Aran had no idea what to make of her yet. Nara vouched for her, and right now that was all that mattered. Still, part of his mind bristled at the little collar of bright runes around her neck. Forcing people to fight seemed to be the Shayan way, and, as a direct victim of that practice, Aran sympathized with Nara's friend. It wasn't right.

Frit was the only other person in their squad without spellarmor, as apparently her species was notoriously difficult to kill. Aran, on the other hand, had no such protection. He wore a simple set of matte black body armor that left his face bare. It might stop an acid bolt. Once, if he was lucky. But it didn't allow him to communicate with the company, or any of a hundred other useful things spellarmor could do.

For the millionth time, he wished he still had his Mark XI. Instead, he had an uncomfortable metal contraption clipped to his ear. A *comm*, Pickus had called it.

Aran leaned around the tree, scanned the manor for an instant, then leaned back. "There are four visible guards, all standing along the wall ringing the inner manor. Standard Mark VII armor. All tech mages, I'm betting. The real talent will be inside."

"How do you want to play this?" Nara whispered. Her helmeted face turned in his direction.

"Quick and dirty. We've only got a few minutes until Ree hears about this. The instant that happens..."

He trailed off as a cluster of spellfighters screamed into view overhead. The golden fighters came in hot, blazing away at the manor with their spellcannons. Wood exploded along the upper level of the veranda, abrupt screams quickly drowned out by the explosions.

Several fat light bolts sizzled into the defending tech mages, obliterating a pair of them. The fighters continued past and out of sight, the whine fading as they turned for another pass.

At least a few of those screams probably came from innocent servants. Aran could confront Ree about it, but she would simply chalk it up to collateral damage. There was no reaching her through the wall of thick, Shayan superiority.

"That woman just loves ruining my day." Aran rose and turned back to the rest of the squad, raising a fist in the air. He could have used the comm. Pickus claimed it was difficult to decrypt comms, but he admitted it was possible for anyone listening to pick up the transmission. Aran just didn't trust the damned device.

Nara sketched a *dream* sigil, then interwove a *fire*. A cloud of dazzling motes zipped off into the house.

"What was that?" Aran asked, not recognizing the spell.

"If Grahl is here, that spell will find him for us, so I can guide us. You ready to move?" She crouched on the other side of the root.

Aran briefly considered waiting, but Crewes and the others would have to catch up. They didn't have time to wait, not after Ree's little stunt. "Let's do this."

Aran sprinted from cover, using a bit of *air* to vault over the high outer wall. He gained just enough clearance to sail over the top, then landed lightly on the mossy forest floor inside the manor grounds.

Nara landed on the wall above, her silver staff now clutched in one hand. A thick, purple nimbus burst from the onyx at the tip as she pointed it toward the manor's second level, the part of the veranda that had survived Ree's volley. "Both guards retreated inside that doorway, and my spell followed."

"Let's get in there." Aran sprinted between redwoods, weaving a path toward the manor.

A line of light bolts stitched their way across the forest floor, forcing him to break to the left as they blasted chunks of wood from the manor house. Aran frowned up at the departing fighter as it disappeared out of sight.

"You think it's Ree?" Nara asked with a note of amusement.

"Nah, she'd never be that petty," Aran muttered sarcastically. He leapt up to the second floor, grabbing the edge of the balcony and swinging onto it. He crouched outside a pair of smoking doors that led into a dining room with a long redwood table. Gold flashed as one of the departing guards disappeared deeper into the house. "Looks clear." He kicked the door just under the handle, and it flew inward with a crash.

"Subtle." Nara drifted in after him.

"We don't have time for subtle. Ree saw to that." Aran moved as he explained, quickly crossing the room and pausing at the doorway the guard had disappeared through. "If Grahl is here, he knows we are, too, and he's going to scurry into hiding. If he gets away, we'll never catch him."

He dropped prone, peering under the door. A single cold eye stared right back, and for one eternal moment they just stared at each other. The eye disappeared and claws scrabbled on stone on the other side of the door.

"Contact!" Aran rolled backward as the door exploded inward. He reached into his void pocket, snatching his spellblade as he rolled back to his feet.

The enforcer cradled a spellrifle in both hands, the weapon scored and scratched from long use. The creature snapped off a hasty hip shot, and a glowing white ball streaked toward Nara. Her hand shot up and she sketched two quick sigils. The white ball exploded millimeters from her chest.

Aran leapt into the air, enhancing his leap with a bit of *air*. He planted a foot on the barrel of the spellrifle, kicking off as the enforcer's claws slashed through the space he'd just occupied.

He pulled *void* and *air* from his chest, and his blade crackled with void lightning. The blade heated of its own accord, growing white as the tip plunged into the enforcer's right eye. The creature screeched, both hands shooting up to the hideous wound.

The spell crackled into the eye socket, cooking the draconic creature's brain inside its skull. The rifle clattered to the ground, and the beast joined it a moment later. Aran landed next to the body, panting.

"He's here," Nara said excitedly. She moved to the doorway, peering cautiously through. "My spell found him in the basement, three levels down. I can feel magic down there. Powerful magic."

Aran scooped up the enforcer's rifle and tossed it through the doorway, into the next room. It sailed over a railing, disappearing out of sight. Several white balls streaked up at the weapon, though the rifle was untroubled by the spirit bolts. They'd only harm the living.

"Looks like they're dug in." Aran glanced back the way they'd come. "I'll cover the doorway. Guide the others in. As soon as they're here, give us an invisibility sphere."

He hated the delay, but rushing an entrenched Krox position sounded like a terrible idea—for him, anyway. Kez and Crewes were another story entirely. They could break the Krox line.

Aran leaned cautiously through the doorway, jerking back an instant later when a spirit bolt slammed into the wall beside his head. Yeah, waiting was definitely smarter.

Nara had disappeared back out onto the veranda to escort the company in. Aran peered cautiously through the doorway, deeper into the manor, but took care not to present a target to the snipers within.

The manor wall above a pair of enforcers exploded

inward, and the nose of a golden spellfighter punched into the room. The cockpit opened, and two war mages encased in golden spellarmor leapt out. There was nothing to distinguish the two, but Aran recognized their styles instantly.

The first figure dropped down toward the Krox lines, raising a glowing blue spellshield to deflect the flurry of spirit bolts. The second figure landed in a crouch behind the first, snapping her rifle to her shoulder.

That would be Ree.

She fired a pair of three-round bursts, each loosing a volley of life bolts. Both sets found their targets, and though Aran couldn't see the damage, he heard the agonized shouts as the spells cooked flesh.

Another enforcer leapt into the room, carrying an enormous spellcannon. He aimed at Ree's companion, who raised his spellshield defensively. A terrible green glow built in the enforcer's barrel, and the spellcannon launched a cloud of green gas. It flowed around the spellshield, surrounding the armored war mage.

Somehow the gas found a crack, or perhaps the spell allowed it to pass through armor. It disappeared inside, and the effect was immediate. A yell came from the figure, and its hands shot to its face as the yell became a scream, then a shriek.

Then silence, as the lifeless figure crashed to the floor.

"No!" Ree shrieked. She sprinted to her companion's body, and dragged it back into cover.

3

IN CHARGE

Nara darted back out onto the still-smoking veranda, where little streamers of smoke rose into the air from the huge gaps in the wooden ceiling. She spotted the company below and waved at the others to catch their attention. Kez was in the lead, as usual. She leapt the wall, kicked off a tree, and sailed into the air onto the veranda. Her gleaming armor crashed down a few meters away, the floor splintering, but somehow holding the drifter's massive weight.

Kez clutched her hammer in one gauntleted hand. The head of that hammer was large enough to flatten Nara in one shot. "Come on, Bord. We don't have time to wait for you to pick flowers."

Bord attempted to replicate Kez's jump, but the apex left him about two meters short of grabbing the edge of the balcony. Nara sketched a quick *void* sigil, and her gravity magic pulled him up far enough to grab it.

"I could have made that jump," Bord protested as she set him down. "But, uh, I wanted to give you a chance to shine, is all."

Crewes fired the thruster on his bulky armor, landing on her other side with a heavy thump. "Play time's over, kiddies. There's baddies inside. Get your game faces on. No more of this godsdamned chit-chat, or you'll get to meet angry Crewes. Do you want to meet angry Crewes?"

"No, sir." Kezia and Bord chorused together in sing-song voices.

"A little help in here, people," Aran called from the next room. His spellrifle fired a moment later, quickly answered by a pair of spirit bolts. He pulled back into cover, and moved his gaze to Crewes. "Sergeant, Ree's in trouble down there and we're going to bail her out. I need you and Kezia to push their right flank, hard. Make it collapse, then set up a defensive position right where they were squatting. I'm going to help Ree."

Nara thought Aran wore command well, and she didn't mind admitting that it enhanced the attraction she already felt for him. He'd come a long way these last few months; they all had. They'd had to. Saving the drifters had earned them a lot of unwanted attention, and everything they did was scrutinized.

"Nara, you have that invisibility ready?" Aran demanded, leaning out of cover long enough to squeeze off a void bolt.

"One sec." Nara glanced back the way they'd come. Frit waited on the grass below the veranda, staring anxiously up. Nara waved, and Frit gave a tense nod. If anything happened to her, it would be Nara's fault. Eros had given her charge.

She wrapped a hand around the control rod in her pocket. Theoretically it allowed her to limit Frit's magic—or, in an emergency, to amplify that magic—but at a cost of permanently burning the ability out of her. It was a monstrous tool, and one that would never leave her pocket. She hated even touching the thing.

Frit shifted into a cloud of smoke and brimstone, rising rapidly to the veranda. She pooled just outside the doorway, shifting back into a flaming girl a moment later. Her hair pooled around her shoulders, heat shimmers rising from every fiery strand.

"What do you want me to do?" Frit whispered. Her features had a determined cast, but her breathing was rapid. Fast puffs of smoke came from her mouth with every breath.

Nara took a deep breath and considered her answer. Aran and the rest of the company was the hammer. They'd smash the Krox lines. She and Frit were the artillery. If they were allowed to free cast, they'd be able to cook the backlines.

"We're going to rush the next room," Nara explained. "I'll stealth the front line, and they'll engage the enemy. Once they do, I'll fall back to the balcony. I need you to hold that balcony. Counter anything they throw in that direction." She threaded a path through the wreckage toward Aran's position. The others had all clustered around him, in preparation for her spell.

Frit gave a tense nod, then followed, but she kept a meter or two between her and the others. Nara could talk to her about confidence later. Right now, they had work to do.

"Get ready." She raised a hand and sketched the invisibility sphere. *Dream* and *air* mingled, rippling outward to cover them. "We're good."

"On three." Aran raised a hand, ticking down fingers as he spoke. "Three. Two. One."

He leapt off the balcony, plunging out of sight. The move was doubly impressive because he wasn't wearing spellarmor, which not only meant he was outclassed, but that he'd need to rely on his own magic to cushion his fall.

Kez leapt next, giving a joyous whoop as she fell. Crewes jumped a moment later, his spellcannon already tracking targets. Nara leapt off, using her gravity magic to guide the armor. She zipped down, struggling to maintain the perfect position.

She needed to be equidistant from all targets. If anyone slipped out of the spell radius, they'd become visible too soon. It was exactly the kind of finesse that made her love this job.

She maintained the spell as they fell into a large dining room. Three Shayan tech mages in Mark VII armor were using the table as cover, exchanging shots with a figure in golden spellarmor. Ree, Nara guessed.

Ree had taken cover behind her fighter, huddling protectively over the body of her companion. She was pinned down, with no way out that didn't expose her to enemy fire.

Behind the enemy tech mages stood a quartet of Krox enforcers. Two carried garden variety spellcannons, and were no different than the dozens they'd fought before. The last pair, however, were clearly figures of importance.

The first wore midnight spellarmor, stylized to enhance his draconic nature. He wore a spellblade belted at his side, and cradled a sleek spellrifle in both arms. A war mage, then.

The second Krox wore no armor, and carried no visible weapon. He did wear a strange sort of golden headdress, and ceremonial robes. He hadn't cast yet, but Nara could sense the tremendous power emanating from that Krox. This wasn't merely a true mage, but a powerful one.

Nara waited for Aran and the others to slam into the ground, then she shot skyward as they began their assault on the Krox line. They rippled into view as they left the radius of her spell, and the enemy's attention, thankfully, focused on them.

She zipped back up onto the balcony, where Frit huddled. Bord stood a meter or so away, apparently trying to comfort her. That shouldn't be surprising. She might have fiery hair and smoldering skin, but if you looked past that, Frit was gorgeous. And Bord wasn't picky.

"Trust me lass, we're in the safest place. It's my job to ward the lot of us. If a spell gets up here, I'll make sure you're fine," Bord's ingratiating voice came from inside his mirrored helmet.

"Frit," Nara said, landing next to her friend. "It's time."

"What do you need me to do?" Frit asked, rising slowly to her feet. She peered nervously over the railing at the combat playing out below.

Nara kept her attention off it, for now at least. It was the first time she'd had to look after anyone in a fight, and before she found her own targets, she needed to make sure Frit knew what to do. "Concentrate your spells on the left side of the room. Wipe out the smaller targets, especially the tech mages. Once they're all down, you can help us deal with those enforcers."

She tried to sound confident, though privately she was more than a little worried. Aran made short work of most enforcers these days, but they hadn't run into a group as tough as this one in any of their missions. The war mage and the true mage were of great concern.

"I can do that." Frit gave a tight nod, and her gaze focused on the combat below. She raised a hand and began sketching—first a *fire* sigil, then a *void*, then another *fire*. Intense magical power burst up around her, a towering inferno of purplish void flame.

Frit pointed at the table where the tech mages sheltered, and a river of purple flame rained down on the defenders. Everything it touched sizzled and hissed as the *void* magic weakened the internal structure, then the flames ignited whatever had survived. The spell was devastatingly effective, and when the flame passed, three of the tech mages didn't rise. The table was nothing more than a smoldering pile of embers, and their armor was blackened and warped.

"Nice work." Nara clapped Frit on the shoulder. "Keep up the pressure." Then she leapt off the side of the balcony just in time to dodge a spirit bolt. It zipped past her shoulder, toward Frit's face. A brilliant white ward burst into existence, deflecting the bolt.

"Stick with me, fire girl," Bord said, moving closer to Frit. "You roast 'em, and I'll keep 'em from roasting you back."

Nara briefly considered staying to look after Frit, but Bord could handle it. She had other work to do. Much as Nara might dislike her, Ree was an ally.

Nara turned back to the combat, dropping down into cover near Ree. "Are you all right?"

Ree's golden armor was scorched along the left side, though she was still moving. She'd taken shelter behind her fighter, but every few moments another spell zipped past.

"I think so." There was a quaver in Ree's voice. She cradled the corpse of her companion to her chest. "They killed Marcus. I've never seen a spell like that."

"Keep it together, or they'll kill us, too." Nara dropped to one knee, peering under the nose of the fighter. Part of her pitied Ree, but mostly she was appalled. Ree represented one of the best armed and trained houses on Shaya, but their shining star had seen so little of real war that any death at all rattled her.

"What was that spell you just cast?" Ree asked, scuttling over to join Nara. She still held her spellrifle, at least.

"That wasn't me. I brought an Ifrit, on loan from Eros. We didn't know you were going to be here to punch a hole in the wall." Nara didn't bother to hide her displeasure. She didn't want to Ree dead, but she was fine with just about anything short of that. "This would have been a lot easier if you hadn't come blazing in here, ruining our ambush."

Ree froze. Nara couldn't see her face, of course, but she liked to imagine a chagrined expression.

"You can lecture me later," Ree replied coldly. "Let's get back in the fight."

4

TARGET NEUTRALIZED

Wood splintered as the enforcer landed in front of Aran. The creature had longer reach with its wickedly curved sword, and it used that reach to devastating effect. The blade flicked out toward Aran and he parried, but the move forced him backward a step and away from the enforcer.

The enforcer launched another blow, and another. By the time the fourth fell, Aran had read his movements well enough to anticipate the next. He launched himself over the slash, scything his foot out toward the enforcer's face. The enforcer foolishly allowed the blow to connect, and Aran smiled grimly.

Some things never changed, and one of the constants he most loved was how often the Krox underestimated humans. Aran channeled *void* and *air* down his leg, into his foot. The twin energies crackled around the outside of his armor, slamming into the side of the enforcer's face in a spray of magical lightning.

That energy took the enforcer's eye, blinding it on the right side. Aran pivoted smoothly into the blind spot, bringing his blade around in a low slash. The blade heated, vibrating eagerly as it pierced the scales just above the knee. The enforcer gave a draconic screech as Aran's sword completed the grisly work, severing the leg and sending the enforcer fluttering away with frantic flaps from its leathery wings.

Aran's chest heaved, and he took a moment to survey the room. There was no sign of Grahl, but he hadn't expected there to be. Nara's spell put the Caretaker in the basement, which gave Grahl time to use any magical items he might have to effect an escape.

"Human!" A draconic voice roared from further in the room. "Try me."

An enforcer in stylized spellarmor stepped from the enemy ranks, heedless of the combat flowing around it. Its fierce eyes fell on Aran, and from the hatred he read there, Aran guessed he'd just killed someone important. An apprentice maybe?

But the apprentice hadn't been wearing spellarmor. This guy was.

Man, why couldn't it ever be easy?

Aran backpedaled, but there was nowhere to go. The enforcer's wings thrust out from either side of the armor, the only unprotected part of the creature. It raised its spellrifle, taking careful aim as it glided closer. In that instant, Aran caught sight of another enforcer, this one wearing strange ceremonial robes. It stood near the back of the room, and had begun sketching a spell.

Then the rifle fired, and Aran flipped out of the path of the spirit bolt. The spell splintered into mana shards as it exploded on the ground. Spirit bolts didn't do much damage to physical objects, but if one hit him, it would pass right through his armor, either killing him instantly or at least making him wish he were dead.

By the time he rose, the enforcer with the sword had interposed himself between Aran and what he guessed must be a true mage.

"Crewes, Kezia, get on the enforcer with the face paint," Aran roared into the comm. "Don't let it open a Fissure."

Crewes shifted instantly, his cannon bucking as it lobbed a flaming hunk of magma at the Krox true mage.

Then Aran lost sight of them as his opponent crashed to the ground a few meters away. A drop of saliva fell from its jaws, sizzling as it hit the wood. "You're quick, little human. Are you him? The one who so vexes mother?"

"Yeah, I vexed your mother just last night." Aran sprinted forward, drawing from *fire* to increase his speed and strength. He used *air* to further increase his momentum, then came down at the Krox in a blur.

Somehow the Krox hopped backward in time to parry Aran's blow. Aran delivered another, and another. The blade flared to life in his hands, its magic further enhancing his strength. He could *feel* its eagerness to kill.

The Krox gave a surprised grunt, reluctantly giving ground as Aran pushed him steadily toward the wall. By the fifth parry, he knew he couldn't get through the Krox's defenses, but right now that wasn't the mission. He needed to neutralize this guy, sure, but only long enough for the rest of the company to kill the true mage and find the Caretaker. All he needed to do was buy the others time.

"You will not separate me from my brother." The enforcer suddenly reversed his stroke, forcing Aran to duck under the blade...right into the enforcer's kick. The heavy, armored foot caught Aran in the midsection and flung him into the air.

Time seemed to slow as he tumbled end over end, barely retaining a grip on his spellblade as he came down hard atop the nose of Ree's fighter. His bones rattled, and he groaned in pain as he tried to recover.

He sat up quickly, but the Krox was already moving. It leapt into the air, its wings flaring out on either side of it as it aimed at Aran. His hand shot up instinctively, and he sprayed blue motes of *water* magic at the Krox's right wing. Then he channeled *air*, grabbing the enforcer's right wing.

The water hardened into ice, and the Krox began to list to the right. It tried to recover, but Aran yanked down hard with his *air* tendrils. The Krox's graceful flight turned into an ungainly fall, and Aran leapt up to meet him.

He thrust his blade at the Krox's chest, channeling a third-level void lightning spell into the weapon, even as the weapon added its own internal *fire* magic. Somehow the Krox twisted, but not enough to avoid the attack. The blade punched into the creature's right shoulder, discharging the spell into the wound.

The Krox roared, then kicked Aran hard in the knee. Pain exploded through him as the knee shattered, and Aran was knocked into a heap at the enforcer's feet. He gritted his teeth and summoned *void*.

This time, he used gravity magic. He brought his blade down in a quick strike, ramming it through the Krox's armored foot. It pinned that foot to the ground, and the gravity magic made the weapon impossibly heavy. Aran rolled backward, narrowly dodging the Krox's return strike.

Out of the corner of his eye, Aran saw Frit casting above him. He rolled further away from the Krox, in time to avoid a torrent of void flame. It washed over the Krox's armor, obscuring it entirely. When the rush of flame was over, the armor smoked, but no other damage had been done.

The floor didn't fare nearly as well, and the ancient timbers burst into hungry flames. The Krox's enormous weight, aided by Aran's sword, crashed through the floor.

Aran extended a hand, removed the enhanced gravity from his weapon, and wrapped a tendril of *air* around the hilt. He yanked it back into his grip, forcing himself to his feet as he peered down into the hole.

He used his free hand to fish a glowing healing potion from the nylon bag sewn into his belt, and upended it into his mouth. The taste of grapes filled his mouth as the golden energy flowed through his body, down toward his wounded knee. The relief was immediate, but it was also his only potion.

The Krox burst up from the hole, shoulder-checking Aran out of the way. The creature's mighty wings pumped as Aran tumbled back to his feet, but the Krox had glided toward the corner where the true mage was erecting a Fissure.

"Remember me, human," the Krox roared. "My name is Tobek, and mine will be the hand that chokes the life from you."

Kezia and Crewes were pushing hard, but the true mage had erected some sort of translucent spell wall that was keeping them at bay. The space behind the true mage split and veined as the Fissure opened, and both Krox dove through. The Fissure snapped shut in their wake, and Aran's grip tightened painfully around the hilt of his sword. It pulsed with rage, an echo of the emotion smoldering inside himself.

Aran looked around hurriedly. Every other enemy combatant was down.

"Anyone have eyes on Grahl?" Aran asked over the comm.

"Over there." Ree extended a gauntleted hand, indicating a table in the relatively untouched corner of the room. Her voice quavered, whether from exhaustion or grief he wasn't sure. Probably both.

Aran glanced down at the far side of the room. A distinguished man matching Grahl's description lay slumped over the table, a dagger clutched limply in his lifeless hand. A curtain of blood coated his chest, shed by the hideous self-inflicted wound in his throat.

"All right, people, clean this up. Then let's get back to the *Talon*." Aran leaned against the wall, gritting in pain. His armor did almost nothing to stop kinetic force, and he was fairly certain it would take weeks for the bruises to heal unless he sought out magical healing.

Aran massaged his neck with a free hand. Who had that enforcer been? Aran wasn't sure he could take him in a fight, certainly not with the enforcer having spellarmor and Aran not.

He'd gotten lucky here. If not for Frit's timely spell, Aran would be dead.

Was Nebiat their mother, and if so why was she leaving her children to take care of her work? That implied she was working on some other plot, and that terrified Aran.

They'd won here, but it certainly didn't feel like it.

5

REINSTATED

Voria scarcely recognized the Tender's palace. It wasn't simply that the damage from the confrontation with Nebiat had been repaired. No, the whole meaning of this place had changed. Before, with Aurelia, it had been a place for their high priestess to commune with their goddess. Solitary and remote.

Now, it was a war camp. Couriers came and went via spellfighter, or clunky Ternus shuttles, vessels like the one she arrived on.

She stepped off into the fierce wind, the only part of all this that felt familiar. A dozen guards lined the fortifications that had been added to either side of the door leading deeper into the palace. No doubt the Shayan nobility found such things distasteful, as there was no way to disguise their placement. They were squat, ugly barricades, clearly made for war.

"Major," a feminine voice said as she approached. The woman was encased in golden armor, but she inclined her helmeted head. "You are expected."

"How is he today?" Voria didn't even know the woman's

name, but over the past few weeks they'd developed a
banter. They were both soldiers, and they respected that
about each other even if they didn't know anything else.

"He's in a foul mood. His attempts to harness the
mirror...aren't going well." The captain moved to open the
door for Voria, and Voria nodded gratefully as she stepped
through.

They said nothing further to each other, no awkward
goodbyes, or empty platitudes.

Voria passed several nobles she didn't recognize, all
hurrying out with pale faces. Eros wasn't known for his
patience at the best of times, but if he'd been working with
the mirror again, what little he possessed was probably long
squandered.

She glided past more couriers, and several clouds of
nobles. Each cloud gravitated around a Caretaker, and the
largest gathered around Ducius. The odious man stepped
into her path, folding his arms in challenge as he eyed her.

"Where is Caretaker Grahl?" Ducius demanded. He
thrust a finger toward the balcony to their right. "We can see
the flashes from the 3rd branch. We know there's fighting.
We demand to know what's going on."

"Oh," Voria replied, blinking. "I'm so sorry, Caretaker
Ducius. I didn't realize you'd enrolled in the Confederate
Military. And to be granted a rank so quickly, that you can
order a major about. Why, that's quite impressive."

She swept past him, ignoring his squawk. Let the
bastard complain to the other Caretakers about how rude
she was. She needed every scrap of patience to deal with
Eros, Neith help her. Ducius called after her, but Voria
merely quickened her pace.

No one else met her gaze as she approached the wide
double doors leading to the Mirror of Shaya. They'd been

black ever since Neith's magic had obscured all divination. The rest of magic seemed to have returned to normal, but those doors were as unchanged as ever.

Voria remembered how they'd appeared the first time she'd come to the palace. Aurelia had the dragon scales arrayed in a perfect representation of Shaya, right down to the gently swaying branches. Yet Eros couldn't even shift a single scale. Somehow that summed up their current situation, summed up everything they'd lost.

She rested a hand against the door and pushed gently. Eros could lock the doors, but he rarely did so. The door opened silently inward, revealing a dim interior lit by four magical braziers. A mystic circle had been drawn around the slowly rotating Mirror of Shaya, which pulsed with divine strength.

"I'm busy," Eros snapped, without looking in her direction. The Tender's gaze was focused on the mirror, its sheen illuminating his too-handsome features. Eros raised a finger, sketching half a dozen sigils so quickly Voria could barely follow.

"Doing what, precisely?" Voria demanded.

That got his attention. Eros shifted to face her and the anger faded from his features. He looked so tired. "What do you want, Voria?"

"What do *I* want? You summoned me, Eros." She folded her arms, watching him expectantly. Everyone else might toady for him, but in her mind Eros was the same pompous ass he'd always been, and an infusion of divine magic didn't change that, even if it had transformed him into an immortal demigod.

"You're being reinstated." Eros walked from his spell, his shoulders slumping. He waved a hand and a goblet appeared in it. He drank deeply before speaking again. The circles under his normally perfect eyes were quite dark today. "The Confederacy has finally made their ruling, and we've agreed to abide by it."

"Reinstated? What does that mean, exactly?" Voria asked. She already had her rank back, but for the past three months she'd been left to her own devices, with no word on a ship, or any other command. If not for Davidson, she'd have no clear understanding of how the war was progressing. Poorly, of course.

"We're giving you back the *Hunter*. She's undergone a lengthly refit, and is spaceworthy. For the most part." Eros plucked at his sleeve. He glanced quickly at her, then away. He'd been that way ever since he'd been bound. "But that isn't why I called you here."

"Of course it isn't." Voria rolled her eyes. She loathed this man, even as she pitied what he'd undergone at Nebiat's hands. "What do you want, Eros? What is the *Hunter* going to cost me?"

"Well, to begin with, your command only extends to the ship." Eros licked his lips. "Ternus has agreed to give you a battalion of their best marines, but you won't be leading them."

"I don't understand." Voria cocked her head, genuinely puzzled. "I'm in charge, but I'm not? Why not give full command to whoever leads the marines?"

"Because Major Davidson refused the command." Eros finally turned his full attention on her, sizing her up with those liquid blue eyes. "He asked that you be given the *Hunter*, to run orbital operations. He further asked that Lieutenant Aran be attached to your command, and given the *Talon*."

"The *Talon* isn't yours to give." Voria's gaze narrowed. "Or anyone else's. She's mine. Given to me by a goddess, Eros. Do you really want to test that?"

"No, no I don't. I said that he asked, not that we granted." His tone had gone sour. "You can do what you want with your precious little ship. But you've been selected for a mission, and that's why you're here."

"Why aren't I hearing this from Nimitz?" Voria asked. It galled her that the Confederates were so disorganized they couldn't even pass proper orders. The chain of command was more like a gordian knot of command. She didn't even know who in the depths she reported to.

"You are to report to Virkon, where you will seek out the Council of Wyrms," Eros explained, as if relating the weather. "You will explain our situation regarding the Krox, and attempt to broker an alliance against them."

"You're sending me to Virkon? To forge an alliance?" She started to laugh, but then stopped herself. She watched Eros careful, eyes widening when she realized what was happening here. "This is a cover story."

"I'm glad to see you're not totally deficient. I miss speaking with competent people." Eros shook his head. "We're sending you to locate the first Spellship, Voria, the one you told us about. Virkon won't give us so much as a pile of dragon dung, and they certainly won't allow you to search their world for a ship that was, very likely, created by their sleeping goddess. But they know we are desperate, and so you are going to show up, hat in hand, and you are going to beg."

Voria gritted her teeth. No real support. Davidson not under her command. This got better and better, and they hadn't even left yet.

6

HONEYBUNS

F rit very nearly bolted from the cafe. It was the first time she'd ever been permitted in a Shayan establishment, and if they discovered her true identity she'd be forcibly returned to her master, and he'd be fined.

Eros would love that.

"Can't we just go to the park?" she whispered to the woman she was following.

Nebiat wore a black form-fitting dress, just tasteful enough to be daring rather than garish. She glided through the restaurant as if she owned the place, shooting a wink over her shoulder at Frit. "Come along, cousin. You'll enjoy yourself, trust me."

Frit reluctantly forced herself forward. Nebiat led her to a private booth in the rear of the restaurant, with a gauzy curtain that could be pulled for additional privacy. Nebiat slid into one side of the booth, so Frit dropped into the other.

The wood beneath her began to heat. It wouldn't be long before it started to warp. Her being here was costing this shopkeeper.

"Miss," Nebiat called, raising a hand to flag down the server. A gorgeous blonde hurried over with a smile. "Two cups of lifewine, and a pair of glazed honeybuns."

"Of course, mistress." The woman doffed her small hat respectfully, the smile widening prettily. "Is there anything else I can tempt you with?"

"Frit?" Nebiat turned to her.

Frit froze as the server's gaze fell upon her. She licked her lips, the flames coating them. The woman could see nothing of course. She probably saw Frit as a teen out with her aunt.

"N-no, thank you." Frit mimed removing her hat like the server had, and felt a fool doing it since she wasn't wearing one.

"Of course. I'll be back in a moment." The woman curtsied, and hurried off toward a pair of dark doors that led into the kitchen. They opened briefly, and a wave of heavenly smells wafted out, pushed by the wall of noise. That noise disappeared the instant the door closed, so quickly Frit was certain a dampening spell was involved.

"You should relax." Nebiat rested her arm on the back of the booth, smiling languidly. "These people have enslaved not only you, but your entire race. Don't you think it fitting that you enjoy being served for the space of an afternoon?"

"What if they find out who we are?" Frit asked in a low voice, her attention still on the door. It hadn't opened again.

"They won't. This place possesses no magical wards, and any respectable mage wouldn't dare be caught this far down." Nebiat gave a soft laugh, her smile growing wicked. "They are blind, Frit. Blind to their enemies, and blind to their flaws. Don't believe me? Watch. Enjoy your lunch. You dine with a dreadlord in the heart of Shaya's capital, beneath her very branches. Yet no spellfighters are descending. No war mages are bursting through the door. This, despite them turning every resource they possess toward hunting us. Eros has invested everything in this inquisition of his, and yet here we sit. Why is that, do you think?"

Frit didn't answer, but she couldn't stop herself from thinking it. *Because they can't stop her.* Because the Shayans were so convinced of their own superiority, they didn't even consider the possibility they were being blatantly deceived.

Nebiat leaned across the table, dropping her voice. "Mere hours ago you participated in a raid, one that showed the Shayans the Krox are on their world. Yet no one here suspects. They know nothing of what transpired above. And when we leave the restaurant, no one outside will suspect either. Don't take my word for it. Watch, little cousin."

Frit shrank back in the booth and gave a weak smile. Thankfully the door opened, and the server hurried back over carrying a large tray. She expertly unloaded a pair of steaming cups, sliding one to Frit, and the other to Nebiat, then set down a plate heaped with flaky pastries. They'd been drizzled with a sweet-smelling glaze, and Frit's mouth began to steam.

"Do you require anything else, mistress?" The server gave another beatific smile.

Nebiat smiled up at the woman. "No, thank you."

The woman smiled back, then she left. She'd detected absolutely nothing, or if she'd had she'd done a fine job of hiding it.

"Go ahead, try one." Nebiat plucked a bun from the pile and nibbled on it.

Frit eyed them careful, then finally picked one up. The glaze warmed to liquid in her hands, but she wolfed it down too quickly to care about the mess. When she'd finished the bun, she realized her mouth and hands were covered in sticky sauce. She laughed.

"What's funny?" Nebiat smiled warmly at her.

"It's just— I've never been allowed to eat before. I mean, I've stolen a snack here or there, but nothing like this." Frit reached for the napkin, and cleaned her hands quickly. She realized she wanted another bun.

"They don't feed you, because it isn't required for your kind to survive," Nebiat explained. She nibbled on her bun. "It isn't necessary for mine either, but we dine because eating is pleasurable. For humans, and for my kind, eating is a social activity. An activity you deny only two classes of being. Pets—"

"—and slaves," Frit realized aloud. She set the bun down uneaten, her appetite gone to ash. She realized now why Nebiat had brought her, the lesson she'd been meant to learn.

She wasn't a real person—not to the Confederacy, and certainly not to Shaya. The question, then, was: why impart the lesson? Why would a dreadlord seek to teach Frit? What terrible thing did Nebiat expect her to do?

There was an ulterior motive, of that Frit was certain.

Worst of all, why did Nebiat continue to be so damned pleasant? The dreadlord had done nothing untoward. Nothing to directly bind her. Nothing but ask questions, really.

"What is it, child?" Nebiat asked. She leaned closer again. "You look like you just had a troubling thought."

"Why did you bring me here?" Frit demanded. It was a tone she was unused to, as far as she could get from the servile role she'd been taught.

"Because." Nebiat popped the last of her pastry into her mouth, chewing dramatically for several seconds. She picked up her cup, taking a sip to wash down the pastry. Finally, she met Frit's gaze. "I want you to understand your people's plight, Frit. No one will speak for them. No one will help them. You must help yourselves, if you are ever to be free."

7

RELIC HUNTER

Aran set his helmet on the shelf between his canteen and a smooth black rock he'd taken from the world where they'd met Neith.

He stretched, thankful to be out of his armor. Unlike spellarmor, the conventional stuff felt heavier the longer you wore it. And it made his back ache. Maybe he'd speak to Bord, though he should be grateful for what the specialist had already done for him. The pain had been a lot worse an hour ago.

Conversation came from outside his quarters, Kezia's lilting voice followed by a loud laugh from Bord. Aran smiled and moved to the door. It shimmered out of existence at his approach, a handy magic he was already growing to appreciate.

Kezia and Bord stopped at the top of the ramp that led out of the *Talon*. Both had packs slung over their shoulders, and neither was carrying a visible weapon. They were talking with Nara and Frit, though all four turned in his direction as he moved to join them.

Nara's cheeks dimpled as she delivered a dazzling smile.

Her dark hair framed her face, and the soft, magical light drew out her freckles. Damn, it was good to see her.

"Oh, he's got it bad. Look at him stare," Bord quipped, elbowing Kezia.

"Are you two heading back to the dims?" Aran interjected quickly, steering the conversation in a safer direction. His cheeks were on fire.

"Yeah, we're due for some leave. I figure we've joost got done wiping out that bolt hole, so they'll probably give us a day or three." Kezia grinned up at him through a mass of blond curls. Her hair had gotten longer over the last few months, and the fact that Bord liked long hair wasn't lost on Aran.

"What about you two?" Aran asked, turning to Nara and Frit.

He wasn't sure what to make of Nara's "apprentice," if that was the right word. She'd mentioned Frit several times, but the day's battle had been the first time Aran had seen her in action. Her magic had been terrifyingly effective, and he'd instantly wondered why he didn't see more Ifrit. Nara could theoretically learn to do the same thing. So could he, if he studied long enough. But neither would be as devastating as Frit or one of her people. Half a dozen Ifrit using void flame could wipe out most opposition quickly, even opposition that had magical defenses.

"I have to report to Eros. You know how he's been ever since he was bound." Nara offered a heavy sigh. "He'll want to know how things went, and I'm sure he'll have some fun things to say about us letting those enforcers go. His paranoia is...bad. He may even suggest someone on our side let them go intentionally. He's positive there's a spy close to him."

Frit stiffened at that, which didn't surprise Aran. She

worked closely with Eros. More closely than any sane person would risk, though it wasn't like she had a choice. Aran's eyes narrowed when they landed on her collar.

"We didn't let them go. They opened a depths-damned Fissure. Into the depths. What were we supposed to do?" Bord protested. "I mean, we did kill the Caretaker. Well, he killed himself, but that's basically the same thing. I wish more targets offed themselves. Really quite considerate when you think about it."

"Yes, very," Aran replied dryly. "I don't have to be Nara to know that they silenced him for a reason. We thought their work with the Caretakers and the Shayan political structure was their real target here. Given what we saw today? I think this is just the beginning. I've never fought enforcers like those."

"They're both very nearly Wyrms," Frit said, her voice little more than a whisper. It was the first time she'd spoken to anyone but Nara, as far as Aran was aware. "They'll go through their first molting soon."

"It makes sense that enforcers would get stronger as they age." Nara pursed her lips, cocking her head as her gaze went unfocused. Aran had learned to recognize when she was tapping into the abilities Neith had given her. He wondered what she saw.

"Won't help 'em none," the sergeant boomed as he strode into the room. He wore a plain black t-shirt and a pair of jeans that struggled to contain his massive legs. He had a battered leather pack slung over his shoulder. "I'm off to my mom's for a few days."

"I thought you hated staying there," Aran pointed out. "We've got the run of the *Talon*."

"Yeah, but his place don't have a gym. If I don't have any Krox to crush, then I need to lift some heavy things. My

kingdom for a squat rack. It's therapeutic. You should try it."
Crewes punched him hard in the arm as he passed. "See you
all in a few days."

"You're already working out again?" Aran blinked.
"You've only had the new leg for a couple weeks."

"I started lifting again the day after I got it." Crewes gave
a proud smile. "Skin's a little too pink, but it works just as
good as the old one ever did. But that's only cause I keep
working out. You should think about that, LT."

Aran nodded, and Crewes clapped him on the back.

Everyone exchanged goodbyes, and a few moments later
Aran was left standing alone in the *Talon's* mess. Even
Pickus, the one person who never seemed to leave the ship,
was gone. He'd been transferred to the *Hunter* several weeks
back, which at least suggested they might repair the aging
battleship.

It was, Aran realized, the first time he'd been alone in
weeks. And, for the first time in months, he had an entire
day to relax. Not a single person in the world had an expec-
tation of him today. He turned in a slow circle, considering.
How should he spend his rare day off? He could go train,
like Crewes. He didn't enjoy working out as much as the
sergeant, but it *was* therapeutic.

Then he grinned and headed down the ramp into the
mess. Kez had been trying to get him to check out a holodrama, something he'd never seen before. They'd watched
the first episode of something called *Relic Hunter*, and the
animated cartoon had left him laughing so hard his
side hurt.

Aran summoned himself a cup of coffee and a plate of
eggs, then headed back to his quarters. It was odd seeing the
ship so empty, but it was also kind of freeing. For the first
time in a long while, he felt like he didn't need to be "on."

He moved to the scry-screen in the corner of the room. The device was strange, not unlike the holo-unit in Pickus's old room. He could use *fire* magic to activate it and tap into the ship, seeing what the *Talon* saw.

But in this case he was interested in the slot on the base. It was hexagonal, matching the shape of dragon scales. He retrieved the blue scale Kez had given him and inserted it into the base of the scry-screen. It flared instantly to life, the show's upbeat music filling his quarters as the screen showed the show's main character, a bespectacled archeologist in a wide-brimmed hat who somehow managed to be handsome despite the ridiculous outfit.

Aran was about to settle into the hovercouch, but hesitated.

He didn't know what warned him. Maybe it was a movement in the air. Maybe it was some instinct imparted by Neith. Whatever the reason he rolled suddenly to the right, just in time to dodge a vicious kick that hummed through the area where his face had been.

He spun to see a woman in a dark, form-fitting mesh suit. The shimmering material was clearly enchanted, though Aran had no idea what it did. It was the sword she carried that he was concerned about. The wide spellblade was longer than his own weapon, and heavier. It was a chopping sword, meant for killing blows.

"Who are you?" he demanded, taking a cautious step back to gain room to maneuver. Thankfully, his quarters were spacious and he knew them well. He could make her sword a liability, if he was careful.

The woman raised her sword. "Telling you would be pointless. You'll be dead in a few moments, traitor."

8

ASSASSIN

Aran extended a hand, and his void pocket slid open. The woman made no move to attack, though rushing him while he was drawing his weapon would have been the smartest play. She could have taken him right then, if she'd wanted to.

"You're letting me arm myself." Aran slid into Drakkon stance, and was surprised when she matched it perfectly. His hand settled around the hilt of his spellblade, and it thrummed eagerly in his grip. "That suggests a certain amount of honor. But you also broke in to my ship, and ambushed me in my quarters."

"Ambushed? Virkonna no." The woman barked a harsh laugh. "This isn't some sort of assassination. This is an execution. I was even kind enough to wait for your companions to depart before administering justice. There's no need for them to pay for your crimes."

Aran followed her words down several paths. Clearly, she was from Virkon. He didn't recognize the accent, but the reference to Virkonna, and the fact that she used Drakkon stance were highly suggestive. She's come a long way, apparently, to find him.

"And are you going to tell me what crime I've supposedly committed?" Aran circled slowly to the right, toward the bed. It hovered half a meter above the floor, enough to present a minor obstacle if needed.

"You are a dragonslayer." Her words were tightly clipped, edged with pain. "The fact that you do not know that suggests there is truth to the rumor you were mind-wiped." She adjusted her stance, moving smoothly to interpose herself between him and the door. The only way out was through her.

"I have no idea what you're talking about, but I guess you're right. It doesn't really matter. If you're here to kill me, then we may as well get on with it." Aran drew deeply from *fire*, enhancing his strength and speed. His blade began to glow, and the weapon thrummed again.

His attacker hesitated, and though he couldn't see her features behind the mesh mask, he could almost feel her surprise.

"You've learned much, it seems. Let's see if it's enough." Her blade burst into crackling brilliance, tendrils of electricity shooting at Aran from several directions at once.

Aran's free hand shot up, and he caught one of the tendrils, the energy pooling in his hand. He deflected another with his blade, sending it spinning into the bed, which burst into flame. The third and fourth tendrils, however, struck him full on.

The first hit him in the chest, every muscle seizing as electricity coursed through his body. The second hit him in the crotch, and he dropped prone beside the bed with a grunt.

So it was that kind of fight, then.

She sprinted forward, jabbing her blade down at Aran's back. He rolled under the bed, slashing awkwardly with his spellblade. The move forced her to hop away from the bed, and he rolled out the other side, and back to his feet.

She was already moving, leaping over the bed and aiming a kick at his face. Aran reached out with *void*, but instead of a void bolt he summoned a ball of glowing black energy, similar to a spell he'd seen the major use. He flung it at the woman's foot, and it clung like glue.

Aran funneled more magic into the spell, greatly enhancing the weight of her foot. It redirected her flight, and he pivoted to adjust. Aran easily dodged her strike, then countered with a wicked slash. Somehow the woman brought her blade around in a desperate parry.

He tried again, but she slapped his spellblade away with the back of her hand and lunged with her own. The tip sank into his arm, just below the bicep. Adrenaline masked the pain, but he knew the wound would slow him.

She followed up with another slash, and Aran knocked her blade away just as she'd done with his. He rammed his sword at her chest, and she tumbled backward out of the way. Aran summoned *water*, a thick ball of ice around his left foot.

He judged her trajectory, then launched a kick. His much heavier foot slammed into her gut, flinging her atop the still-burning bed. The woman rolled away from the flames, patting at her clothing to put them out.

Aran charged. He leapt over the bed and poured *void* and *air* into his blade. Void lightning crackled around the superheated steel, and he thrust the weapon at her throat. She dropped her spellblade, flipping backward out of the path of the attack.

She came up fast, flinging a book from the table. Then another. He dodged both, moving to keep himself between her and her weapon. Losing her blade wasn't much of a disadvantage in close quarters, and he couldn't afford to underestimate her. His arm ached, the flow of blood a reminder that time wasn't on his side.

Aran reached out with *air* tendrils, but the woman extended a hand and met him tendril for tendril. He rushed her then, leaping over her and bringing his blade down in a brutal slash. This time it caught her across the thigh, though she dodged the worst of the blow. A line of slick, shiny blood marred her suit there.

She favored her right side, where he'd landed the kick. Maybe he wasn't so bad off as he thought.

"Aran?" Nara's voice came from the entryway, no more than thirty meters away.

Aran's eyes never left his assailant, he was positive of that. One moment she was there, and the next she was gone. There was no visible use of an invisibility spell, no teleport that he could see.

He backed up slowly, putting his back to the wall as he scanned his quarters for any sign of her. There was nothing, no breathing, no footsteps. He had no idea if she was there, or she'd fled. Unfortunately, the scry-screen was still playing —not loud, but loud enough to cover an invisible person trying to sneak off the ship.

His weapon vibrated eagerly in his hand. It tugged at him, urging him to swing. Aran resisted the impulse.

"I'm in here," he yelled. "Be careful. There's an assassin." He strode boldly from the room, blade at the ready as he entered the main chamber.

Nara stood there, staff in hand. Her finger came up and she sketched a *fire* sigil, then a *dream*. Her eyes began to glow as she slowly scanned the room. "I don't see anyone."

Aran leaned against the wall and propped his sword against it, within easy reach. He put a hand over the wound in his arm, which was still bleeding freely. "Where's Bord when I need him?"

"They really got you." Nara hurried over and bent to inspect his wound.

Aran kept his attention on the room around them, in case his assailant came back. "She was from Virkon. She fought like me, but better."

"Well, she can't have been that much better. You're still alive." Nara moved to the medical supply cabinet Pickus had installed along the wall and removed a role of gauze. The ship's internal magic accelerated healing, but something this bad would still take a day or two to fully heal. She began wrapping his arm in gauze. "You sure do have a knack for making friends. Do you have any idea why this person wanted to kill you?"

"I have no idea. She called me *dragonslayer*, so maybe this is about Khalahk." Aran tested the arm. It wasn't too bad off. He looked Nara in the eye. "I think I'm out of time. My past has caught up with me, like it or not. I need to find a way to Virkon, before this assassin—or another like her— catches me in an off moment."

Nara bit her lip. "I'm supposed to go meet Eros, but I can blow that off so you aren't alone. Or you could go with me."

"I appreciate that, but you've got work to do. I know Eros is hard enough to deal with. I hurt the assassin, so that's probably given me a little time. I'll head to Ree's Kamiza until I can figure something out." He pulled her into a hug with his unwounded arm, and she returned it.

In spite of everything, he couldn't ignore her scent. Or

the attraction he felt. Of course if he gave in to that, it would provide just the kind of opportunity the assassin was no doubt after.

Nara disengaged, and smiled up at him. "I'll stick around until then. I can be a little late."

9

WELCOME HOME

Voria felt a swell of pride as she entered the makeshift space dock. A veritable army of techs swarmed around the *Wyrm Hunter*, adding armor panels, or welding patches in place. A steady flow of hover transports moved in and out of the cargo bay, loading munitions and other supplies.

She had no idea who'd paid for all this, or who'd authorized it. The work had clearly been going on for weeks, judging from the differences since the last time she'd seen the *Hunter*. The cracked keel had somehow been repaired, and she was beginning to resemble a space-worthy vessel once more.

A line of Inuran hovertanks rolled into the bay, the lead vehicle one she recognized. She hadn't seen Davidson's tank since Marid, but it was unmistakable. Larger and sleeker than the others, and with a powerful magical signature she could sense even at this distance. The cannon was long, almost comically so, and extended beyond the body of the tank. The range must be incredible, and would make Davidson's hovertank a threat, even to capital ships.

Voria hurried up the ramp, making for the aft entrance. That was the fastest way to the battle bridge, and she was fairly certain that was where Davidson would head as soon as he'd parked. She had no idea what he thought of the situation, though the fact that he'd recommended her was very promising.

"Sir," Pickus said as the lanky private detached himself from the wall. He fell into her wake, following her inside the ship. "I was hoping we could talk, sir. About the, uh, tree magic?"

"Tree magic?" That brought Voria up short. She stopped and gave Pickus her full attention. "What are you on about, Private?"

"Well, uh, you said I was supposed to go talk to the tree and it would give me *life* magic, right?" He blinked at her from under a mop of red hair, as much sheepdog as man.

"Precisely. Is there some problem with that? This isn't like most Catalysts. Your chances of dying are very low," Voria offered. She wasn't used to having to convince people to accept enormous power.

Pickus's already pale skin went even more white, and he blinked owlishly. "Wait, there's a chance I could die?"

"It's remote," Voria offered. She took a deep breath, trying to extricate herself from the situation she'd created. "When you peer into the mind of a god, there is a temptation to drink too deeply, to claim too much magical strength. Our minds can handle far more than our bodies, and the amount of magic you bring back can incinerate you if you are not careful."

"So how do I know if I should turn back?" Pickus asked. He stuffed his hands into his pockets. "I really don't want to die. I mean, I'd like to be able to heal people. And I want to peer into the mind of a god. That sounds fascinating. But, you know, I'm kind of a coward."

Voria smiled as a wave of affection for the Ternus tech bubbled up. "You will do fine, Pickus. You are intelligent, and you have good instincts. You saved the dims. You've faced the Umbral Depths and lived to speak of it. I'd hardly call you a coward."

"Thank you, sir." Pickus clenched his fist in front of his heart. "Well, then, I'm going to go meet the tree. I'll let you know how it goes, sir."

"Shaya's grace to you, Private." Voria returned the salute, and watched proudly as Pickus trotted back the way they'd come. These last several months had taught her how much of her identity was wrapped up in command, and, like it or not, she needed these people as much as as they needed her.

She needed to be needed. Helping people like Pickus didn't just make her feel good and useful, it defined her. And she didn't think that was a bad thing.

Voria continued through the ship, expertly tracing a path through the chaos of recommissioning, stepping over wires, and around chatting technicians. She was acutely aware that every last one wore a Ternus uniform, not a Confederate one.

Finally, she arrived at the battle bridge. This room appeared to be the eye of the storm, empty and wholly intact amidst the storm of activity covering the rest of the vessel. And, as she'd guessed, Davidson was already there.

His blond hair was still military short, but he'd added a thin beard along the jawline. It aged him, though not as much as the weight in his eyes. Marid had changed them both, but him more than anyone else who'd survived.

"It's a pleasure to see you again, Major." Voria walked around the primary spell matrix, joining Davidson near the scry-screen. He was much taller than her, though she wasn't a tall woman. "I'm told we'll be working together. I am also told you are the reason I was given command."

His stoic expression softened into something approaching a smile. "I'd forgotten how blunt you are, Major. It's good to see you as well. You're wondering why I didn't accept command?"

"Indeed." Voria gave a tight nod. It was refreshing how frank Ternus officers were, after having dealt with so many Shayans recently.

"Listen, six months ago magic was just a concept to me." Davison raised a hand, and a soft glaze of ice appeared around his fist. "Now I'm a tech mage, whatever that means. I'm learning all about these fancy new powers, but the problem is that my world doesn't have a large body of knowledge on the subject. In short, we don't know squat about magic."

"So you want me here as some sort of teacher?" Voria asked. She wasn't sure how she felt about that. Training mages, especially new mages, took a great deal of time and attention.

"Partly. But you also know how to run combat using a battleship like the *Hunter*. Can you imagine someone as green as I am trying to pilot her through combat?" Davidson gave a self-deprecating chuckle. "Ternus command doesn't even understand magic well enough to know that I'd need *void* magic to really make the most of this vessel. They're fed up with Shaya, and they want to run this vessel themselves. Nimitz really pushed for that."

"But you realize engaging the Krox with a single tech mage running this vessel would be suicide?" Voria shook her head with a smile. "Both our governments are bad at this whole military thing, I think. We need the best part of both, not the dregs of each."

"There's good news on that front, at least," Davidson offered. "My Marines all have experience battling Krox. They know what they're dealing with. Some come all the way from Starn. They've drilled with those tanks, and they've fought with them. They'll give as good as they get when we need them to."

"You're aware of our current mission?" Voria asked. She wasn't sure how far Eros trusted Ternus. She doubted Davidson knew more than the cover story, and perhaps not even that much.

"Sort of. I know we're going to Virkon, and Virkon is run by dragons. They're on the other side of the sector, so we haven't had a lot of dealings with them. They haven't told me why we're going, other than to establish some sort of diplomatic relations." Davidson stroked his beard. "Honestly? Sounded like nebulous bullshit to me, and I know you don't do bullshit. There's something important going down on Virkon, and though I don't know what it is, I do know you'll be at the heart of it. For whatever it's worth, you've got my full support."

Something eased in Voria, a weight she hadn't realized she'd been carrying. First Pickus, and now Davidson. It was as if she were returning to herself, cleansed of all her preconceived notions and ready for the war she'd been shaped to fight.

"It's damned good to have you back, Davidson. Welcome home." Indeed. Welcome home to them both.

10

WYRM FATHER

Nara rapped sharply on the thick shayawood door, waited a precise three seconds, then opened it without waiting for an answer.

Eros paced along the back wall of the study, oblivious to their entry. His dark robes were rumpled, no doubt slept in again. That had happened often, of late. He muttered to himself, quietly enough that she couldn't make out the words. Part of her was glad.

"This should be fun," Frit whispered from behind her.

"At least you won't be the focus of his attention," Nara whispered back. "So where did you go after you left the ship? I heard he was looking for you."

"Nowhere." Frit's face instantly lost all emotion, and she eyed Nara sidelong as they approached Eros. "We'll talk about it later."

Nara sighed. She had no idea what Frit was hiding, but did she have any right to pry? Frit was a friend, and it stung that she was keeping secrets.

Not that Nara had any room to talk. She kept her fair share, and besides, she knew for a fact she'd been a terrible person before the mind-wipe. She didn't have any right to judge anyone else, and was just grateful not to be "pirate girl" anymore.

"Master Eros?" she called hesitantly, when the new Tender continued to pace without acknowledging them.

"Hmm?" he turned abruptly in their direction. "Oh, it's you. I'm not pleased with either of you. Frit, I'm told you couldn't be located. I will not have you haring off on goddess knows whatever fancy takes you. Now, how did today's raid go? I'm told Grahl is dead. How did it happen?"

Nara licked her lips, composing her words carefully. That came much more quickly with Neith's gifts, and she'd found herself adept at conversation since then. "Ree's fighter squadron alerted the enemy to our presence before we were ready. We engaged, as ordered, and successfully neutralized most of the defenders."

"Most?" Eros demanded, eyes snapping into focus, on her. "We do not deal in *most*. Who survived? And why?"

"Two enforcers, both on the cusp of Wyrmhood," Nara admitted. She squared her shouldered and forged on. "They were able to open a Fissure and escape. Both enforcers possessed strong magic, and one was a true mage. I don't know if he was the one who bound Grahl."

Eros's nostrils flared, and his eyes reflected his disappointment. "How did the Caretaker die? I'm told our mages are unable to communicate with the spirit."

"Ritual suicide." Nara shook her head. "He was already dead by the time we forced ourself into the room."

"So his last act was ensuring we couldn't learn what he was up to. It could be anything," Eros growled. He began to pace again.

"Or it could be nothing," Nara countered. "We know the Krox are here. We know they're binding politicians. We don't know why, or how. And we're expending resources hunting them. That could be exactly the kind of distraction they're after. What are we not seeing while we focus on their activities here? We've focused everything here, and that means we are blind everywhere else."

Eros froze, and shifted a critical eye in her direction. "A keen observation, pirate girl. Very keen indeed. I am disappointed you failed to eliminate these Krox. Unfortunately, you will not be given another chance to catch them."

"Why is that?" she asked. He was about to deliver big news, she could tell by his self-important expression.

"You're officially assigned to the *Talon*, under the command of Lieutenant Aran. You will be representing the House of Enlightenment, and Shaya in general. I trust you will not embarrass us."

"I don't know if I'd trust that," Nara muttered. Frit giggled beside her and Nara gave her a covert smile. "Master, what's our mission?"

"I suppose you have a right to know, but I must insist you discuss this with no one." Eros frowned. "We know there are spies everywhere, and I am positive there is at least one close enough to learn secrets no one should have access to."

That sent Nara reeling. They'd taken great care to make sure the entire palace was warded. Anyone with even a minor binding would set off alarms long before they made it inside. Any magic of any kind was tracked, and dealt with ruthlessly where necessary. There was no way for a binder spy to make it this far inside, not anymore. And that meant if there was a spy, they were serving the Krox of their own free will.

"You are heading to Virkon, ostensibly to forge an alliance," Eros explained he rolled his eyes. "A flimsy cover, since all know the Wyrms are too proud to consider us equals."

"And the real mission?" Nara asked. She hated how Eros drew everything out, prolonging his importance as long as he could.

"You will be recovering this First Spellship of Voria's. Since she will have to pretend at this alliance, we expect you to do the bulk of the searching." Eros folded his arms, studying her for a response.

"If you expect me to find this ship, I need to understand a great deal more about who created it, and what the galaxy was like when they did," Nara said, thinking aloud. "I'll need to understand the spell hiding it, and whatever else we can determine about its origins and capabilities."

She noted that Frit had become very interested, a welcome surprise. Frit was usually much more interested in blowing things up, or talking about their latest respective crushes. She didn't care much for history or magical theory, beyond how it would help her torch her enemies.

"I can give you a starting point, at least. I understand that your historical knowledge is badly lacking, and you may not know about the dragonflights." Eros oozed the casual arrogance he probably didn't even realize had become his hallmark. "How much do you know of them?"

"I know that Virkon is called the last dragonflight, but I've never heard of the others," Nara admitted. "What are they?"

"The dragonflights ruled this galaxy for countless millennia. Our sector was ruled by eight in particular, all children of the same goddess," Eros explained. "You've already met the ghost of Marid, Wyrm Mother of the *water* Wyrms. Now you've met this Keeper of Secrets, the Wyrm Mother of *Fire*. Virkon is called the last dragonflight, because it is the last to follow their ways. Humans are treated as chattel, and only those who distinguish themselves in battle are elevated into serving them directly. We, of course, are also considered beneath them. At one time the whole of the galaxy was enslaved by dragons, though they would call it honorable servitude."

"I'm sure their culture is fascinating, but it's also likely to be quite vast, especially if I'm searching through millennia of myths." Nara felt overwhelmed, and she'd scarcely begun. "Where should I start?"

"I will send you with several knowledge scales about the flights. Most of it is unusable myth, since much of our knowledge was lost at the end of the godswar." Eros shook his head sadly. Only a tragedy as great as losing knowledge could inspire him to emotion. "Pay particular attention to the fact that there is never any mention of the *life* Wyrm Father."

Nara's eyes widened. "Enchantment requires *air* and *life*. In order to construct the Spellship, they'd have needed both. Virkonna, and whoever this Wyrm Father is."

"Precisely. Find this Wyrm Father, and you may find the answers you seek."

11

CHOICES

F rit experienced the most awful surge of guilt watching Eros and Nara talk. The things they were speaking about—this hidden goddess, and this mysterious First Spellship—were secrets they'd clearly not shared with anyone.

Yet they were willing to discuss it in front of her.

Nara did that because they were friends, and Nara trusted her. Eros probably assumed Frit was too much of a *thing* to ever be self-aware enough to pass information to his enemies. Something she hadn't yet done, though she knew Nebiat was after precisely this information.

"What do we know of this *life* Wyrm Father?" Nara asked. She moved to one of the chairs in front of Eros's massive desk, and sat lightly on the edge.

Frit envied her passion for knowledge. It wasn't as common as most would assume, not even in the heart of the most scholarly organization on Shaya.

"Nothing, which in and of itself tells us something." Eros wore one of his expectant looks, the kind he wore when he meant a student to make a logical leap. Frit almost always failed such tests.

Nara's eyes widened and a pleased smile burst onto her face. "If there is no knowledge, then someone must have gone to great lengths to remove all mention."

"Precisely, which is why I recommend the *Codex Draconis* as a starting point. There are myths about the *life* Wyrm Father, which I believe survived because they never directly referenced him," Eros said, speaking with the same passion.

Both had forgotten her presence. Frit sat in the other chair, next to Nara. Nara didn't even glance at her. Frit didn't blame her, not really. Nara just wanted the same approval every student was after—the difference being that she actually received it, whether she knew it or not.

"What commonalities do the other Wyrms have?" Nara asked, pursing her lips. "How were the flights similar to each other?"

"Astute questions, but ones to which we lack the answers. Were you to come to me as a student, I'd send you to Virkon. The archivists there would most certainly have the answers." Eros rubbed his hands together slowly, and adopted a distinctly uncomfortable look. "That presents certain challenges, however. The archivists from Virkon consider us to be...upstarts at best. They're even less flattering in their opinion of Ternus, though that is small consolation."

"She won't have any trouble convincing them to help her," Frit muttered. Louder than she'd meant to evidently, as they both looked at her. "I, uh, only meant that Nara's resourceful. I'm sure she can find someone there to help her understand about these Wyrms. I mean, she is asking about their culture. Most priests like talking about themselves, but they *love* talking about their religion."

"That's an excellent point." Nara snapped her fingers, turning back to Eros. "Aran is from Virkon. I can bring him with me. Maybe they'll talk to one of their own."

"Certainly worth the effort. Your Outrider friend will be quite the curiosity on their world, I imagine. The citizens of that world rarely leave it for long, and he's been gone for some time." Eros returned to the bookshelf at the far side of the study, and began browsing the spines. "Hmm. Yes, there's one more book I'd send with you. It's a treatise on the dragonflights. It's mostly just chants, but those chants appear to be ancient prayers. And I believe they are still in use on Virkon, so if you can memorize a few you might impress the local clergy."

Frit sighed. They'd already forgotten about her again. She raised a finger to her collar, touching one of the runes. The pain made her grit her teeth, but part of her understood that even those teeth had been fashioned by her captors.

She endured the pain, and thought about all that Nebiat had said.

12

A PLAN

Voria blinked rapidly as her eyes adjusted to the
Talon's much brighter lighting. She leaned on
Ikadra, taking in the battle bridge once more.
She'd spent less time here than she had on the *Hunter*'s
bridge, but being on the *Talon* afforded her a satisfaction
she'd never felt on another ship. She hadn't built the *Talon*,
but she *had* reclaimed it.

If the First Spellship were it on a grander scale...well she
could only imagine the majesty. What was that lofty vessel
capable of? What would it bring to their cause that made it
so vital, so worth all the work they'd done, and would do, to
find it?

"Sir." Aran was the first to acknowledge her presence. He
rose from the command couch, and stepped from the matrix
to offer a crisp salute—a salute she very much appreciated.

Voria softened into a smile.

"Officer on deck, wipes," Crewes barked. The sergeant
snapped a salute as well, and Bord and Kezia joined him a
moment later. He turned a wide smile her way. "Welcome
back, sir. You've been missed."

"Don't get used to my presence, Sergeant. Where's Nara?" Voria asked, not seeing her anywhere on the bridge.

"She's in the library." Aran pointed at the ramp leading into the main meeting room at the center of the ship.

Voria raised a hand and sketched a quick missive. The spell flitted down the passageway. She straightened her jacket with her free hand, waiting patiently for Nara. The girl didn't disappoint. She emerged moments later, hurrying in with a book still clutched in one hand. The *Codex Draconis*? Interesting. Probably given to her by Eros.

"Ah, excellent, you're here. We can begin." Voria was about to do exactly that, when Ikadra's sapphire began pulsing wildly. Since he was unable to speak, he'd rapidly learned this was a way to annoy her into asking what he wanted. "Yes, Ikadra?"

"I forgot what I was going to say," Ikadra said in a deflated tone. The sapphire dimmed.

Voria stifled her sigh, and turned back to the others. "I cannot stay long. I'm only here to deliver our orders, and I didn't want to risk a missive."

Their faces grew sober, even Bord's.

"We've been ordered to Virkon, as we hoped," Voria said, allowing a smile. The others shared it, but politely refrained from their usual antics. "But there is still much work to do. We need to find the Spellship, and that's not something I can tend to directly. For that reason, Nara will be dispatched to locate the ship. She'll have any resources she needs."

"What will you be doing?" Aran asked. Voria noticed a bandage peeking out of his jacket. Had he been wounded in the raid? If so, she hadn't heard of it.

"I will be meeting with the Virkonnian government, and so will you," Voria explained. "The Confederacy believes your return will be a matter of great importance."

Nara frowned and gave Aran a worried look. "And also a monumental distraction. A risky one. Have you told her yet?"

"Told me what?" Voria tensed. News like this was rarely good.

"An assassin boarded the *Talon* without being detected, and ambushed me in my quarters," Aran explained simply, with no preamble. She liked that directness. "She used Drakkon style, and fought me to a standstill. When Nara appeared she vanished. I didn't recognize the magic. There was no visible spell effect."

"And I couldn't see her with a *pierce invisibility*," Nara added, shaking her head slowly. "Whoever she was, she had access to magic we're unfamiliar with."

"I'd give much to see this suit she was wearing," Voria mused. "I'd wager that's an eldimagus, and the source of her stealth. There are other means of hiding besides invisibility. One of the more insidious methods is a kind of binding. It forces observers to ignore you. Their minds can no longer accept the fact that you are there, in essence rendering you invisible—to that person at least."

Aran resumed his seat in the command matrix, and the others followed his cue.

Nara cleared her throat. "So how would you fight against something like that?"

"If someone wanted you dead, I don't know that you could stop them. You'd need a ward of some kind, something that would trigger when such a spell was used." Voria looked up at the sapphire. "Ikadra, do you know of any defensive magics that could be used to defeat such a spell?"

"Uhh, probably." Ikadra pulsed slowly. "A nullification field doesn't really work, because then you lose all other magic, like my awesome voice. I'd be mute, which is a pretty terrible side effect." He pulsed more quickly. "Wait, doesn't the handsome guy have a pet sword? I know it's still just an imprint, but it's been to a few Catalysts now. It has to be developing a mind."

"You're talking about my weapon?" Aran reached into his void pocket and removed his spellblade. The sword was a meter and a half, but no more than three fingers wide. Fast and slender, with a dark, glittering finish to the metal. Perfect for a man with increased speed and strength.

"Yeah, which you need to name by the way. I don't want to sound judge-y, but you're a terrible parent." Ikadra pulsed a little more slowly. "You might not be able to see this assassin, but your sword can. You just have to tell it what you want it to do."

"That's useful, but if her being cloaked were a problem, I'd already be dead," Aran pointed out. "She stopped using it when she fought me, and she fought fairly, for the most part." His hand dropped to his crotch.

"The fact remains that an assassin attempted to end your life, and that assassin hails from the world we are about to journey to. I find that very troubling." The last thing Voria needed was more problems, but at least new ones no longer came as a surprise.

"Sir," Nara ventured. "You realize this means if we put Aran on public display it will be even easier to assassinate him?"

"I am painfully aware of that." Voria sighed heavily. "We'll need to deal with it, but not right now. We're to leave tonight. Dock the *Talon* inside the *Wyrm Hunter*. Aran, I'd like you to report to the battle bridge once you are situated."

She could tell them now, but she'd rather do it when she was alone with Aran. He had a right to know the command situation, and would be discreet in telling the others.

13

THE COUNCIL OF WYRMS

Kaho leaned on his long, black staff as he slowly entered the chamber. Every time his staff met stone it echoed up the steep slopes, all the way to the eight perches near the top of the cavern. He didn't need the staff, but bringing it served twin purposes. First, it showed that he valued such objects. These were *air* Wyrms, and such Wyrms valued enchanted objects more than any other. They coveted them, and were fantastically curious when presented with a new one.

The staff also showed humility. It said *I am still a hatchling. I am beneath you, and I understand that.* His brother had argued that such a posture would weaken Kaho's position, but Kaho understood the truth: They had no position here.

"Speak, child," rumbled a massive male, from an alcove on the left. His eyes smoldered with blue lightning, and sparks leapt from his nostrils with every breath.

Kaho delivered a low bow, which flared his wings to the side and curled his tail around his feet. He held the bow until he finished the introduction. "Greetings, most exalted Wyrms of the last dragonflight. I have been dispatched by

my grandfather, Guardian of Krox. We have come to offer
praise to Virkonna, our aunt."

"Does your mother think us fools, child?" A female
moved to the edge of another alcove. Her face was ancient,
craggy grey lines etched into her scales. "Your grandfather
wouldn't insult us with progeny. How long have you even
been out of your conniving mother's egg?"

Kaho wasn't certain how to answer that. "Respectfully,
Wyrm Mother, I *am* merely progeny. I have only been out of
the egg for eighty-seven years. I will undergo my first
molting soon." He wasn't sure why he added that, and
regretted it immediately. "My mother sent me here, and I
did not hear the words from grandfather's lips. I merely
relay her words."

"I thought as much," the Wyrm Mother rumbled,
settling back into her alcove. She eyed him with those
lantern eyes. "Now tell us why you have really come. In your
own words."

This part Kaho had been ready for. He knew why his
mother had sent them here. He knew what she hoped to
accomplish. And he knew exactly how much to tell Virkon
so they'd know he wasn't lying. They'd suspect he was
holding things back, of course, but if they thought they
could guess the Krox plans, they'd grow complacent.

"The Confederacy considers Wyrms a 'galactic threat.'
They've killed countless elder Wyrms in their short existence. They inspire all mortals everywhere to take up arms
against us, their rightful masters." He paused for a moment,
but he couldn't see if his words were having any effect. No
way out but forward. "Most recently, they killed my uncle
Kheftut. Shortly thereafter, they killed Wyrm Father
Khalahk."

A great rustling of wings echoed through the chamber.

None of the Wyrms spoke aloud, but Kaho could sense the agitation. He must tread carefully, lest they vent their wrath on the messenger.

"You ask why I have come. I have been sent to see that justice is done," Kaho explained. He finally rose from the bow, and looked up to meet the eyes of the great Wyrms above. "My mother asks that I present evidence that the Outrider Aranthar, one of your own, murdered Wyrm Father Khalahk. It was his hand that guided the ship. His hand that fired the *disintegrate*."

The rustling intensified, and one of the Wyrms, a matronly female, leapt from her perch and soared out the top of the chamber. It took many moments for the commotion to subside, and when it did, all seven Wyrms glared down at him.

"Speak quickly, child, or I will vent my rage upon you," the first male rumbled. Kaho had never met Aetherius, but he knew the Wyrm Father by reputation. Kaho was certain the horned male was he.

"Please, I beg your indulgence, mighty Wyrms," Kaho offered humbly. He bowed again, though not so low. "I am happy to relate the entire tale, exactly as my mother told it to me. You can perform your own seeings to verify my words."

"I can see why your mother sent you," the elderly Wyrm rumbled. She slithered to the edge of her alcove. "If we find fault with your 'evidence,' then all she loses are a couple offspring."

Kaho sincerely hoped they did not find fault with his evidence.

14

GOOD NEWS AND MANY POTIONS

The *Talon* zoomed under the eighth branch, slowing as it approached the space dock where they'd parked the *Hunter* what felt like a lifetime ago. Aran still remembered the battleship coming to rest like an aging wolf lying down for the last time.

Bord had already proved resurrection was possible, and seeing the *Hunter* now drew a swell of pride up through Aran's chest. It said that, somehow, they'd survived the worst the sector could throw at them.

"I can't believe it," Nara murmured. "They fixed her."

"Every last rivet." Bord gave a whoop from the corner of the room where he'd started an impromptu game of *Go* with Kezia.

"It's good to see her whole. The old girl ain't never gonna quit," Crewes said, wiping at the corner of his eye.

The *Hunter*'s hull was discolored, but the awful rents caused by Kheftut and the battles that had followed were all repaired. The last armored plate was being lowered into place as they approached, levitated by a pair of *void* mages.

A tech mage in Mark V armor rose on a plume of flame, raising a rivet gun to bolt the piece into place.

Aran guided the *Talon* low, slowing further as they approached the docking bay—the same docking bay he'd been taken to from the Skull of Xal, toward an uncertain future. So much had changed in so short a time.

"Is that Davidson's tank?" Nara asked as she thrust a finger at the scry-screen.

"Damn, that thing looks nasty," Kez said as she started packing up the game pieces. "Glad it's on our side."

They still hadn't seen it in combat, since Davidson had been separated from them almost immediately after they'd Catalyzed. Aran wondered what ability Marid had given the tank. The ice block his armor had received had proven immensely useful.

Which, of course, made him think of his armor. The whole fight with Dirk replayed in his mind often, but the nightmares always ended with the *void* magic eating his armor. With him tumbling out the back as parts of his suit dissolved. He'd lost the suit in the resulting explosion, and hadn't been prepared for how hard that had hit him.

It wasn't like a pair of boots you could just replace. Even if he had the funds a new set of armor...well it wouldn't be his old armor. That armor had been a living thing, a child, of sorts, that had grown alongside him.

"Looks like they're rolling out some sort of honor guard," Crewes rumbled. He sounded unsettled, which fit. The sergeant didn't love attention of any kind.

Aran set the *Talon* down in the corner of the bay, where a number of troops in parade dress were assembling. Their uniforms weren't Confederate blue. They were the olive green of Ternus, though both militaries used gold as a highlight color.

"Well, the good news is that you get to stay here," Aran said, extricating himself from the command couch. He ducked through the spinning rings, and headed for the ramp down to the mess. "I've got orders to meet with the major, but the rest of you are free to do whatever."

"And here we just packed up the pieces." Bord reached for the *Go* set and started unpacking stones again. "Come on, Kez. I'll let you win."

"You let everyone win, Bord. Because you're joost bad at this." Kez sat down and began setting up her own pieces. She hummed happily to herself.

Aran looked up and found Nara's gaze. They shared a brief smile over Kez, then Aran ducked past her. He turned back to Crewes. "Sergeant, you've got the conn."

"Yes, sir. I'll keep the rugrats in line." Crewes settled back on his couch and reached into the pocket of his cargo pants. He fished out a silver can with a stylized logo on the side. "But seeing as we are nowhere near a combat zone, I'm gonna use a chemical fix to make Bord's jokes a little more tolerable."

Aran chuckled at that, then headed down the ramp. He continued down the second ramp that led to the airlock door, which dissolved before him as he approached. A shimmering blue ramp appeared, sloping down to the deck below.

The instant Aran stepped onto the ramp, every marine, probably a hundred plus, snapped to attention. They didn't use the Confederate fist over heart, but instead snapped their hand to their brow in a tight Ternus salute.

"Welcome back to the *Hunter*, Lieutenant," a familiar voice called.

Aran trotted down the ramp, and his face split into a grin when he caught sight of Captain Davidson. "What happened to your face? You look a botched morph between a human and a golden retriever."

"Seriously? You're going to dog on my beard?" Davidson raised a hand to stroke the coarse blond. "Yours makes you look like the dread pirate cliché."

"Nara likes it," Aran pointed out, a bit more self-consciously than he'd have liked to admit.

"Well, that explains it." Davidson slugged him in the shoulder. His face shifted to serious, and he glanced at the waiting marines. "Listen, this isn't the place to have a long chat, but I at least want to give you the facts on the ground. This war isn't going to be like Marid. My unit is attached to the *Hunter*, but we operate independently. I have full say. Voria is in charge of the ship only."

That hit Aran like a hammer. It meant a lot more than the major losing some authority. It meant Ternus was less invested in the Confederacy—not that he blamed them, or that he himself was invested. Far from it.

But the Confederacy was what they had to stop the Krox, like it or not.

"Maybe we can find time to catch up later? I don't know what you've been up to over the last few months, but you remember Marid...what we saw inside her head." Aran paused as he struggled for more words. "It's bigger than we thought. I don't know all of what I can tell you, but you're involved."

"I hate this cloak and dagger crap." Davidson heaved a sigh. He turned to the marines, and snapped a crisp salute. They returned it, then relaxed when he did. "Why don't you go chat with the major? Figure out what you can tell me, and we'll meet for a beer later. I'm sure we'll have plenty of time in the depths while we sail all the way to Virkon."

Aran clapped him on the shoulder, then cut a path

across the hangar. The whirring of servos, and the yells of techs were so much louder than they'd been before. This was what the *Hunter* was like with a full crew.

Ternus hadn't just brought their marines. They'd brought everything, including munitions, if the crates in the corner were any indication.

He left the cargo bay and threaded through several hallways, finally arriving at the battle bridge. Unlike the rest of the ship this place was still empty. There were no guards, and he only passed one tech.

Voria stood within the command matrix, and nodded at his entrance. Ikadra bobbed up and down in midair just outside the slowly rotating rings.

Pickus gave an excited wave from the offensive matrix. He raised a hand. "Check this out, man!" A brilliant golden glow built around his fist, the same brilliant glow that built around Bord when he healed.

"You have *life* magic?" Aran blinked. "When did that happen?"

"Yeah, the major got it approved. I got to talk to the tree lady and everything," he said, all in a rush. "I saw into her mind, like whole planets being built and stuff. It was amazing. Not at all like talking to that creepy-ass spider. That thing made my ears bleed."

"Pickus, would you mind going down to the mess and fetching us some lunch?" Voria asked. It wasn't like her to make a menial request, unless she had some other motive.

"Of course. I'll be back in a bit." Pickus ducked out of the matrix and trotted out of the room.

"What's your read on our newest tech mage, Lieutenant?" Voria asked mildly. Her face was bathed by the faint glow of the sigils on the matrix's rings, and her eyes were far away.

"I'm still surprised you got him to enlist." Aran moved to the offensive matrix, and stepped inside. He tapped a *fire* sigil, bonding himself to the ship. She was different than the *Talon*. Slower, more ponderous. And far, far less aware. "He's intelligent. And he's not afraid to experiment. Taking control of the *Talon* during the fight with your father saved a lot of lives."

"But?" Voria asked.

"But he's green. He's never been in real combat. On the... dark planet he was a liability, and we all knew it," Aran said. He was glad Pickus wasn't there. The words were honest, but they would shred the tech's confidence. "I think, in time, he could be a serious asset. I think if you limit his responsibilities, he'll master them quickly. But I'd keep him out of direct combat."

"I agree completely." Voria gave him a faint smile. "I've drafted Pickus to work comms. We need someone to replace Crewes, since he'll be aboard your vessel."

"My vessel? You're making me the *Talon*'s captain? I was always under the impression she was yours, sir," Aran said, more than a little uncomfortably. He loved being in command of the *Talon*, and felt like he was good at it. But he hadn't been given Ikadra; the major had. By rights, the ship should belong to her.

"She is most definitely your ship, Lieutenant." Voria stepped from the matrix and approached Aran. She stopped a meter away, eyeing him soberly. "Our whole purpose in going to Virkon is to find mine."

The matrix chimed softly, and Aran tapped a *fire*, then a *dream* sigil. His jaw fell when he realized what he was seeing. "Sir, we've just received a missive."

"From who?" Voria asked curiously.

"It's from your brother. Kazon just docked."

She gave a broad, excited smile. "Well, that's a welcome surprise. We'd best get down there and find out what he's brought us. Good news, and many potions, I hope."

15

A PRESENT

Aran spent the walk back to the docking bay wondering. How did Kazon know they were here? And why had he come? They hadn't spoken since Marid, and Kazon could have come to Shaya at any time during the last few months. Why show up on the exact day they were departing for Virkon?

It was all a little too convenient, which put his guard up despite being excited to see a man he considered a brother.

By the time they arrived, Davidson's marines had mostly cleared out, as had the newly minted major himself. Their tanks dominated the south side of the room, flanked by boxes of munitions. Davidson's larger tank stood over the others like a protective older sibling.

A little ways away sat the *Talon*, and next to it an unfamiliar ship. It was, to put it bluntly, a floating black brick. It was a long rectangle with a smooth hull and no obvious weaponry of any kind. No spellcannon, or even gauss rifles. Either it was purely a shuttle, or it utilized a different kind of weaponry. The metal had an oily sheen to it, bending the light in uncomfortable ways.

"What is that vessel, sir?" Aran asked. They'd nearly reached her, and he now stared up at the hull. It appeared to be one solid piece of metal, with no seams or joins.

"I don't know." Voria raised a hand and touched the metal. "It's magical, whatever it is. Some sort of new Inuran alloy?"

"Probably," a voice boomed from directly behind them.

Aran spun to see Kazon, the man's beard even more unruly than it had been the last time they'd spoken. The big man lunged forward, seizing Aran with tree-trunk arms. "It is good to see you, brother."

Aran tensed, then relaxed into the hug. Two in one day. They were going to yank his man card.

"It's good to see you, Kazon." Aran disengaged and shared the big man's infectious grin. "So what brings you all the way out here? You must be pretty important to the Inurans judging by the fancy new ship."

"She's incredible, the first in a new line." He patted the hull affectionately. "And you are not wrong. Outside of Mother and Skare, it turns out I might be the most important person in the Consortium."

"Well, I can see your smugness has returned." The major wrapped Kazon in a brisk, official hug. "It's good to see you. I'm guessing this isn't a social visit, however. Why are you here, Kazon?"

Kazon burst out laughing. "You're looking for the hook. Jolene said you would."

Voria began massaging her temples. Ikadra hovered in midair next to her. "Can you blame me? Every time the Consortium has been involved, I've paid a higher price than I've wanted. This time we might not need your help, though. Davidson and his marines are well armed."

"But my brother isn't." Kazon snapped his fingers and a

deep hum built inside the ship. Nothing else occurred, at least not immediately. "The holo-scry of Aran's fight with Dirk has gone viral throughout the sector. I've watched it a couple dozen times myself. They set it to the most incredible music. Simply epic. And I couldn't help but notice that Aran came out of that fight missing his armor."

A large black crate materialized on the deck a few meters away.

"You didn't." A swell of emotion rose in Aran, and he seized Kazon in another hug.

"I will always see that you are armed, brother." Kazon gave a booming laugh. "Now see what I've brought you."

Aran inspected the crate, circling it until he found the side with the red button. He stabbed it with a finger, and the crate began whirring as its components retracted into the base.

It exposed a set of armor quite unlike his Mark XI— quite unlike any spellarmor. It was smaller, for one thing, just a bit larger than conventional body armor. That meant less protection, theoretically. The armor was made from the same oily metal as the ship, rippling under the light almost like a liquid. It had a faint magical...odor wasn't quite the right word, but there was a kind of bitter flavor to the magic.

"What is it?" Aran asked, raising a hand to the chest. He could feel the power pulsing from it, restrained chaos, barely held in check.

"I don't really know, to be honest. Jolene won't say anything about how it's constructed. I believe she doesn't know herself. Skare invented it." Kazon moved to stand next to Aran. "It's really quite impressive. The metal is naturally resistant to magic, of course, but there's more." He turned to scan the hangar. His gaze fell on a trio of marines who happened to be crossing the bay. "Hey, you there. Do you have a moment?"

The marines eyed him curiously, but moved over to join them. The one in the lead had the same dark skin as Crewes, putting him from Yanthara. "Sir?"

"You've got a sidearm, I see. That's a slug-throwing weapon, right?" Kazon asked.

"Yeah, it fires bullets," the marine confirmed, a bit cautiously.

"Can you fire one of them at this armor here? Anywhere you'd like. All three of you." Kazon waved encouragingly at the armor.

"Are you sure?" the marine asked.

"Please." Kazon gestured again, expectantly this time.

All three marines drew their sidearms. The pistols came up, almost as one. All three weapons barked, filling the air with the sharp scent of gunpowder as the barrels kicked. Bullet after bullet slammed into the spellarmor.

Instead of deflecting the bullets, like his old spellarmor, the armor merely rippled and the bullets shot out the other side, into the wall.

"What am I seeing?" Aran asked. He circled the armor. He'd felt a surge of *void* magic from the armor each time a bullet had struck.

"The armor is using complex *void* magic to teleport the bullet. It never actually touches the armor, and is instead redirected out the other side. Kinetic projectiles are much less of a threat, until the armor's reserves are depleted at least." Kazon grinned at Aran. "The best part? This stuff might be slow to produce, but it's also much cheaper to produce than our current line. You give us a year or two, and we'll have these available on every market. In the meantime, you're a step ahead of the rest of the sector."

"Uh, sir, are we done here?" the marine asked.

"Yes, yes. Thank you for your assistance. Here, for your trouble." Kazon reached into his pockets and produced a handful of glittering golden scales. He handed one to each of the marines. "Spend it unwisely. If you can remember the night, you didn't do it right."

The marines thanked him gratefully, then hurried off on whatever errand Davidson had set them. Aran barely noticed, focused instead on his new armor.

"Well, give it a try!" Kazon prompted.

Aran sketched a *void* symbol over the chest, and the oily metal went translucent. He slipped inside, bracing himself as the metal darkened around him. It was only for a moment, but he felt like he wasn't alone in the darkness.

The armor solidified and the faceplate lit up, showing him the cargo bay. The HUD was nearly identical to his Mark XI, though the potion icons had been updated. He cautiously channeled a bit of *void* magic into the armor, and it rose into the air.

"This thing has *nine* potion loaders?" Aran asked through the suit's speakers. As he focused on the potions, a list blinked into existence on his HUD, cataloguing each potion with a little color-coded icon.

The icons were broken into *green* for support, *red* for offensive, and *blue* for defensive, grouped like matrices on a typical battle bridge. All three defensives were counterspell potions. The supports were, thank the gods, healing potions, and the offensives were an unfamiliar red potion.

"It has many more tricks to offer. You'll notice it does not include a spellrifle," Kazon called. "Aim your fist at something, and cast a spell."

Aran did as Kazon asked and aimed his fist at the bulkhead. He drew enough *void* for a level one bolt, and was pleasantly surprised when it zipped from his fist, hissing into the wall with no obvious effect.

The ability to fire ranged attacks from your hands was impressive, though Aran doubted this thing had anywhere near the range of his spellrifle.

"There is one final trick. When you land, sketch the sigil for exiting. You will be presented with an option. Choose storage mode." Kazon's grin had, if possible, gotten even bigger. He looked like a toddler who'd just delivered his first present.

Aran landed next to Kazon, and sketched the *void* sigil inside the right gauntlet. The armor vibrated and a sigil appeared on his faceplate. As promised it had two options: exit, or storage mode. Aran chose storage mode.

The armor vibrated again, then gave a high-pitched whine. Aran lurched, disoriented as the armor flowed around him in a river of metal. It slid down his face, and when he could see again he watched as every bit of liquid metal flowed down his arm. It formed a wide silvery band around his wrist—warm, and practically weightless.

There were no obvious spell sigils on the device, making it different from every other magic item Aran had worked with. He wasn't an enchanter by any means, but he could recognize a technological leap when he saw one. Somehow the Inurans had found, or developed, something vastly superior to what they'd been using. This could change the face of warfare.

"And you say this is cheaper than traditional spellarmor?" Aran asked. He held the bracelet up for inspection. It looked so innocent. He could wear it into any bar in the sector, and no one would look twice at it.

"By an order of magnitude, apparently. Its only downside appears to be the time to manufacture." Kazon shrugged. "I haven't looked too closely into it. I've been occupied by...other matters." His voice dropped with the last two words.

"Other matters?" Aran also lowered his voice. He glanced around. The marines were gone, and apparently so was the major. At some point she must have returned to the bridge.

They were alone, or as alone as they could get on the *Hunter*.

"I have a certain number of responsibilities now, but my free time has gone toward learning how we ended up under Yorrak's care," Kazon explained. He leaned forward, all amusement gone. "Aran, I was hunting for a Catalyst. Whoever stopped us wiped out an entire station to prevent me from telling anyone about it. They killed a full Wyrm, *your* Wyrm as I understand it."

"Who is 'they'?" Aran pressed. He didn't try to suppress his eagerness. Kazon had the resources to find real answers, and it looked like he'd accumulated a few. To finally have a target for his anger...it was about time.

"That I don't yet know. They're very secretive, and given everything I've seen I'd guess they were the ones who contracted Yorrak to remove us. Because I was investigating this Catalyst." Kazon looked around the hangar, only speaking again when he seemed certain they were fully alone. "I found a missive that referenced Nara. It was one of Yorrak's conversations."

"Where did you get this information?" Aran asked.

"I went back to the Skull of Xal." Kazon shuddered, and Aran mirrored it. The mere thought of that place made his skin go to gooseflesh. "I found Yorrak's ship. It was still drifting, and he had several knowledge scales. Most were drunken recordings, but a few had interesting bits. Most of those bits had to do with Nara. Apparently, whoever Yorrak worked for had plans for her. They called her a 'long term investment.'"

The implications were unsettling. "You think they might still have plans for her?"

"They might. But that wasn't what worried me." Kazon rested a hand on Aran's shoulder. "Listen, brother. You know I dislike Nara, and you know why. When I say this, I don't want you to think that's coloring the information. Nara wasn't a good person. At all. She was eager to work with Yorrak's employer, but apparently he kept preventing it out of jealousy. If she gets her memories back, she won't be the sweet girl you've gotten to know. Be careful, Aran. She is an unstable ward, ready to detonate."

"I'll keep an eye on her," Aran said, and meant it. He had feelings for Nara—for the woman she was now. But that woman she'd been before? "I've got bigger concerns at the moment. You've heard where we're going?"

"I've been told." Kazon nodded. He extended a hand. "Be careful, brother."

Aran took it. "I will, brother."

16

INTO THE DEPTHS

Voria was curiously troubled as she returned to the battle bridge. It was good to see her brother, though she didn't really know the man he'd become after the wipe. There were similarities, of course, to the man he'd used to be.

But this Kazon was going out of his way to distance himself from his old identity. It was as if he didn't want to be linked to the man he'd been. The one brief missive she'd received from her mother had harped endlessly on that point.

"Private Pickus, inform me when the Inuran vessel has departed the docking bay." Voria swept onto the bridge, making for the familiar comfort of the command matrix.

Ikadra's sapphire pulsed.

"Yes, Ikadra?" she asked absently, still considering Kazon and this new ship of his.

"I've been scrying the vessel that docked on your ship." Ikadra's sapphire flickered rapidly. "I cannot see inside. My magic is completely blocked. That shouldn't be possible with the sector's current, primitive armaments."

"Intriguing," Voria allowed. "Can you tell me anything else about the ship?"

"I don't trust it," Ikadra replied immediately. "It reminds me of someone, but I can't put my finger on who."

She didn't want to ignore Ikadra's misgivings, but if there was something wrong with the vessel it wasn't as if she could do anything about it. She made a mental note to inspect Aran's armor, just in case.

"Kazon isn't staying, so you won't have to see it again." Voria's mind was already turning toward Virkon. She had so much planning to do. Would the Council of Wyrms even receive a Shayan? The Confederacy had never sent a delegation, and she had no idea how they'd react to her arrival.

"Private, how do you feel about taking us out?" Voria asked. She could do it herself, but the fastest way to get new officers wet was to throw them in the water. This was the shallows.

"Uh, I can do that, sir. Make for the planet's Umbral Shadow?" Pickus asked. He raised a hand, but didn't tap any sigils.

"Please." Voria exited the command matrix, and gestured for him to assume her place.

"Oh, that's right. I need to be in that one to fly the ship. I'm used to the *Talon*." Pickus blushed furiously as he entered the command matrix, but Voria studiously ignored his discomfort. "Do we have any other backup? Or is it just us two running the whole battle bridge?"

"We can call upon Captain Davidson in an emergency, but other than that, yes, it's just the two of us to run the *Hunter*." Voria didn't like that situation, but she also knew it was the smartest allocation of resources. And it was better off than she'd been when Thalas had been around.

Having Aran and his company on the *Talon* was simply

too useful to give up. That sort of rapid response team had already proven devastatingly effective, and she needed that kind of tool in her arsenal.

"Take us to the Umbral Shadow," she ordered. "When we get there I'll open a Fissure, and you'll pilot for the first leg of the trip. Just steer right through."

Pickus gave an eager nod. He learned quickly; that was part of why she liked him so much, and also part of why she needed to take a step back. She couldn't afford to get attached. Numbers didn't lie.

If this mission was anything like their last few, most of these people would never make it home. It was her job to make sure everyone who could be saved was. And she was going to do exactly that, whatever it took.

They were coming back with the First Spellship. She tapped the first *void* sigil and began casting her Fissure.

17

WRONG SIDE

F rit clutched her cloak tightly about her. She wasn't
supposed to be down here at the space port. Not
that Eros would care, unless he needed her to do
something. Even then, he wouldn't care where she was, only
that she wasn't where she was supposed to be.

That thought gave her the strength to keep going. Frit
ducked past a pair of men in flight suits, one of whom eyed
her appreciatively. She smiled back, just for a moment.
Then she clutched the cloak even tighter and hurried to the
little park Nebiat had told her about.

As promised, it was absolutely beautiful. Towering
redwoods stretched into the sky, swaying gently in the stiff
winds. Ravens called, chatting in the higher branches. A few
couples walked down the well worn paths, the orange
mulch staining their shoes.

Frit enjoyed the last few dozen meters, now that she was
certain she wasn't being followed. Being here helped crys-
talize her resolve, because it showed her one more thing she
wasn't allowed to have. One more thing any normal Shayan
—or even human—would take for granted.

Sitting on a park bench. That was denied her.

She stopped in front of a young redwood with a hollow at the base. Frit clutched the scale in her pocket, considering. If she did this, she crossed a line that could not be uncrossed. She could never go back to being the dutiful slave.

Worse, she'd no longer be fighting for the same side Nara was. She loved Nara. Nara had been the only student to treat her like a person instead of a thing. But that had only happened because Nara was ignorant of the social rules here.

Nara was on the wrong side. Nara supported the very people who had enslaved Frit and her people.

And it wasn't as if she were giving Nebiat any personal information about Nara. She'd left out everything about the Spellship, because there was too much chance Nebiat might intervene, and Nara could get hurt.

Telling Nebiat about which Caretakers Eros had met with, and what they'd talked about? Now *that* she had no problem passing along. If Nebiat could find something of use in their oppressive ramblings, she was welcome to it.

Frit stuck her hand into the tree, and dropped the scale. She felt a momentary surge of *void*, and there was a tiny whoosh as the scale was sucked through the Fissure Nebiat had installed here.

"I'm committed now," she whispered to herself. She was anxious, of course, but she was also glad. She's just committed a tiny act of defiance. It proved she wasn't powerless. Maybe, if Nebiat was right, the day would even come when she was free.

She, and all her sisters.

18

BATTLE STATIONS

There'd been a time when Voria couldn't think of a punishment worse than two weeks in the Umbral Depths. The endless, smothering darkness wore on the stoutest captain, eroding her will, and fraying her nerves.

But Voria had journeyed to the heart of the Umbral Depths. She'd fought there. Been changed there. This was, in some disturbing way, a kind of home for her now. And so when Voria tapped the final sigil to her Fissure, she felt none of the usual relief at exiting the depths.

Voria guided the *Hunter* through into normal space, turning to their guest. "Thank you for coming, Major Davidson. We'll take all the help we can get."

"I'm not sure how much help I'll be," Davidson said. He approached the defensive matrix, eyeing it like it was a strange animal. "What do you want me to do?"

"If we need you to cast a spell, I'll walk you through the process. For now, simply enter the matrix and stand ready." Voria braced herself, focusing all attention on the scry-screen as the Fissure closed behind them.

Very few ships came to Virkon, and most did not return. There was a real possibility they were about to find out why.

The world below was ordinary enough, a simple purple orb. There were no asteroids, and no visible defenders. They were over the night side of the world below, yet there were startlingly few lights below. No large cities, at least none she could see.

"Major, I'm not much of a scryer, but, uh, I don't think we're alone out here." Pickus pointed at the scry-screen. "Look at that patch on the bottom right. I'll zoom in."

The scry-screen showed a patch of apparently empty stars, backlit by the purple clouds of the distant Erkadi Rift, the home of the infamous Krox. Something slithered through the darkness, the light from the stars glinting off scales.

Voria hesitated for only an instant, but it proved her undoing. She wavered between sending a missive and launching an attack, and by that time the largest Wyrm she had ever encountered was hearing down on the ship.

"Brace yourselves!" she roared, stabbing a *void* sigil three times in rapid succession. The vessel hummed as it prepared to blink away, but the Wyrm's mouth clamped down around them with a tremendous crash.

Voria was thrown against the stabilizing ring, barely catching herself as the ship spun crazily. The scry-screen showed nothing but darkness now, broken only by a sea of fangs.

"Holy crap, did that thing just swallow us?" Pickus whispered. There was a quaver in his voice, but he was holding.

"No. The beast is holding us in its mouth." Voria realized aloud. She rose to her feet. The shaking had stopped.

"If it bites down, we're done," Davidson pointed out. "Is there anything we can do? Maybe launch the *Talon*?"

"Captain, this Wyrm is larger than Drakkon, and by a significant amount. I seriously doubt any of our spells will harm it." She considered his suggestion. "I will alert Aran, at the very least."

She tapped a *fire* sigil, then a *dream*. The missive fired, and Voria waited until the scry-screen shifted to show Lieutenant Aran's concerned face.

"Sir, this looks bad. What do you want us to do?"

"I want you to stand by," Voria instructed. "Have Nara ready to blink you outside. But don't do it unless our situation worsens." She paused, praying internally that she was right. "If I am correct, we're being brought to whatever authority runs the last dragonflight. This thing, as large as it is, is some sort of watcher. I believe it guards the Umbral Depths."

"And what leads you to that conclusion?" Davison asked. "Because I got none of that from the thing attacking us the moment we hit the system."

"If it wanted us dead, we'd be dead," Aran pointed out. "I think the major is right. If this thing bit down, whatever problem we pose would be solved. So it must be taking us somewhere. We'll stand by, Major. Any other orders?"

"No, just be ready to move and have your company suit up," Voria ordered.

Aran nodded, and the screen went dark.

She left it that way, rather than show their predicament. "Davidson, you're relieved. Please see what you can do to organize your men. I hope it doesn't come to a fight, but if it does, we should be ready."

"Beats this spinny-ring crap." Davidson ducked out of the matrix and hurried from the battle bridge. That left her alone with Pickus.

"Pickus, get the scry-screen up. Show a view of the

planet below us." Voria folded her arms, her mind in turmoil as the blue world sprang up on the monitor. They were descending into the shadowed part of the world, so it was difficult to see much.

They were descending to a point in a mountainous region, with massive peaks stabbing many kilometers into the air. Deep crevasses disappeared into shadowy darkness, hiding whatever might lay at the bottom. Hundreds of winged shapes flitted between the peaks, with many smaller winged shapes on the lower slopes.

Voria's mouth went dry. She'd seen perhaps fifty dragons in her day, maybe a hundred if she searched her memory. Below them were thousands—literally thousands—of dragons. All united, apparently, into one culture.

And they were being dropped right into the middle of it.

The titanic Wyrm carried them gently through the atmosphere, and though the hull groaned, it wasn't the tortured scream of metal buckling. All things considered, the Wyrm was being remarkably gentle.

It dropped lower, descending toward the largest mountain at the center of the range. The Wyrm winged toward the peak, which proved to be hollow. A volcano then. The beast landed near the middle, and set the *Hunter* down on a relatively flat lava field.

The stone cracked under their weight, but after one stomach-lurching moment they righted and the ship settled.

"Pickus, get me on with the entire ship," Voria ordered. She took several deep, slow breaths to compose herself.

Pickus tapped *fire*, then *dream*, then *fire* again. He glanced at her. "You're on, sir."

"Attention all personnel, this is Major Voria. We have arrived on Virkon, if not in the manner of our choosing." She paused then, considering what to tell them. What

should they do? Sally forth in a show of strength? Or ready
for the inevitable assault? "We cannot assume our captors
are hostile. Please, stay calm, but be ready to fight. If we are
threatened, then we will show them our teeth. Get to your
battle stations. Major Voria, out."

19

HOSTILE WELCOME

"Pickus, I want you to stay here near the command matrix," Voria instructed as she slipped through the stabilizing ring.

"Yes, sir." He gave an absent Ternus salute and slipped into her place.

Voria hurried from the room and made her way to the belly of the ship, down into the cargo hold where Davidson would be mobilizing. She still had no idea what to expect of these Wyrms, but she doubted a show of force would achieve anything.

She needed to make sure Davidson understood that, particularly given their overlapping authority. He could claim this was a ground op, in which case she'd have to cede authority. That could be catastrophic. If indecision and squabbling paralyzed them, the Wyrms would end them easily.

The cargo bay was a flurry of activity. Hovertank crews disappeared into hatches. Squads checked the action on their rifles, and some tucked extra magazines into pockets.

Davidson stood on top of his tank at one end of the room, barking orders to a lieutenant Voria didn't recognize.

"What's up, Major?" he called as she neared.

"I wanted to see about a plan," she said, sketching an *air* sigil. She rose up to land lightly next to the captain, Ikadra clutched in one hand. The magic use was over the top, but these marines needed to respect her, and that began with them understanding what she was and what she could do.

"What do you have in mind?" Davidson asked. He wore his skepticism openly.

"We send out one tank, yours. I stand on top of it." Voria left it at that. She could explain her reasoning, but it would be better if Davidson arrived at the same conclusion on his own.

Davidson eyed her curiously. He stroked his beard, studying her for long moments. "I'm just going to come right out and ask. Are you doing this to atone for Marid? Sparing the marines at the expense of the officers? Because, while that's laudable, it's also bag-of-rocks stupid."

"Don't worry, Captain. I'm as cold-blooded as ever, I assure you." Voria raised an eyebrow. "I'm not foolish enough to sacrifice us both just to preserve the rest of your command. That would leave the survivors leaderless, and at the mercy of the Wyrms here. I'm doing it because I believe any show of force will be met with much greater force. We need to be humble, Captain."

"That I can agree with. Are you going to alert Lieutenant Aran? I feel like bringing him and his company wouldn't be a bad idea," Davidson suggested. "That's still not much force, so they aren't likely to get their scales all ruffled. And if we need to get out in a hurry, Aran is the only way that's going to happen."

"True, and given his past here it might be a good conversation starter." Voria looked at the *Talon*, considering. If she brought Aran, that meant revealing she'd brought him, whatever the consequences.

Besides, if he was here and they got into trouble, he might be able to get them out. If not, he could still escort Nara in their quest to find the Spellship—though she strongly suspected they'd need Ikadra. She wondered if she should leave the staff behind. Their enemies hadn't learned of it yet, as far as she knew.

But leaving it behind carried its own dangers, particularly in light of the fact that someone could so effortlessly sneak aboard the *Talon*.

"Sir?" Davidson asked.

"We'll bring him." She sketched a *fire* sigil, then a *dream*. The swirling missive shot into the *Hunter*, disappearing from sight. "I doubt it will take them long to get ready."

A translucent blue ramp descended from the vessel, and Aran burst out in his disquieting new armor. The way it reflected the light made it hard to look at, which might be an advantage in combat.

Voria remembered Ikadra's warning, but she wasn't one for feelings and hunches. She'd monitor the armor, and study it carefully. If there was anything they needed to be aware of, she was confident they'd find it. And, to be frank, they needed the firepower. Aran was much more effective, both as a soldier and as a commander, if he had access to spellarmor. She certainly couldn't have afforded to purchase him a set.

The rest of his company followed—Nara next, of course, then Crewes, followed by Kez and Bord. They moved as one, each taking their cues from Aran as they prowled toward her.

"What's the situation, sir?" Aran's voice boomed from the armor. He landed on the tank a meter away.

"Have your squad fly honor guard for Davidson's tank. We're going to meet our...hosts," Voria explained. Davidson had already disappeared into the tank, and she gave a relieved sigh when the engine rumbled to life.

Not because she was eager for what was about to happen, but rather because it was finally happening. She considered tapping into her extra senses. Examining the timeline could prove useful, but it would also leave her disoriented for some time. If they were bringing her to anyone of authority she wanted a clear head when dealing with them.

The blast doors rose, giving them their first look at the new world. A sharp wind howled through the gap, chilling the room instantly. Voria's teeth began to chatter, and she briefly wished she had a set of her own environmentally controlled spellarmor.

The tank lurched into motion and rolled through the doors. It hummed over snow and rock, up a small rise that afforded a good look at the crater around them. It was far smaller than the one on Marid, and much less hospitable. The entire field was coated in dull grey, lifeless rock. An ancient lava field trampled by the elements for centuries.

They'd only made a few hundred meters when a shadow passed over them. Voria shaded her eyes, tracking the Wyrm's flight. It was large, but nowhere near the size of the Wyrm that had plucked them from orbit.

The sun prevented her from seeing the color, but she had the impression of white scales as the creature winged by overhead. It entered a steep dive, and she tensed as it fell toward them. Aran and his company fanned out around them, preparing for combat.

Stone surged up into the air in a huge wave as the Wyrm crashed into the earth no more than thirty meters away. It bellowed a challenge, its nostrils flaring as lightning crackled about its eyes.

"I am Sentry Daygon. Who are you and why have you come to Virkon?" The creature's voice rattled Voria's teeth, though after hearing Neith she was considerably less impressed than she otherwise would have been.

"My name is Major Voria, of the Shayan Confederacy. I've been dispatched to meet with the Council of Wyrms, on behalf of my people." Voria paused for a moment as the Wyrm's long neck stretched closer. She was very cognizant of the rows of teeth a mere three meters away. "We're hoping for an alliance, or at the least an exchange of information."

The creature studied her as if trying to puzzle out whether or not she were serious. The Wyrm's head shot up, and it began to laugh. "Very well, mortal. Bring your little honor guard and follow us in your earthbound vehicle. I will conduct you to the council. But take care with your tongue. They are not a patient lot."

20

AUDIENCE

The trek across the lava field drove home how insignificant they were. Wyrms dove and wheeled through the sky, banking suddenly to avoid colliding. An entire cloud followed their tank, shadowing their agonizing progress across the crater floor.

The Wyrm who'd offered to guide them glided a little ways ahead, stopping occasionally to preen as he waited for them to catch up. His scales glistened in the sun—now silver, now white. Otherwise, he looked much the same as Khalahk, with impressive horns jutting from his head. Voria couldn't begin to guess his age. Three centuries? Four? Definitely less than a millennia.

"Why do I feel like we're walking toward our own execution?" Aran muttered over the comm.

Voria jerked, startled by the sudden disruption to the tense silence. "You are not alone in that feeling, Lieutenant. There are more Wyrms here than we faced on Marid, by a hundredfold."

Crewes barked out a harsh laugh. "Notice none of them scaly bastards has gotten too close, though, 'cept for that guide." He feathered his booster, and his armor rocketed to the head of their little caravan. "They might be able to kill us, but I'm betting word got back about Khalahk."

"I'm not sure that's a good thing, Sergeant," Voria countered. She shaded her eyes. They were approaching a cliff face with a wide slash down the middle. That slash disappeared into darkness, though she could see light filtering down inside, probably from some sort of open roof.

They crossed the last few hundred meters in silence and followed their guide inside the cavern. The walls sloped up high above them, disappearing into the shadows. The center of the ceiling had been carved away, allowing light from above. It would also allow a dragon to fly out, if they chose.

Something massive moved in one of the shadowed alcoves above, and several fist-sized rocks tumbled down to spill across the path. Davidson paused the tank and only moved on when the debris had stopped raining down.

More shapes moved above, each keeping to the shadows. Their eyes blazed, so very much like Khalahk's had been, lurking in the darkness when they'd left Shaya aboard the *Big Texas*.

Hostility radiated down from above like heat from a star, the full fury of creatures more ancient than the oldest living Shayan. They didn't want her here, or any lowly bipedal race. That was clear without a word being uttered. Voria was meddling, and these Wyrms did not like meddlers.

One of the Wyrms, a long-necked female, crawled into a shaft of light. She stared imperiously down at Voria. "I am Wyrm Mother Olyssa, and, at present, I stand first among the flights. You address the Council of Wyrms, little Shayan. Tell us, why have you come to our world?"

Voria sketched an *earth* sigil, then a *spirit*. The amplification spell swirled around her for a moment, then disappeared. It would raise the volume of her voice, but not enough to be a challenge to the Wyrms.

"I've been dispatched by the Shayan Confederacy, to bring you troubling news." Voria kept it simple. "The Krox are stirring in the Erkadi Rift, and have begun invading our space. We believe this war will quickly spill across the entire sector, and once the Krox have dealt with us they will turn their attention toward you."

Deep, booming laughter came from several of the alcoves, though not from Olyssa. Her scaly face tightened, and her eyes flashed.

Another Wyrm moved, this one smaller than Olyssa. Her eyes were dull and rheumy, and her scales had faded to a soft ash-white. "Yes, I thought that might be your argument. The Krox representative arrived some time ago, and made very similar arguments about you. They claim you will come for us, if not stopped. The difference is that you've killed one of our oldest Wyrm Fathers, whereas the Krox have done nothing to harm us. Why should we listen to you, morsel?"

Wings rustled in several other alcoves, and Olyssa dipped her head deferentially to the wizened Wyrm. Voria considered her answer with great deliberation. How did one admit to murdering a powerful member of this society, without having them perceive you as an enemy?

"If you're referring to the death of Khalahk, then what you've heard is true," Voria admitted. There was no sense denying the truth. They could ferret it out magically, if that was even necessary. They could see it on her face. "We were attacked, and we defended ourselves. Not once, but twice. In the end we had no choice but to kill Khalahk. Would any of you have done differently if assaulted by a Wyrm of Khalahk's strength? Would you have gone willingly to your death, or would you have fought back for your own survival, as we did? His death was a regrettable tragedy, but Khalahk left me little choice."

There was more rustling, then whispers in a language Voria didn't recognize. The Wyrms hissed back and forth to each other, the matron arguing with Olyssa. A massive male slithered to the edge of his alcove, glaring down at Voria.

"I am Aetherius, and Khalahk was my mate," he boomed. "He was the Wyrm Father of our flight. You come here after murdering him, and you seek our aid? Are you mad, little humans? I understand that your tree goddess is flighty, but have you so little connection to reality? You may have been defending yourselves, but if you think I will thank you for killing my mate, you are sadly mistaken."

"Why would Khalahk have attacked you?" Olyssa demanded. Aetherius's head snapped up and he glared hard at the Wyrm Mother. She met his gaze evenly, her tail swishing behind her in what Voria guessed might be a challenge.

Aetherius flicked a forked tongue across his teeth, but said nothing.

"I don't know," Voria said, and it was the simple truth. She'd guessed it might be connected to Aran, but sensed that bringing it up would be a monumentally bad idea.

"Because," Aetherius roared, "the vessel carried a dragonslayer. We already know this. The Krox have presented their evidence, and we have found it sufficient. Khalahk sought to kill Aranthar for the death of Rolf, and instead an Outrider turned upon his master and slew him."

Voria wished, however briefly, that she'd never left Shaya. She didn't really understand what significance Outriders played in Virkonnian society, but she guessed they were a bit like tech mages on Shaya. Useful servants perhaps, but that wasn't quite right. She suspected these Wyrms saw their Outriders as pets, and that changed the equation.

You fired a servant who disappointed you. But if a dog turned on its master, you put the dog down.

"Is it true your vessel carries an Outrider?" Olyssa asked.

Voria had the sense Olyssa knew the answer, and the answers to all her questions.

"It did," Voria admitted. "We brought Lieutenant Aran, the Outrider Aranthar, home. We were unaware he was being considered for murder, as, again, we were merely defending ourselves from assault." She didn't mention that Aran was hovering a few meters away. A bead of sweat dampened her cheek.

"He is here?" Aetherius roared. His wings flapped, sweeping stones and debris down upon them. Voria sketched an *air* sigil, and a translucent umbrella appeared over the tank. Rocks the size of fists rebounded off with enough force to have crushed a human skull. Without magical aid, any one of them could have been killed.

"Lieutenant, perhaps you should remove your helmet," Voria suggested once the barrage of stone had subsided. She didn't know what else to do. Instinctively, she reached for the *seeing* Neith had given her.

Possibilities stretched out before her. Aetherius swooping down and swallowing Aran. Aran killing Aetherius, then dying to the rest of the Wyrms. There. A possibility flitted by, different from the rest. She pursued it.

A woman she didn't recognize detached from the shadows at the base of one rough cliff faces, and addressed the Wyrms. Olyssa listened to this woman, and Aran lived.

Voria came back to reality with a sharp shake of her

head. Aran was just now removing his helmet. Thankfully, only a few moments had passed.

"No," Olyssa howled. She retreated into the shadows, her voice feral, and weak. "I refused to believe it. But I cannot deny it with my own eyes. One of ours, a dragonslayer."

"He is from your flight, Olyssa," Aetherius roared. "What is his fate?"

Voria spun around, looking to the shadows from the timeline. Sure enough, someone moved there. A master of stealth, but one who was too interested in the proceedings to conceal herself fully.

Who was she? And what could Voria do to get her to intervene?

"Aran," she whispered into the comm. "Stall. Tell them a story. Keep them busy."

Aran shot her a murderous look. "Stall? Some days I really hate this job."

He flew into the air and drew the attention of every Wyrm in the room. Voria took the opportunity to study the woman in the corner.

She wore shimmering cloth that covered her completely. Voria sketched a *parse aura* spell and was unsurprised to see the heavy enchantment interwoven through the cloth. It flowed and pulsed...like a living thing. Her armor was alive.

It also matched the description Aran had given of the person who'd tried to assassinate him in his quarters. If she wanted him dead, why did the possibility exist that she would intercede on his behalf? That meant there must be a great deal of internal conflict.

You didn't have an internal conflict like that for a mark, so she hadn't been paid to kill him. Which meant she was killing him for another reason.

Virkon was supposed to be all about honor. Had that been it? Had she been honor bound to kill him?

Perhaps she was a superior. Or a mentor. Or a family member. Whatever the relationship, part of her didn't want to see Aran die.

Voria took a deep breath. She sketched one more spell, since everyone was focused on Aran—a simple missive, with a single sentence.

If you do nothing, he will die.

Aran's mouth dried like he'd just inhaled a fire bolt. He stared up at the Wyrms above, both awed and terrified to be the focus of their attention. He had no idea what they wanted to hear, but when all you had was the truth, that was what you led with.

"I am an Outrider, I think. Several months ago I was mind-wiped, and I can't remember anything before that moment." He guided his new armor a little higher, his dark helmet tucked under one arm.

Several of the Wyrms shifted restlessly. He halted his rise. Maybe that was taboo. He was only a lowly human, after all.

The Wyrm they'd called Olyssa prowled back over to the mouth of her alcove. She stared coldly down at Aran, and he read murder in those slitted eyes. "Do you think not remembering a crime absolves you of it?"

Aran's hand flexed, reaching instinctively for his spellblade. That was understandable. He felt more in control with a spellblade in his hand, and he desperately needed to feel in control right now. Because he knew he wasn't.

"No, I suppose it doesn't," he admitted. "But if you're going to try me for a crime, will you at least tell me what it is?"

"Try?" Olyssa asked. She cocked her head, her neck bringing it closer.

"He's talking about a March of Honor," a clear, feminine voice echoed through the cavern. "On Shaya, the world he's been hiding on, they talk about crimes. Sometimes, they punish them. But they do not force their people to fight for their convictions, or to defend themselves from the consequences of their actions."

Aran's eyes widened when she stepped into the light. It was the woman from his quarters, still wearing the same flowing uniform. He couldn't see anything, only her eyes. She wore her spellblade belted at her side, and walked as if it were an extension of her. He hadn't developed that, he realized, because he always stored his blade in a void pocket.

The woman walked slowly forward, and dropped to one knee at the very center of the caravan. "Wyrm Fathers. Wyrm Mothers. I ask your leniency. Your Outrider left this world. Only a shell has returned. A shell that does not remember its own actions. If it is to be judged, then let Virkonna judge him."

"So you believe that your brother should be given the honors of an Outrider, even after murdering Khalahk? We may very well see war between the flights, and that's a direct result of Aranthar's actions." Olyssa leapt from her perch, swooping toward the ground. She slammed into it with a crash, sending up a spray of stone and grit that knocked the woman in the suit back a step.

The woman coughed once, then pulled off her mask. Dark, shoulder-length hair spilled out, framing a face not so different from Aran's. She was pretty, in a severe way. Her eyes bored into him, in open challenge. He stared right back, meeting that challenge with the same ferocity he had when she'd attacked him on the *Talon*.

The woman waved a hand to clear the last of the debris floating through the air. "That is precisely what I am saying. My brother served the dragonflight loyally for his entire life. He never had a black mark, until Rolf was killed. And, from the report he himself sent, we know Aran was dealing with forces he couldn't possibly overcome. He was the junior Outrider, not the senior. How can you hold him to account for that?"

Olyssa reared up, her wings extending high above her. "It is only your past service that prevents me from ending you, human. We are not here to debate what happened with Rolf. We are here to talk about Khalahk."

"Khalahk attacked Aran." The woman walked boldly toward Olyssa's towering leg. "Aran defended himself. He did so in ignorance, with no knowledge of his people. He can't know what a crime he has committed. If you devour him here, he dies confused, and that is not justice. He is a victim in all this."

"So what do you advocate?" Aetherius boomed from above. Other Wyrms called similar questions.

"Let Virkonna judge him." She slowly raised her arm and pointed at Aran. "Let the Wyrm Mother decide. Aran makes the March of Honor. The odds of his survival are almost none. Those of you with a vested interest in his death still get it, but he gets to die fighting."

Olyssa kicked off with a mighty flap of her wings, and the rush of air knocked Aran's armor several meters back. She soared up to her perch, and landed agilely. The Wyrm clung to the rock, peering down at Aran and the woman they'd called his sister.

"What say you, Olyssa?" Aetherius rumbled. "He comes from your flight." He gave a vicious grin. "We could dismember him here. Fastest dragon gets the morsel."

"No," she snapped. "My anger and grief are overpowering, but this woman's words hold a bit of Mother's wisdom. We should let her decide. I call it to a vote. Who will allow this Outrider to take the March of Honor?"

"What if he survives?" the wizened Wyrm called. She crawled into a shaft of light, which glinted off her dull eyes. "If we allow a dragonslayer to live, then we invite a hundred hundred fools to follow this one. They'll be rising up all over the planet, calling for Virkonna knows what."

"She speaks true," Aetherius pointed out. "We cannot allow him to live. End it now, Olyssa, before this grows into a problem that must be solved with much greater violence."

Aran was grateful for the brief moment where he wasn't the subject of their attention, and the more time he had to think, the better. Anything he said would only make it worse, so he said nothing.

"A vote has been called," another Wyrm called. "The subject must be settled."

"I will trust you, Olyssa," Aetherius said. "But if this human comes back to bite my tail this will be the last time you have that trust. You had better be right. I vote to allow the Outrider to take the March of Honor." He whirled, then disappeared deeper into his alcove.

The other dragons murmured their answers, one after another. Aran wasn't sure how their voting worked, but when it was over, each Wyrm flapped into the air and soared out of the top of the cavern.

Once all had disappeared, Aran was left hovering there,

alone save for the Company and the woman who'd spoken on his behalf.

He floated down to stand next to her. "I guess we haven't been properly introduced. I'm Aran." He extended a hand.

She looked at it, and rolled her eyes. "Come on. We have work to do, little brother."

"Wait, I don't even know your name," he protested.

"Astria. Now keep up, or we're both dead." She turned and trotted deeper into the cavern.

22

MARCH OF HONOR

A ran replaced his helmet, feeling the tiniest surge of relief as it hissed shut and his HUD lit. The armor wasn't noticeably different from the Mark XI in terms of comfort, but it wasn't the comfort that made him feel safe.

There was just something about having a suit of enhanced spellarmor between you and your problems. That was especially useful when your problems had a two-hundred-plus-meter wingspan.

"Major, I'm going to follow my sister." Aran hovered above Davidson's tank. He kept one eye on Astria's retreating form. "Whatever this March of Honor is, it sounds like it can serve as the perfect distraction for you to locate the Spellship."

"Aran, that's suicide," Nara protested. She zipped up beside him in her Mark V. His armor reflected back at him from her mirrored faceplate. "It sounds like they're going to hunt you like an animal. Did you hear the way those Wyrms were talking? We're not even pets to them. We're cattle."

"It isn't suicide," Voria countered. Her eyes had gone unfocused again. "There is a chance he will die, of course. I see many possibilities where Aran does not survive. But I see a strong possibility that he does. And he is right. We will never have a better opportunity. Lieutenant, go with your sister and participate in this March of Honor. Check in each evening by missive."

"Major, she tried to kill him." Nara stabbed an accusing hand at Astria's retreating form. "We can find another distraction."

"No, we can't," Aran said. "Not quickly enough, and you know it. You know it better than any of us."

Nara's armored shoulders slumped. "We should at least send someone with him."

"Hey, Davidson," Crewes barked. He jumped thirty meters, and landed right outside the tank. "How much you charge for babysitting?"

"For you? A case of brew and we'll call it square." Davidson's words were followed by an amused laugh.

"Sir, how about I tag along with the LT? It's not that I don't trust that lady, but I don't trust that lady." Crewes fired his thruster, and rose to join Aran.

"Glad to have you along, Sergeant." Aran spun to face Astria. She'd reached the far side of the cavern, and stood at the very edge of the shadows. That suit of hers made her nearly impossible to see, and that was before she activated it.

A missive request came from Nara. He accepted it, and her face appeared in the lower corner of his HUD. "Hey, I know you like to play hero, but be careful, okay? It feels like this whole world wants you dead."

He gave her a wry smile. "That's not too different from Shaya."

"It is. Ree doesn't want you dead. She wants you miserable," Nara quipped.

They both laughed at that. Aran smiled as a swell of affection rose up. "I'll be careful, I promise. You do the same. It's not like you're going to be hanging out on the ship. Finding the Spellship will take work, and you know the gods will have made finding it lethal. So I'll turn it back on you. Be careful, Nara."

Her cheeks dimpled as her smile widened. "See you on the other side." Her missive window disappeared.

Aran triggered a Company-wide channel. "All right kids, you behave for the nice captain. Davidson, have them in bed by nine."

"This is bullshit," Bord protested. He hopped down off the tank, his silvered armor sending up a puff of dust as he landed. "We're always getting left behind while you and the sarge are off doing cool stuff."

"So staying with me is a burden? Is that what I'm hearing?" Kez demanded frostily. She gave a small sniff, and her armor turned away from Bord.

"You know it isn't like that, Kez..." Bord trailed off. He looked up at Aran. "Fine, go on then. I'd rather stay here, anyway."

Aran delivered a salute, and the Company mimicked it instantly. Then he turned and flew after Astria. The sergeant fell in beside him, but unlike the others, he stayed silent. Crewes understood, and that meant a lot.

He landed a few meters from Astria, who stood just inside the mouth of a narrow tunnel. Far too narrow for any of the Wyrms, though enforcers could probably squeeze through. She turned without a word and trotted up the tunnel.

Aran glided behind her, with Crewes hanging back a

good ten meters. They continued down several twisting tunnels, and each time Astria took the left branch.

"You rely too much on that armor," Astria said abruptly. The sudden comment caught Aran off guard.

"Yeah, I don't know anyone who relies on a magical suit." Aran had dialed the sarcasm up to eleven, but Astria didn't react.

The tunnel finally ended, spilling them into a valley sheltered on three sides by ridges of the massive volcano. Squat adobe houses lined a packed-earth road. Most of the traffic on the road was pedestrians, but here and there a cart was pulled by...a dragon?

"You use dragons as beasts of burden?" Aran asked. How did that square with worshiping the Council of Wyrms?

"Those aren't dragons, idiot." Astria removed her mask and eyed him like he'd just said the stupidest thing she'd ever heard. "Drakes are *animals*. They're the lowest form. They come directly from the primals that find their way to our world. Most are feral, and extremely dangerous. Some are taken young, at an age when they can be trained. And yes, they are used as beasts of burden."

Aran noticed more than the drakes pulling carts. Smaller drakes, some no larger than a house cat, sunned themselves on thatched roofs. The entire village was straight out of a *Relic Hunter* episode. It was like looking at world lost centuries in the past. None of the modern amenities Ternus had introduced were used here, at least not that Aran could see.

"This way." Astria threaded a confident path through the traffic, which led them past one of the drakes.

The stench burned Aran's eyes, and he blinked rapidly as he quickened his step. The crowd parted before Astria, and almost everyone murmured something and pressed two fingers to their forehead when she passed. Most eyed him curiously, but looked away quickly if his helmet faced their direction. What must he look like to these people?

High above, a Wyrm screeched, and the crowd collectively flinched. Most relaxed immediately, continuing with their business as if nothing had happened. But that moment had been telling. He read the fear there, and understood it.

"This is my home." Astria led him to a simple adobe building. She pushed open a thick curtain of dark leather and ducked inside.

Aran followed and sketched the *void* sigil inside his gauntlet. He chose storage mode, and the armor began flowing down his body. It was still disorienting, but he knew what to expect now. He counted slowly down, noting that it took four seconds. If donning the armor took the same amount of time, that would be useful to know in a combat situation.

"You can simply hide your armor?" Astria asked. She folded her mask carefully, and set it on a beautifully carved marble bench. She sat on the bench next to the mask.

Aran looked around the room, but other than a narrow cot there was nowhere else to sit. He put his back to the wall and slid into a sitting position. "The armor is new, but yes, I can hide it."

"That is a small, but very important detail. Tomorrow, when you begin the march, you will only be allowed to take what you can carry. Since you can carry the armor, you can take it." Astria rose and stretched. She moved to a small cupboard, also carved from marble. "I am going to make dinner. Nothing fancy, mind. Not like the decadence of Shaya."

Aran laughed at that. "Most of my meals are MREs the Confederacy made twenty years ago. That's what I've got packed now. You could boil rocks, and I bet it would taste better. So, can you tell me about this March of Honor? What is it exactly?" He folded his legs and rocked back and forth until he was comfortable.

Astria removed a small knife and a pile of green tubers and began expertly slicing them. "The March of Honor, sometimes called the march of atonement, is reserved for an Outrider who wishes to be punished for a crime."

"Hey, you guys in there?" Crewes called from outside the curtain.

"Inside, Sergeant," Aran called back. He turned to Astria. "I hope it's okay that one of my men came?"

"It is not." Astria's chopping stopped. She set the knife down, and fixed Aran with a glare. "I will remind you that you know nothing of our world. Nothing of our customs. If you wish to survive the next few days, then you cannot make arbitrary decisions. You must listen to me."

"So, uh, can I stay?" Crewes asked as he poked his head through the doorway. "Cause I ain't had dinner, and it looks like you're about to."

"You may stay, but you must make your armor disappear." Astria's chopping continued.

"Uh, only his armor does that. I can take it off, I guess."

"There's no point. If you leave it in here it will only take up more space, and if you put it outside the scavengers will make off with it long before dawn." Astria scooped the tubers into a bowl then sprinkled orange dust on top of them. She took a handful, then passed the bowl to Crewes. "Sit, and don't break anything."

"I'll be careful, ma'am." Crewes slowly lowered himself to the ground. His armor took up almost a third of the room, and he gave a sheepish smile. "Thank you." He took a

couple generous handfuls of tubers, then passed the bowl
to Aran.

"You were telling me what this march was," Aran
prompted. He took a handful and tried an experimental
bite. The tuber tasted almost exactly like a potato, and the
orange stuff reminded him a lot of garlic.

"It's very simple, really," Astria explained as she
munched on the end of a tuber. "You must reach the Temple
of Virkonna, the same temple where you and I gained our
magic. Your enemies, anyone who feels you have wronged
them, will attempt to kill you before you can reach it."

"What kind of force can they bring to bear?" Aran asked.

"Anything they want, but honor dictates they only send
enough to finish the job. More is seen as distasteful, and
lessens the honor for those who participate." She chewed
thoughtfully for a moment before continuing. "Most of the
time, they'll send just enough to kill you. Since they don't
know you, some will underestimate you, and some will over-
estimate you."

"Can I go with him?" Crewes asked.

"No. You can stay until he departs, but even I cannot go
with him. He must do this alone," she explained.

Aran munched thoughtfully. At least he knew what he
was dealing with. People trying to kill him was just another
normal day.

23

ISMENE & PYTHO

Nara pulled the strange cloak more tightly about her. On a good day, she felt naked without her spellarmor, but the weird, flowing dress made her feel worse than naked. She kept tripping over it if she walked any faster than a glacially slow amble.

It irked her that the major had sent her to do this, knowing it meant Nara would be the one who had to wear the dress. Mostly, though, Nara was worried about Aran. That sapped a lot of the anger. What right did she have to complain about minor discomfort when Aran was doing some sort of march designed to kill him?

She threaded through the crowd as she tried to find the most expedient way to the Temple of Virkonna. The building wasn't hard to spot. It was the only building carved entirely of stone, a beautiful elder sister surrounded by ugly younger siblings.

A trickle of traffic flowed through a wide gateway. Each potential entrant was screened by a pair of war mages in white. Both uniforms had blue trim, but the patches on their arms were slightly different. She didn't know enough about local politics to know how or why, but committed both symbols to memory so she could investigate them later.

Nara slowed her pace and aimed for dignified as she approached. She landed somewhere closer to a stumble and her cheeks heated as she approached the war mages. Damned dress.

"Name and reason for entering the Temple?" the war mage on the right asked. He was tall, though not quite as tall as Aran.

"Nara from the Temple of Enlightenment on Shaya," she explained simply. She dropped her eyes to the gravel path. "I'm here to learn. I'd like to ask the Archivist some questions, if that's allowed."

She glanced up to see what sort of reaction she was getting. The guard eyed her thoughtfully. He ran a hand along his bald scalp, and gave his partner a shrug. "I don't think it's breaking any rules. You can go inside. But I can't promise anyone will speak to you, least of all Archivist Jocasta."

"Thank you." She tried another curtsy—badly—and hurried up the path toward the building. She only tripped twice on the way.

She passed under an arched doorway into a room dominated by rows of marble columns. They held up a massive stone ceiling, and she was nervously aware that, if it crashed down, all the books lining this room would be crushed instantly.

Nara scanned those shelves, noting she saw only scroll cases or actual books. There was not a single dragon scale anywhere. Books were fine, but one of those shelves was also far, far less efficient than a single knowledge scale. Perhaps the Wyrms didn't allow them.

A pleasant-looking girl just out of her teens approached. She wore a dress similar to Nara's, though hers was the same white with blue trim they all seemed to love so much on this world. The girl would have very much fit with the other students back at the Temple of Enlightenment.

"Drake-tide, stranger," she said as she bobbed a quick curtsy. "I am sub-archivist Ismene. Is for short, or Meanie if I just pulled a prank on you." She gave a brilliant smile, and brushed a lock of thick, blond hair over one shoulder. Bord would have been salivating.

"My name is Nara. I'm from Shaya." It wasn't strictly true. She wasn't from Shaya. But explaining the whole story was more trouble than it was worth.

"Shaya?" Ismene blinked. "That's wonderful! You've come so far, across nearly the whole sector. Did you meet Cerberus? He's the guardian of the depths."

"Oh, yeah, we met him." Nara raised a hand and mimed the dragon engulfing their ship. She considered using an illusion, but wasn't sure if using magic publicly were a good idea. "He carried us down and just sort of dropped us off."

"We? There are more of you?" Ismene blinked her large eyes.

"A whole ship of us," Nara admitted. She'd briefly considered lying, but it was too easy to verify the truth. "We're parked on the ridge northwest of here, on the edge of the crater."

"And they sent you to us?" Ismene cocked her head. "Why? What are you looking for?"

"Ismene," a voice cracked from across the room. Ismene's posture snapped erect, and she spun to face the woman who'd spoken. The approaching woman had silvering hair pulled back into a severe bun, and age had added a sour set of lines to her face. "What are you doing, child? You are meant to help people find things, not interrogate them."

She strode across the room at a fast walk, apparently untroubled by the miserably stupid dress. The woman stopped next to the pair of them, and took in Nara with the kind of glance Nara was used to getting from Eros. It said everything the woman didn't.

"What does this urchin require of us?" she demanded.

Nara extended her right hand and summoned her staff from her void pocket. She tapped it lightly on the marble, rising to her full height. "I don't *require* anything. I came because I'm told you have access to knowledge from the age of dragons. I had some specific questions I was looking to have answered, and the archivists on Shaya seemed to believe you might help."

Jocasta raised an eyebrow at the staff. She eyed it distastefully. "Ah, a Shayan. That explains a great deal. I'll be certain to lower my expectations. Ask your trivial questions, and I will see if we can find a tome with small enough words. If you're certain you don't want to go find a tree you can sob on. That's how you pray to your dead goddess, is it not?"

Nara was shocked by the outright hostility. The Shayans were all about subtle jabs. They made it clear they were superior, and they did it in a hundred different ways—not one of them overt, or ever coming right out and saying it. Any proper Shayan scholar would be horrified by Jocasta's behavior.

Nara, on the other hand, didn't care. *Oh, hey look, another group of uppity scholars. What a shock.*

"Yes please, small words with large print. Lots of pictures, if possible." Nara affected her best imitation of Shayan arrogance. She even tried on a little accent. "I'd like to know about the original flights. There were eight, yes?"

"Of course," Jocasta allowed. She folded her arms.

Ismene looked like she wanted to slink away, but hadn't yet found the right opportunity. Having been on the receiving end of Eros's temper more than once, Nara completely understood the desire.

"Unfortunately, most of the books on Shaya are nearly all pictures. We struggle with words, as you know." Nara kept her tone completely serious. It wasn't easy, but it was rather fun. "I can't seem to find a picture, or a real name, for the Wyrm Father of *Life*. All the rest are accounted for, but not that one. Can you tell me more about him, or provide a book that can?"

"I'm unsurprised you know so little about the dragon-flights. Your own goddess was merely a servant of a Wyrm Mother, after all," Jocasta said, her tone all innocence. "Oh, I'm sorry, did you not know your goddess was the divine equivalent of a nurse?"

Nara laughed at that. She couldn't help it. Where was this woman the last time Eros had droned on about his "lady"? He'd become obsessed with the tree since he'd been named Tender. She'd love to see Jocasta take him down a peg or three.

"I didn't," Nara said. "If you have a book on Nurse Shaya, I'd be happy to read that, too, but can we start with one about the Wyrm Father or Wyrm Mother of *Life*?" She kept her tone sweet, and it wasn't all that hard.

If Jocasta was being rude because she disliked Shayans, she wasn't losing any points with Nara for it.

"Ismene, help this poor ruffian find what she needs. I have more important work to tend to." Jocasta gave an exasperated sigh and glided off with that fast little walk she did.

"That was amazing," Ismene whispered. She eyed Jocasta out of the corner of her eye. "You wielded sarcasm like a spellblade, and I don't think she knew what to do about it. Sorry about her. She can be a little, uh, abrasive. Especially toward Shayans. I don't know why she hates you so much, but you were really good-natured about it. Thank you for that. I didn't want to have to throw you out, and she'd have made me do it."

A winged form drifted down from the ceiling like a falling leaf. Nara took a large step backward and her hand shot up instinctively to cast a defensive spell. She hesitated. The drake couldn't have been larger than a meter from tail to snout. It landed gently on Ismene's shoulder and nuzzled her with its scaled snout.

"Nara, meet Pytho," she scratched behind the drake's ears, and it pressed its head into her hand. "He's afraid of mother, too."

"I can't blame him." Nara forced herself to relax, a little at least. It was hard not seeing every dragon—and anything that resembled one—as a threat. "So can you really help me find the books I need?"

"Of course. I've already picked out the first one. Mother could have done that immediately. Follow me, and we'll get you some answers." She gave Nara a warm smile, and hurried off between rows of shelves.

Nara hurried after. At least she had a starting point.

24

FIRST STEP

A ran slept fitfully that night, despite how comfortable his armor was. He dreamed of being chased, and of darker, more nameless things. He finally rose a little before dawn and started cleaning his gear.

The sergeant snored softly in one corner, while Astria lay unmoving on her tiny cot. She rolled over suddenly, and the whole cot creaked. "You move quietly, at least. That will help you out there." Astria rose, stretched, and headed to the chopping counter. She withdrew another bunch of tubers and began slicing.

"Can you give me any other advice? It would be helpful to know the terrain, and the local fauna. Are drakes the only thing to watch out for?" Aran asked quietly. Might as well let the sergeant sleep as long as possible.

"Primarily drakes, in the beginning," Astria said. "They are the dominant predator in this area, and the larger ones are quite dangerous. They're also highly aggressive, and if you start fighting one, others will come to investigate. But drakes are also lazy. If one attacks you, flee. Make it chase you. But stay low. Drakes can't resist aerial targets, and if they see you flying you're done for."

Aran considered all that. "So hug the ground, and if a drake comes after me lose them as quickly as possible. Will using spells draw their attention?"

"Only if the spell is particularly flashy." Astria scooped the tubers into the bowl and passed it to Aran. He accepted it gratefully.

"When do you think my 'enemies' will attack?" Aran asked. "Who are they, even?" That last part was the most troubling, because it was difficult to prepare for an attack by unknown assailants.

"Most will come from Aetherius's flight. They are the most vocal critics of our flight, and of our Wyrm Mother, Olyssa."

Aran passed the bowl back to Astria and began munching a tuber. He chewed as he considered how to attack the problem. "It sounds like Wyrms are unlikely to intervene directly, because they consider Outriders beneath them."

"We are beneath them," Astria corrected. "But yes, they are unlikely to intercede directly."

"So they'll send other Outriders, and what else? Enforcers?" Aran asked.

"Enforcer?" She asked, cocking her head.

"The bipedal draconic guys that the Krox use. They usually carry spellrifles. Most are war mages, but I've run into a true mage." Aran wished he had illusion magic. Nara could show Astria exactly what he meant, without sounding nearly as lame.

"Ahh...you mean hatchlings." Astria shook her head in amusement. "I forget how little you know now. Yes, there's a chance they could send a hatchling. That's rare, since the hatchling will get little honor from killing a mere Outrider. In your case, because of Khalahk, some hatchlings may take this personally enough to intercede."

Aran finished the last of the tubers and licked his fingers clean. He dried them on his armor. "Is there anything else you think I need to know before getting started?"

"No. I can lead you to the path whenever you are ready." She set the empty bowl on the counter and dusted her hands.

"Sergeant," Aran called loudly.

Crewes stopped snoring, and his nostrils flared. His eyes snapped open. "I don't want anymore, ma." Then his eyes focused and he seemed to recognize Aran. "Oh, thank the gods. Just a dream."

"I'm taking off." Aran offered him a hand and the sergeant took it. "Take care of them for me."

"You know I will. Good luck out there, LT." Crewes slapped Aran hard on the shoulder, but his armor shimmered and his hand passed through the other side. "Man, that shit is fancy. Hope it keeps you alive."

"I'll be back as soon as I can." Aran rose and walked to the curtain.

Astria followed. "Put that away before you exit. Remember, only what you can carry."

Aran hid his armor, counting the precise four seconds again. He stepped out into the chilly predawn, and was surprised by the level of activity. Dozens of people moved off alone or in pairs, each heading to a different crevasse along the edge of the valley.

Astria led him to the south, up a path that carried them to the ridgeline. It was hard hiking, and Aran enjoyed it. This world had an austere beauty to it. It lacked trees, but the ridges came in a riot of colors, from deep reds to bright purples.

The sun crested the horizon, and those colors leapt into clarity. Dragons winged above, screeching in the distance as they wheeled through the air. The temperature spiked immediately, enough that Aran wished he could put his armor on.

A crowd of people waited at the top of the ridge. They stood clustered around a woman atop a boulder. That woman wore a simple white dress with blue trim. Her long, grey hair had been pulled into a bun, and though her face was lined with age, her eyes glittered powerfully.

She stared hard at Aran as he approached, unblinking and full of judgment. "An Outrider comes before me wishing to walk the path of honor. Is this true?"

"It is." Aran shot Astria a glare. She hadn't mentioned anything about a ceremony.

She shrugged innocently, but her smile was anything but innocent. Welcome to life with an older sister.

"Do you come with only what you can carry and a blade of your own fashioning?" The priestess demanded.

"I come with only what I can carry." Aran reached into his void pocket and withdrew his spellblade. "I guess you could say I fashioned this. I've brought it to several Catalysts."

The priestess's face darkened. She leaned forward and tapped Aran on the chest with a bony finger. "Carry your blade openly, Outrider. Do not hide it away. Others must know you."

"I'll wear the sword openly, then," Aran agreed. He waited to see what else was involved in the ritual.

"Well, go, then." The priestess made a shooing motion. "Get out of my face."

The crowd began to disperse with disappointed murmurs. He had no idea what they'd been expecting.

"Good luck, little brother." Astria tousled his hair. "It's too short now. You used to get so annoyed when I'd mess it up. Especially if one of your little girlfriends was around."

"Astria, I wanted to thank you." Aran considered hugging her, but feared losing a limb. "You've risked a lot to help me. I don't know why you came to Shaya, and I don't know why you changed your mind about killing me. I do know I would have stood no chance without you. So, thanks. I'll try to make you proud out there."

"You'd better." She pointed down into the canyon below. "Follow that ridge into the canyon, and, like I said, keep low. Resist the urge to fly. It will seem like a good idea, because it is so fast, but you do not want to aggravate an entire flock."

Aran activated his armor and counted a precise four seconds as it flowed over him. The instant the HUD lit he dove into the canyon, flying just above the deck.

25

DRAKES

The first few hours had been surprisingly fun. Aran had kept low, as instructed. He'd hugged valley floors, flying a few meters above the ground. He ate up the distance and had made twenty kilometers by the time he stopped for breakfast.

He sat in a hollow behind a pile of boulders, and was fairly certainly nothing could see him from below. If something came by from above, he hoped the shadows would hide him.

Aran removed his helmet and withdrew an MRE from his void pocket. The concept of meals ready to eat had been new to him, but the Ternus marines had made him a believer. Despite what he'd said to his sister, he'd take an MRE over just about any other meal. Especially one of the lasagna packets.

He tore the seal and waited.

The wind played low over the valley, rising and falling every few moments. During one of the lulls, Aran heard something. A *clack clack* of rocks falling. The sound had come from above, not below.

He pulled himself deeper into the shadows and peered up above. He didn't see anything, but that didn't mean something wasn't there.

An urgent vibrating came from his spellblade. Aran dropped a hand to the hilt and could feel the heat even through the armor. "What is it? What do you see?"

There were no words, but he could sense what the blade was feeling. It was alarmed. It detected a threat, one Aran couldn't see.

He froze and strained to catch any sound. Any hint that something was out there.

Nothing came.

Aran waited several more minutes, until a little streamer of steam came from his MRE indicating it was ready to eat. He sat down, fished a spoon out of his void pocket, and began to eat.

Something was out there, of that he had no doubt. But he couldn't detect it, and unless it attacked, there was nothing he could do about it. Besides, he strongly suspected he knew who it might be.

He'd only met one person who could cloak her presence. If she were out there, then she'd reveal herself when she felt like it. Maybe this was her way of helping without helping, since she'd said she couldn't take part.

Aran finished his meal, then summoned a bit of *fire* to incinerate the packaging. He replaced his helmet and started flying through the valley again. The sun hadn't quite come up, but the predawn offered a much better view of his surroundings now. A mighty river roared beneath him, which seemed like perfect cover so long as he flew close to the water.

He dropped down to the deck, zipping over the water as he made his way south. He'd gone perhaps another kilometer when the sun finally crested the horizon. The high canyon walls kept most of it out, but he caught glimpses as he rounded bends in the river.

A scaly creature burst out of the water beneath him in a flurry of teeth and claws. A tail snaked outward to coil around his right ankle, and it yanked him toward the ocean of teeth. Aran pressed both hands together and aimed them at the creature's face. He pulled deeply from *void* and launched a level three bolt at point blank range. It sizzled into the creature's eyeless face, and the beast recoiled with a shriek.

Aran kicked off the creature's bulbous body, knocking it back into the water with a huge splash. He poured more *void* into the armor and willed it to maximum speed as he soared away, and angled his flight to the right until he passed over the riverbank.

He had no idea what that creature had been, but it was possible there were more of them, and steering clear of the water seemed like a great idea.

Aran flew low and fast along the rocks until he rounded another ridge and got his first look at the next valley. Hundreds upon hundreds of drakes in all sizes littered the valley. Some roosted on the lower slopes of hills. Others sunned themselves in the meadows along the valley floor. There seemed to be a hierarchy to the gathering, with the largest drakes toward the center of the valley.

One of the bulls rushed a rival, and the two began to grapple. Boulders were flattened, and their trumpeting calls were deafening.

"Boy," Aran said to no one in particular, "I sure do wish someone was following me so I could ask them whether or not crossing that valley was suicidal."

Astria's disembodied voice answered almost instantly. "If

someone were following, they'd have to stay silent, because no one can help you on this march."

"If that were true, why would someone follow in the first place?" Aran wondered aloud.

There was no answer.

"Fair enough." Aran took a few running steps then leapt into the air. He flew low, as usual, but didn't feel the usual thrill. How had Astria kept up with him? And why follow, if she couldn't or wouldn't help? He didn't want her to break her oaths or anything, but didn't understand what she hoped to gain. Still, he appreciated her support.

He dove into the valley and followed a small ridge along the north side. He skirted the edges to make sure he didn't pass any of the largest drakes. He'd nearly made it to the far side when one of the bulls below looked up. Its head tracked his flight, and it began to flap its wings.

The creature leapt into the air, and half a dozen drakes joined it. The lead bull flapped in Aran's direction. *Crap.* He kicked off a rock and dove into a steep fall toward the water below. The drakes followed—a whole flock of them, now.

Their angry screeches followed Aran up the river, but most refused to approach—most, but not all. The largest bull had nearly caught up and was flying no more than three meters behind Aran.

Evasive maneuvers weren't going to work.

Aran dove into the water. He swam beneath the surface, going as deep as he could. The current was strong, and dragged him along the bottom. He rebounded off a sharp boulder, and a yellow warning light appeared on the paper doll in his HUD.

He grabbed a passing outcrop, and pulled himself beneath it. A shadow passed by above, then another. Aran calmed his breathing, clinging to the rock as he watched. More shadows passed. They were circling.

They'd probably go away soon. He hoped.

The idea that they sent people to do this without spel-larmor made him damned grateful for Kazon's gift. If he survived this, he was sending that man flowers and chocolate.

26

A CLUE

This time when Nara made her way back into the temple she did it by a side door, and she went straight to the table in the back that she and Ismene had used last time. Ismene had made it very clear that the best way to deal with Jocasta was not to, and now that she knew why Nara was here, she was adamant that Jocasta *couldn't* find out.

Ismene was already waiting, Pytho curled over her shoulder, asleep. Little sparks came from the drake's snout whenever she snored. Ismene looked up with an excited smile and waved Nara over.

"I'm so glad you got my missive. You're going to be so excited!" Ismene whispered as she struggled to contain herself. "Come sit down. Take a look at this."

She hurried back to her seat, and Nara hadn't even sat when she pushed a book under her nose. "There. Bottom paragraph."

Nara scanned the contents. It talked about the Wyrm Father of *Life*, and the Wyrm Mother of *Air*. "They were a mated pair?" She leaned back in her chair, staggered by the flood of implications. Her mind flew through possibilities.

"Think of what it could mean!" Ismene's voice had grown louder, and she cringed and lowered it. "It would require both aspects to create a wonder like the vessel you've described. It's very likely the wonder was constructed here."

"That's amazing news," Nara whispered. She reread the paragraph, considering. "If the vessel was made here, what did they do with it? We know it's hidden somewhere on this world. If you're Virkonna, or this mysterious Wyrm Father, where do you hide the vessel?"

"I don't know." Ismene drummed the fingers of one hand on the table, and used the other hand to toy with Pytho's tail. "There's so little about the Wyrm Father, not even a name."

"That confirms what I found on Shaya." Nara pushed the book back with a frown. "It's as if he eradicated all memories of himself, all mention of his name."

"The legends make something like that sound almost trivial to a true god." Ismene stopped drumming. "So let's assume he did. And let's assume he made the ship here, with the Wyrm Mother. I do not possess magic, but I know the theory well. Every sub-archivist does. An eldimagus that powerful would create a signature to match. If you have magic, could you perhaps use divination to locate it?"

"We've tried," Nara admitted. She knew it gave away the fact that she was a mage, but even though she'd only spent a few hours with Ismene, she knew a genuine soul when she saw one. There wasn't a shred of deceit in the girl. "I can't find anything. The only signature of any note on this world is Virkonna herself."

"That's it!" Ismene gave Pytho's tail an excited tug and his eye blinked open. He reached up lazily and bit her ear.

"Ow. Don't do that, Pytho." She punctuated the statement by tugging his tail. The drake bit down harder.

"You were saying about the signature?" Nara prompted. She liked Ismene, but the girl was incredibly distractible.

"Sorry." She released Pytho's tail and focused on Nara. "Well, if we're positive the ship is on this world, then perhaps its signature is hidden under Virkonna's. She's buried in the pyramid your Outrider friend is heading for. This ship, if it's there, could be under the temple, too."

"If it is, how do we reach it? Are there tunnels that run under the pyramid?" Nara prompted.

"Theoretically, yes. They're called the warrens. But they aren't policed. There's drakes down there. Bandits. And worse. And, as far as I know, there's no real map."

"So how do you suggest I get down there? Can I hire a guide?" Nara asked.

"Maybe," Ismene mused. She stroked Pytho's neck. "The problem is that the only people who know those warrens are Outriders with something to prove. They go there to kill drakes, or other trophies. And they don't like people from Shaya any more than my mother does. But I do know someone who might help. He's a little...unorthodox."

"Unorthodox?" Nara blinked. "I don't care if he's got three eyes. If he can help me find the Spellship, than I'd love to meet him."

"He's not that unorthodox." Ismene gave a quiet giggle. "But he's not from Virkon either. He's from Ternus."

"Ternus?" Nara leaned back in her chair, curious now. "What would bring someone here from Ternus?"

"Well, he calls himself an archeologist," Ismene explained quietly, "but I get the sense he's more of a scavenger. He looks harmless enough, but I watched him gun down six people. He's not someone I'd want to piss off."

"All right, how soon can you arrange a meeting?" Nara asked.

"You come back tomorrow at the same time, and I'll make sure he's here." The way Ismene smiled left no doubt as to why she was confident she could get him there. The poor guy probably had it bad for the pretty archivist.

"I'll be here. In the meantime, let's see what else we can learn." Nara pulled the book closer again, and began scanning the page.

27

VORIA GOES TO A PARTY

Voria had no idea what to expect when she arrived at the cliffside balcony near the very tip of Virkon's highest peak. She'd known the stronghold of the Wyrms would be majestic, and it was: all tall fluted spires where Wyrms could perch, with magnificent statues sprinkled below those perches.

She'd dressed the part, with her freshly pressed parade jacket dripping with medals. She'd even used a little illusion magic to enhance her lips and eyes, a conceit she'd never have admitted to, publicly at least.

Curiously, not a single perch was occupied. Instead, the Wyrms had shifted to something resembling a human form. They talked and mingled, every Wyrm taller than she by at least thirty centimeters. Not a single one had hair of any kind, quite unlike Voria's one brief look at Nebiat's human form. Her long white hair seemed a rarity among Wyrms, and that aroused Voria's curiosity.

"Welcome, Major," a tall, dark-skinned woman called. She approached, the sunlight glinting off her bald scalp. She smiled at Voria, but the smile was too wide for a human, and too predatory. "I am pleased you have come. I realize you will not recognize anyone, as we have adopted a more suitable appearance for such a meeting."

"Olyssa?" Voria guessed.

"Indeed." Olyssa placed a hand on Voria's shoulder and guided her through the crowd. There had to be a hundred Wyrms here, all enjoying goblets of a drink that smelled of sharp spices. "Your arrival has occasioned much curiosity. We do not often receive visitors from the Temple of Enlightenment."

"Ah," Voria replied drily. She glanced at Ikadra, which was still clutched in her left hand. Every Wyrm who saw it would realize she was a true mage, and it was natural to assume she must be from the Temple. She had studied there, so it wasn't that far from the mark. "I must admit I am a bit puzzled. I expected a private council meeting, but this looks much more like a party."

They passed by a floating game board covered with intricate patterns of black-and-white scales. As she watched, one of the Wyrms crooked a long finger and a scale flared on his arm. It rose and moved to the board, then clicked into place. The move surrounded a section of white scales, and a bright, magical light flared. The scales disappeared then reappeared in a stack in front of the dragon who'd placed the scale.

"What are they playing? It looks a good deal like *Go*," Voria asked, intensely curious. She paused to peer at the scales. She'd played *Go* back at the Temple; every student had. It was one of the safest ways to test them against each other, and allowed those with less physical aptitude an arena in which to dominate their more scholarly peers.

"It's called Kem'Hedj." Olyssa paused. "It is also known as the oldest game—so old that we do not know when the first game was played. As I understand it, your *Go* is descended from our game. The two games are not at all dissimilar. The primary difference is that our game boards continue to expand as they are played. There is a game on the south slope that has been going on for seventy-four years. It covers nearly a kilometer."

A pair of tall females sauntered over. The taller had her arm draped over the shoulder of the shorter, who huddled against the taller woman's side with an adoring smile.

"That staff you carry," the taller woman boomed. She leaned forward, her focused eyes studying Ikadra. "How did you come by it? He is fabulously old. Countless millennia."

Only in that instant did Voria realize the magnitude of her blunder. She'd brought her staff, because she was a mage and that was what mages did. She hadn't been thinking strategically enough. Ikadra wasn't a mere staff. He was a key—a key to the vessel she sought on this world. She couldn't afford to pique curiosity about Ikadra. She didn't want to draw any attention to him, if she could avoid it. Perhaps leaving him behind would have been the better decision after all. Too late for that now.

"Oh, such artifacts are common on Shaya," Voria lied terribly. "This staff has been in my family for generations. I don't really know where it comes from."

"Would you be interested in selling it?" the tall woman asked. She turned those unsettling eyes on Voria as she awaited her answer.

On the far side of the room, behind the tall woman, stood a pair of hatchlings. Krox hatchlings. Their dark scales glinted in the sun, marking them as the only draconic figures in the entire crowd. Everyone else was old enough to possess the ability to morph.

Her eyes met with those of one of the Krox, the one also

carrying a staff. He held her gaze for an instant, then delivered a slow, respectful nod. Voria considered for a moment, then returned it.

Her attention was pulled to the second Krox, who boomed a raucous laugh and drew distasteful glances from neighboring Wyrms. That one wore a spellblade, and spellarmor. Such equipment marked him as a child in the eyes of Wyrms, as Voria understood it. But that didn't seem to deter him. He downed another goblet of the spiced drink, then snatched a haunch of meat from a passing tray.

They might not be the same hatchlings Aran had encountered recently back on Shaya, but it seemed an awful coincidence for an identical pair to be on Virkonna, at this precise party.

"No," Voria said as she turned back to the tall woman. "The staff is not for sale. My father gave it to me, you see, and he recently passed. Olyssa, I realize this is terribly rude, but would you excuse me? There's an urgent matter I desperately need to attend to."

"Of course." Olyssa's expression went carefully neutral. "We have another party scheduled in two days time. Will you consider attending? Many Wyrms will be disappointed they missed you."

"I'll return for the next party, I promise." And she meant it. But right now she needed to get out of here, and get Ikadra into hiding. She had no idea if the Krox knew what the staff could do, but if they did, and if they now knew she had it, she could expect a response.

28

THE TEMPLE OF VIRKONNA

The shadows circled Aran's underwater perch for over an hour, but thanks to his *air* magic he simply stayed submerged. He waited until the last shadow departed, then cautiously swam to the surface. He was, as far as he could tell, alone.

Nothing bothered him as he guided his armor to the left bank and followed it south. The sun was creeping toward its zenith, but the high walls provided perpetual shade—at least until he reached a break in the canyon.

Before him stretched a long, very open road. It stretched all the way across the next valley, a massive bowl ringed by low mountains. Near the center of that bowl stood the pyramid from his visions. Multi-colored sigils dotted the golden slopes, glinting in the sunlight. It was utterly massive, dominating the center of the valley, and overshadowing every surrounding peak among the hills ringing it.

Aran had pictured some sort of gauntlet he'd have to run. A running gun battle, or ambushes in canyons. He had not expected to see an organized war camp at the base of the pyramid.

"Let's get a better look," he whispered absently, channeling a bit of *fire* into his armor. He zoomed his vision in on the camp, which was mostly made up of humans. They waited on a trio of enforcers—hatchlings, he guessed.

Two wore the black-and-grey of the Krox forces, but the third wore an outfit identical to Astria's. That gave him pause. Did that mean he could disappear from sight? Aran had to assume it did, and he'd need to find a way around it.

"That was really stupid, going into the water," a disembodied Astria said. "You could have been attacked by another fangmouth. The first one almost killed you."

"Hey there, sis." Aran continued flying along the road, following it toward the temple. In a way, it was definitely anticlimactic. No one in the camp moved to intercept him, they merely watched as he approached. "I know you can't help me, and this isn't really help. Why aren't they attacking?"

"Because they have honor?" The way she asked made it clear she thought he had none.

He raised an eyebrow. "So, it's cool to attack me with overwhelming force, just not until I've almost had my face bitten off and have walked across half the planet?"

"Exactly."

"You are just loads of help." Aran risked rising a few meters higher off the deck. He increased his velocity, using a mixture of *void* magic for gravity, and *fire* magic for thrust.

This was the first time he'd really been able to open his armor up, and he was pleasantly surprised to find she was nearly as fast as the Mark XI. Fast, light, small, and powerful. It seemed like the armor had no drawbacks, which meant Kazon was right about this stuff being next-level. It was the future, without a doubt. If there was a downside, he hadn't found it.

Aran continued toward the pyramid, and noted that the humans around the camp had begun moving. Most were trotting toward the pyramid, fanning out by level. He flashed back to the memory Neith had shown him, the one of Aran and his sister battling on those very steps.

He dropped back to the ground and slowed his flight as he approached the base of the pyramid. He didn't know if there would be some sort of formal ceremony, or if people would just start attacking. No one carried any ranged weapons, so there was that small blessing. This would be a very short battle if all his opponents were armed with spellrifles.

"I count fifty-six," his sister whispered from a meter or so away. The words were ripped away by the wind, yet somehow he still heard them. There was magic involved there, he was certain of it. *Air* magic, by the feel.

"I don't see how I can take that many," he called back. Now that he was closer, he could see more detail. Every human was armed, almost all with swords. A few used daggers, and one carried a heavy mace. Every last one had the bearing of a life-long fighter, though their weapons were crude—not the high-end Inuran tech he was getting used to.

"Most do not possess magic, though all will be skilled fighters. They have never seen armor like yours. Use your mobility," she instructed. "The war mages, the real threat, will wait until you have bled yourself on the lesser targets. Then they will finish you."

"So the leader studies how I fight, and hopes I get wounded on the way up. Solid strategy. Worst-case scenario, I have to expend some resources before facing them. Best case, they learn enough to take me down fast." Aran slowed further as he neared the pyramid, then glided into a walk. He slowly approached the steps leading up to the first level.

The three dozen or so combatants on the first level all wore the same white outfits with blue trim. Their faces were uncovered, and they ranged across age and gender. All bore the same hard eyes, though. All stood with the same practiced stance.

His stance. Drakkon stance.

Aran adjusted his spellblade on his hip, still not used to wearing it. He considered using the spellrifle, but if the guy up top was assessing his abilities, he wanted to reveal as little as possible. If these guys really didn't have magic, they were going to go down faster than the slaves had back when Aran and Kazon had faced the tech demons.

He could beat them, but that wasn't the point. The more he narrowed his responses, the less he gave away.

He charged up the steps, and leaped into the air when he neared the top. Three of the swordsmen advanced, their weapons held high. Aran matched their pose. He already missed the extra strength and speed Neith had infused into his Mark XI. He'd have to do this the old fashioned way.

Aran glided forward and brought his blade town in a brutal chop at the first opponent. She rolled backward, but Aran grabbed her with a tendril of *air* and pulled her onto his blade. It pierced her chest, and she staggered backward clutching at her chest.

He was fairly certain the wound wasn't fatal, but there was no way she'd be back in the fight any time soon.

Aran carved a bloody path through the next pair, slicing a hamstring on the first warrior, and crushing the kneecap of another with a savage kick. He was mildly surprised by how easily the men went down. He'd grown used to fighting enforcers and war mages. Un-enhanced combatants didn't have a chance.

He flowed into Drakkon style, dancing from combatant

to combatant. At least two were masters, definitely better than him at pure sword play, but neither had a suit of spellarmor to deflect blows, nor did they possess a powerful spellblade. Aran cut them down ruthlessly, one after another.

Within moments the entire first tier was clear, and Aran stood amidst groaning men and women, panting.

"You know," Aran began as he flicked the blood from his blade, "we could just end this right now." He stared up at the hatchling in the magical suit two tiers above him. "Do you really want me to waste time killing all your buddies?"

"They are merely fodder," the hatchling roared. He flapped his wings behind him and walked to the edge of the fourth tier. "I believe you are entirely too confident. You will not reach me. You've yet to face my war mages, or the two retainers the Krox were kind enough to lend me." He indicated the pair of enforcers on the third level.

Aran tore his eyes away from the hatchling. It wasn't easy. He had used the word fodder—the same word Thalas had used to describe the marines back aboard the *Hunter*.

He'd go down, but first Aran had to deal with the enforcers.

That was probably where Aran would face the most trouble—well, other than the hatchling with the stealth suit. That ability might be the end of him, if he made it that far. But to do that, he'd need to stay focused.

One level at a time.

This time Aran walked slowly up the stairs. He took his time reaching the second level, because he knew no one would attack until he reached it.

A quintet of hard-eyed fighters waited. Each wore the same white outfits as the warriors on the level below, but these all had a patch on the shoulder. A patch just like he'd seen in his vision, just like they wore on Shaya.

The patch of a war mage. A patch he'd still not earned the right to wear, at least, not since the mind-wipe.

"These ones are more dangerous than they appear," Astria breathed into his ear. "Do not underestimate them."

"I won't," he murmured back. Aran had never faced a Virkonnian war mage. Outriders, he guessed. Well, he'd never faced one outside of his sister. And now he was fighting five at the same time.

Of course, this time he had his armor.

Aran surged toward the right flank where the smallest of the combatants waited. Underestimating an opponent based on size was a rookie mistake, but these people had never met him. They couldn't know what sorts of dumb things he might do.

Sure enough, a small, dark-haired man gave an eager smile and rushed forward to engage. Past his companion, unsupported. Aran shifted to the right, keeping the short man between him and his partner.

The little man leapt into the air, soaring several meters over Aran on a plume of *air*. As he darted down, his blade began to crackle with lightning. It was exactly the kind of attack Aran might have used. If the blade connected, the lightning might paralyze him, and that would give the other four war mages time to attack.

Aran shot out a hand and caught the sword. The energy played over his gauntlet, smoking briefly as they fought for control of the weapon. Aran yanked the sword to the side and rammed his own spellblade through the shorter man's heart. He flung the body at the man's partner, rolling to the side to avoid something that flashed in the corner of his eye.

A tall woman had thrust a hand in his direction, and

discharged a thick bolt of blue lightning. It tracked his flight, grounding into his right leg, just above the right knee. The energy scorched a hole through the armor, and Aran roared as it poured into his leg. Tears streamed from his eyes, and all he could do was take short, shallow breaths.

He landed in a heap, rolling desperately back to his feet as he triggered his first healing potion. He breathed easier as the warm glow flowed into the wound. They were already coming for him, and he couldn't afford more than a moment. Thankfully, adrenaline had already begun to mask the lingering pain.

"Cowardly," boomed the hatchling. "You brought healing potions on a March of Honor. You are lower than offal. Finish him, Outriders."

Aran drew upon *void* and fed it into the armor to increase his mass. He dove at the mage who'd hit him with the lightning spell, and used the corpse of her companion as a shield. He slammed into her with incredible force, flinging her violently off the side of the pyramid. She sailed off into nothing, eyes unfocused as she fell.

Had she been conscious she probably could have saved herself. Instead, Aran turned away before the inevitable happened.

The closest surviving war mage was a weathered man with greying hair. He held a larger sword than the others.

"You will pay for killing Esmelda," he said, quiet as death. "Rayd, take him on the right. Saaf, be ready with a counterspell."

Aran's blade vibrated eagerly and the blade flared white as it awakened its internal fire. He sprinted forward and lunged at the grey-haired man. The man's blade came at him, fast as anything Dirk could have managed.

Enchanted steel met enchanted steel, and power flooded

through Aran's weapon. He could feel the touch of Neith, feel the strength the god had infused the weapon with.

The grey-haired man's blade shattered, and Aran's slash continued down. It sliced through the man's shoulder, carving a path all the way to the heart. He yanked the blade free, and began to pivot to face the next target. Too late.

Something punched through Aran's side, a hot poker of agony, just under the armpit. The blow would have been fatal, but his armor shunted the tip away, and it slid into the air on the opposite side of his armor. Kazon had saved his ass once again.

Aran's elbow came up and crushed the man's nose into his skull. He dropped into a crouch, and barely avoided the last war mage's slash. Aran dropped his sword and tackled the war mage. They grappled for a moment, but Aran got his hands around the man's head. He twisted sharply, and the man's neck snapped with an awful crunch.

He rose and walked over to retrieve his spellblade. Aran turned to face the pair of Krox on the next level. Thus far he'd managed to avoid using much magic, but that time had passed. He wasn't sure he could take both, not if they were war mages like the one he'd fought back on Shaya.

Time to find out. Aran started walking up the stairs.

29

SECOND LEVEL

A ran surveyed the enforcers carefully. It helped to think of them as hatchlings, as it put them into perspective. These were baby dragons, with much of the power they'd possess as adults. They could learn magic, of any kind. They could learn to fight. They were stronger, tougher, and almost certainly older than Aran, Voria, or any of the other people he fought alongside.

But he'd also killed a whole lot of hatchlings in his brief career. Some had gone down nearly instantly, though most of the time that had happened he'd gotten the drop on them. These two were waiting for him, and from the way they stood on opposite sides of the stairs they were used to working as a team.

Time to find out what they could do.

Aran started slowly up the stairs, allowing the healing potion to complete the last of its work. He was fully healed for this, though the paper doll on his HUD showed red on the armor's right leg. That lightning bolt had done serious damage, damage that couldn't be fixed quickly. A red tracery of angry lines extended through the paper doll, which Aran assumed meant some of the internal systems were damaged.

Neither hatchling spoke as he crested the last three steps. That was a bad sign. Rookies taunted. Veterans treated combat with the focus it deserved.

Aran drew a large amount of *void* from his chest and fed it to the armor. He crossed the distance to the first enforcer in the space between heartbeats, and his sword flashed down as he sailed over. The blade glowed white, and Aran fed it *air* and *void*, coating the weapon with void lightning.

The tip sank into the enforcer's back, but the armor deflected most of force. He didn't need much, though. Just enough to ground the spell. The purple lightning flowed down the blade like a living thing, surging into the wound in waves.

"No!" the hatchling roared, hopping backward suddenly. He yanked a hammer about the size of Kezia's from a void pocket, and leapt at Aran. From the corner of his eye Aran could see the other hatchling smoothly adjusting to flank him.

Aran ducked under the hatchling's blow, but barely. The hammer hummed past his face, his dark armor reflected in the weapon's pocked surface.

The second hatchling thrust a hand at Aran and flung a spirit bolt at his face. Aran's momentum from the fall was carrying him right into the path. His heart thundered as he reached for *void* in an attempt to pull himself out of the way.

Too late.

The spirit bolt slammed into his chest, the white energy going misty as it met the dark metal. Whatever resistance the armor offered, it wasn't enough. The bolt passed through, and icy numbness wrapped clawed fingers around his heart. His entire body went limp, and he crashed to the ground, sliding across the stone.

Aran struggled to rise, but his limbs refused to respond. It wasn't the same as being paralyzed. That cut off all access to your own body. He had control of his body, but had never felt so weak. Lifting his arm might as well have been lifting the planet.

The hatchling with the hammer brought it down over Aran's head. It slammed into his helmet, and white, frigid pain exploded through his skull. He blinked rapidly, and his vision refocused enough to see the spiderweb of cracks running across the HUD.

"You will never even reach me," the hatchling called from the level above. "You've met your betters, little Outrider. Now we will show you why our species ruled this sector for a hundred millennia."

The hatchling raised his hammer again, while his companion crouched a few meters away, ready to fire another spirit bolt. Aran took a trembling breath and willed the first counterspell potion to activate. Blinding sapphire light burst from his armor, exploding outward in all directions.

It washed away the numbness, and Aran's limbs began to function again. He rolled backward and flipped into the air, soaring several meters out of reach. The hatchling with the hammer kicked off the ground, and his wings extended. He soared after Aran and moved with the kind of precision reserved to those who'd been born with a set of wings.

Astria's voice whispered into his ear from a few millimeters away, though he was positive it was a spell, not her actual mouth. "Drakkon Style is offense. Attack, brother. Make them fear you."

She was right. The more defensively he fought, the more

he gave them a chance to attack. He needed to take down the Krox with the spirit bolts first, then he could deal with the one using the hammer.

Aran reversed his momentum, zipping past the startled hatchling. The creature tried to bring the hammer around, but Aran was too quick. He flashed past, toward the hatchling on the ground. That enforcer thrust out a hand and flung another ball of pallid white.

This time Aran was ready. He activated the second counterspell potion, and smiled grimly when blue energy burst from his armor. The spirit bolt splintered into harmless mana shards, and left nothing between him and his opponent.

A distant part of Aran regretted the need to show so much power, but he knew he needed to end this quickly. Aran summoned equal parts *void* and *fire*. His blade, already a beacon of brilliant white light, flared with purplish flames. He brought it down over the Krox's heart, slamming it into the breastplate.

The enchanted metal screamed, then reluctantly parted for Aran's spellblade. His weapon punched through the armor, through the creature's thick scaly hide. It discharged the void flame into the wound, and the hatchling screeched.

Its wings flapped, and it pulled free from the blade, staggering away in a half-flying half-fall that ended with it lying on the edge of the first step to the next level. The light faded from its eyes as a streamer of smoke rose from the gaping hole in its chest.

Aran didn't hear the hammer until a split second before it caught him in the back. The blow didn't hurt nearly as much as he expected, though it did launch him into the pyramid wall. Aran rolled with the blow, and came up a few meters away from the enforcer. Thankfully he'd retained his spellblade.

"Now, it is a fair fight," the hatchling growled as it took as step closer.

Aran glanced at his HUD to see what kind of damage the blow had done. The armor along the back had gone yellow, but the real damage was clear now: his potion loaders had been shattered. All of them.

There'd be no more healing. No more counterspells. No more of whatever the red potions had been.

He looked up at the hatchling. The Krox had greater reach, but he was a hell of a lot slower. Aran didn't wait for him to approach. Waiting wasn't the way of Drakkon. He was a predator. A dragon. He killed.

Aran flung his sword at the Krox. The blade flared as it left his grasp, the intelligence within fueling the glow with *fire* magic. Aran added *void*, not to coat the blade in void lightning, or void flame, but instead to make it heavier. He added *air* to increase the velocity further.

The blade slid easily through the Krox's armor, directly through the throat. The weapon sank all the way in, until the crossguard finally halted the blade's momentum with a meaty thunk.

Aran wasn't done. He wrapped several tendrils of *air* around the tip of enemy's blade. As he'd hoped, the hatchling's grip relaxed as his body reacted to the hideous damage Aran's sword had inflicted.

He used *air* to fling the hatchling's hammer toward its own face, and the creature's head exploded in a shower of gore. The Krox's headless body twitched once, then slumped to the ground. Aran walked over calmly and retrieved his sword.

He turned to look at the level above, where the final

hatchling waited. Aran had no more potions. His armor was severely damaged, showing just how disappointingly fragile it was compared to his old Mark XI.

But all his opponents were dead, except for one. He knew what he needed to do. Aran met the hatchling's gaze, and noticed that this time...his opponent said nothing.

Aran began climbing the stairs.

30

BOSS FIGHT

A shadow passed over Aran as he mounted the final step. He glanced upward to see dozens of dragons wheeling like birds, all watching the show he was providing them. Well, he hoped they enjoyed it.

He held his spellblade loosely, and the tip drew a line of sparks from the stone as he approached the hatchling. The hatchling merely watched him, with wide, curious eyes in that reptilian face. Now that he was closer Aran could detect no animosity. Had all the bravado been for show?

The creature's own blade was also tip down, the blade plunged a few millimeters into the stone. "Tell me, Outrider, before I kill you, why did you come back to this world? You had to know you would find nothing but your end here. It seems a curious thing, to return to a world you know will kill you."

Aran raised his sword and flowed into Drakkon stance. "I came because my past was taken from me. Because I know nothing of this world, or of your kind. I came for answers." It was true, even if it wasn't the whole truth.

"Can I share a secret?" the hatchling said in a conspiratorial whisper. "I regret the need to kill you. You are a curios-ity, Outrider. And, so far as I can tell, you've done nothing wrong. Nothing save defend yourself. It's a pity you slew Khalahk, but you had no better option."

Aran cocked his head. He wondered idly if this creature was trying to distract him, but he couldn't see any reason why. It held all the advantages, and delaying a few moments to talk seemed motivated by nothing more than genuine curiosity.

"So why are you trying to kill me then?" Aran asked. He raised his blade slowly.

"Pragmatism," the hatchling admitted. "My sire bade me slay you. You cannot be allowed to leave this place, or others will take up your ways. Mortals will be attacking dragons all over this world, and we'd be plunged into anarchy."

"Aren't you afraid killing me will turn me into a martyr?" Aran asked. He considered advancing, but hesitated. The hatchling wasn't the only curious one.

The hatchling blinked, and his spellblade fell a few millimeters. "I hadn't considered that, though I imagine my sire must have. Yes, I can see why, now that I think about it." He gave a toothy smile. "Dead heroes do not inspire other heroes, because no hero wishes to die. If you killed a Wyrm, but were properly judged there is little chance any will wish to share your fate."

"Good point," Aran admitted. If he lived, he might inspire others. But if he died, whatever the cause, no one would want to share his fate. "I guess we should do this, then."

"Indeed. Die well, Outrider. Know that you have my sympathy." The hatchling delivered a respectful nod, and raised his weapon again.

Aran returned the nod.

He blurred forward, kicking off the stone and bringing his spellblade down in a brutal slash. The air hummed, then a tremendous metallic ringing, like a gong being struck, echoed out into the sky over the pyramid.

The hatchling parried the blow, then answered with a short punch that caught Aran in the gut. He staggered back a step, momentarily unable to breathe. The creature's blade flicked at his face like a serpent, and Aran rolled away. The blade flashed down, striking another line of sparks from the stone as Aran came to his feet.

"You move well, but you revealed too much while reaching me." The hatchling moved slowly in his direction, each step forcing Aran a little closer to the edge. He was all too conscious of the long drop. His magic wouldn't save him. Holding himself aloft with *air* would only make him an easier target.

"Time to think outside the box, I guess," he muttered.

Aran thrust a hand at the marble, reaching for *water*. He flung a thin coat of ice in a long line toward the hatchling, who hopped nimbly away. He eyed it contemptuously, which meant his gaze left Aran for a split second.

Aran dashed onto the ice, using a bit of *air* to increase his momentum. He slid across the ice, and by the time he reached the hatchling he must have been traveling at thirty or forty kilometers per hour. His shoulder caught the hatchling in the chest, and even though Aran was lighter the blow flung the creature into the pyramid wall.

It recovered almost instantly, but Aran was already summoning *void*. This time he opened a void pocket directly underneath the hatchling. He'd never tried to do that before, but the yawning mouth snapped open, and the hatchling's feet slipped inside, up to the knees.

Aran's right hand came out, and a globe of water materialized around the hatchling's head, further distracting it. The creature clawed at the water, which wasn't more than a minor irritation. And a conductive material. The tip of Aran's sword brushed the water, and a tide of electricity crackled into it.

The water amplified the electricity, and while the blow didn't do much damage, it did temporarily blind his opponent. Combined with its legs trapped in the void pocket he'd have thought it enough to stop his opponent.

Before he could capitalize the creature's tail snaked around his leg. He was yanked down to the marble, his faceplate slamming into the stone with a tremendous crash. Cracks spiderwebbed across the faceplate, and the HUD winked out entirely.

Aran's blade vibrated in his hand. For the first time Aran could feel a real emotion coming from the weapon. Hate. It longed for the hatchling's death. The weapon was consumed by it. The ferocity of the emotion was more than a little troubling; anything that all-consuming was dangerous.

But right now, Aran needed dangerous. He instinctively reached for the blade's rage and let it flood through him, their minds joining.

He seized the hilt with both hands, and brought the spellblade around in a wide slash. The inferno around the blade flared up, light and heat bursting from the weapon as it sliced through the hatchling's tail, freeing him from its grip.

Aran pressed the attack and rammed his blade toward the hatchling's chest. The blade had almost reached it when the creature vanished. Aran stumbled forward into the space it had occupied, quickly catching his balance and spinning to look for his opponent.

"Your mind will not allow you to see him," Astria's voice whispered into his ear. "I'm sorry, brother."

He spun slowly in place, and sought any sign of the hatchling. Any scrap of sound, or even the scent of charred flesh. Something to betray his opponent's presence. But, if he understood the magic conveyed by the suit, he knew none of that was possible. The spell would prevent his brain from registering any of that.

So how did he deal with this thing? The sudden rage made it difficult to think.

Aran sensed more than saw something out of the corner of his eye. He dove forward, but the hatchling's spellblade found him anyway. It sliced into his kidney, drawing a deep thirty-centimeter cut along his lower back. A cut he didn't have a way to heal. Why hadn't the armor deflected the blow like it had the others? It must be too badly damaged. That should have been clear when the hammer hit, but the rage made it difficult to focus.

He flipped his sword in his grip and rammed the blade backward, toward the hatchling. The tip touched armor, but then the hatchling vanished again. Aran growled wordlessly as he slashed through the space where his opponent had been. Maybe he could get lucky.

"Your technology is impressive," the hatchling called from a few meters away, near the stairs that led all the way to the top of the pyramid, several hundred meters above. "But it is also why you are losing. You draw your strength from this technology, instead of yourself and your own magic. Now that your armor is non-functional, you are helpless."

Aran barked out a laugh. "That attitude is why this is the *last* dragonflight. I spent the last three months fighting without spellarmor. It's useful, but if you think I'm helpless without it then why don't you come finish me."

"Perhaps you have a point." The voice came from directly behind him. Aran flung himself to the right, but the tip of a blade scored the armor along his shoulder, drawing a jarring white scratch in the oily metal.

Aran dropped into a crouch and seized the hatchling's right ankle. He pulled deeply from *water* and created the largest ball of ice he could, completely encasing the hatchling's foot, all the way up to the knee.

The hatchling vanished.

Aran rammed his blade into the space the hatchling had just occupied, approximately where its heart would be. There was momentary resistance, but only for an instant. His blade had probably glanced off the creature's thick hide, but the tip glistened wetly. He'd found flesh.

A keening cry came from one of the wheeling dragons, and others took it up. Cheering? Or taunting?

"You're faring a good deal better than anyone expected," the hatchling's disembodied voice sounded embarrassed. "I am certain my brothers will ridicule me for how long it took me to kill you. So, die knowing that, Outrider. Die knowing I respect you, as much as I can a mere human. I am sorry."

Aran's blade vibrated in his hand. It understood the hatchling's words and was enraged by them. The tip angled away from Aran. It tugged toward a spot several meters away.

"I'm sorry too," Aran said. He gave a deep, reluctant sigh. "Okay, sword. Let's dance. You lead."

Aran turned over control to the weapon. He flowed where it led, gliding across the stone in Drakkon stance. It came down sharply, toward what appeared to be empty air. The blade flared, then tugged him suddenly backward. Aran rolled with the weapon and came to his feet a few meters away.

The blade vibrated more strongly. The rage and hate were total.

Aran closed his eyes. He held the blade before him, every muscle poised to move. The blade trembled and he pounced. Aran's eyes shot open and he poured void lightning down the blood-slicked feathersteel.

The weapon jabbed forward, and met resistance. It sank deep into something, and the void lightning crackled around a roughly hatchling-shaped hole in reality. It disappeared again nearly instantly.

Aran landed and rolled away again. He came to his feet, noting that several puddles of blood now stained the stone. They led to the far side of that level, almost to the corner of the pyramid. He moved slowly in that direction, the blade tugging in an attempt to get him to move more quickly.

The hatchling appeared suddenly, winking back into existence in exactly the way it winked out. It clutched at a hideous wound in its stomach.

It probably wasn't fatal.

Aran brought his blade around in a low slash, severing the creature's wrist and spilling it to the marble in a spray of dark blood. "You fought well. I haven't met too many hatchlings with what I'd call honor. Die well."

His blade sang in his hands, brilliance bursting from the blade as Aran pinned the hatchling's skull to the marble. The blade poured a torrent of white flame through his brain, and the hatching gave a brief shriek. It twitched once, then lay still.

That was definitely fatal.

He slumped to his knees and struggled to catch his breath. Every part of him hurt, and he knew the adrenaline would stop masking that soon. But, theoretically at least, he'd won.

"What now?" he asked quietly. Hopefully Astria was still here.

"Now, you will be judged," she answered, just as quietly.

Thunder rumbled from above. Aran glanced up to see the sky darkening ominously. Bolts of lightning stabbed down—first one, then a dozen...and then a hundred. They crashed down on the pyramid from above. At first Aran assumed they were random, but every bolt found the body of one of the fallen. Those bodies were incinerated, only a light dusting of ash on the stone where they'd been.

The final bolt crashed into Aran.

31

JUDGED

Aran had no time to react as the final bolt plunged from the sky, and caught him on the crown of his head. The magical energy surged through him, scouring away all conscious thought in a tide of pain that lingered for an eternity before rolling away.

When the whiteness faded, Aran sought to understand his surroundings. He blinked away afterimages and realized he couldn't feel his body. It was remarkably similar to how he'd felt when he'd wandered through the mind of Xal.

Aran's vision returned and he found himself hovering in space, above Virkon. He recognized the purple world from their arrival.

A vast, endless cloud of Wyrms swam among the stars around that planet, more dragons than Aran would have guessed had ever lived, across all the ages. They ranged in size from hatchlings, to Wyrms larger than Cerberus. Being in space should have prevented hearing, but their sad, keening dirge echoed through his mind.

"They are mourning Mother," a disembodied voice rumbled. It was so powerful, it thrummed through his body, rattling his teeth. The voice of a goddess, just like Neith. At least he could still feel his body.

Aran spun around slowly, noting a very human-looking woman hovering a few meters away. Her hair flowed down around her, a river of crackling lightning. Tiny storms played across her cornea, but they were not the only sign she wasn't human. A pair of draconic wings extended from her back, and a long, prehensile tail curled behind her. She was, in some strange way, a cross between human and dragon.

"Are you...Virkonna?" Aran ventured hesitantly. He wasn't entirely certain what had happened, but the pieces were suggestive. He was in the mind of a goddess, again, which meant the bolt of lightning must be a catalization. She'd picked him, again, just as she'd picked him in the vision Neith had shown him of his past.

"Mother's death was so unexpected." Virkonna, if that was who she was, continued as if Aran hadn't spoken. "She didn't see the possibility, none of us did. Not even Neith, and she sees more truly than any of us. I still do not know how Nefarius managed it."

Aran didn't respond. Virkonna didn't seem like Marid, or Xal. This wasn't a fragment of a dead mind. But she didn't seem like Neith, who'd been easy to converse with instead of offering this maddeningly cryptic *I'm a god, and it would be too easy if I just told you* crap.

"I don't know what to do now." Virkonna's voice took on a forlorn tone, and her crackling eyes softened to the color of the sky after a storm. "It is wrong for me to hide. Wrong for me to give up. But if Nefarius can manage this, what does any of what we do matter? What if he has anticipated the Spellship? What if his children subvert the vessel? That possibility is as strong as the other. As time passes, it will become stronger still."

Aran's ears perked up at the mention of the Spellship. He didn't understand everything she was saying. Aran had no idea who Nefarius was. If anyone were going to "subvert the vessel" he'd expect it to be the Krox. They were the ones who'd come here to oppose the Confederacy. So what the depths did Virkonna mean?

It was like being given half the puzzle pieces and told that some of the pieces were actually for a different puzzle entirely. He didn't have enough context to understand, and it bothered the piss out of him.

"Can you tell me more about the Spellship?" Aran asked. He hoped she could hear him.

"Mmm?" she asked. Her gaze fell on him. The full weight of it was terrifying, and if he could have fled, he probably would have. The storm returned to her eyes. "The time has finally arrived. The possibilities narrow. I cannot do much, but I can do this. You already bear my mark, Outrider. But now you bear it fully. Go to your destiny armed with every tool I can give you. When the time comes, give in to the song. Become *air*."

Twin streaks of lightning shot from her eyes, crackling over Aran. They rushed through his entire nervous system, the magic playing through him in ways he couldn't begin to understand.

Aran dimly remembered the memory Neith had shown him, of his body being lifted into the air as Virkonna's magic had infused him. It had been his very first catalization, and when it had ended he'd been returned to the pyramid. He could only hope that would be the case now, too—that the pain would eventually end and he'd be restored to his former location. Hopefully with the tools to find the Spellship and stop the Krox.

"No," Virkonna rumbled, an impossibly vast distance away. "You will not be returning to your friends. Or even your own time. This spell was laid countless millennia ago, ready to trigger when you finally arrived. Go now, to where you need to be. To *when* you need to be."

The pain ceased, and Aran found himself tumbling backward into darkness.

32

WESLEY

Nara returned to the temple on the third—and, she hoped, final—day. She'd spent most of the previous evening worrying over Aran. There'd been no word, which she supposed meant he was still alive. If he were dead, Aetherius and his flight would no doubt call off their hunt and start bragging about it. And it was fear of that kind of news that had kept her awake, distracting herself with tomes about the age of dragons.

She'd had several cups of caf, enough to fortify her for today's meeting. She had no idea what to expect of this archeologist. If he couldn't help her, she didn't have a lot of options. The major had been skeptical, at best. She had apparently heard of an order of archeologists from Ternus. They were basically, in Voria's words, playing at magic by poking magic things with a stick and writing down the results.

Slender hope, however, was better than no hope at all. Ismene seemed certain the man could help, so Nara would remain cautiously optimistic. She entered the temple through the side door, and crept to their usual table.

This time there were two occupants. Ismene sat smiling up at a very interested man. Her finger twirled a lock of her hair, which Pytho was trying to bite.

The archeologist was dressed very strangely. He was a youngish man with a battered hat with a wide brim, kind of like the logo on the *Big Texas*. His jacket was dark leather, and his pants were a simple pair of dusty denim. The only thing ruining the image was the pair of small spectacles perched on an unfortunately prominent nose. They drew attention to it, and with a nose like that, attention was never something you wanted.

"Wes, this is my friend Nara." Ismene rose and waved at Nara.

Nara smiled warmly and offered Wes her hand. He pumped it furiously, much like Pickus did. What a strange custom.

"A pleasure." He sat again, then scooted his chair closer to Ismene. His face lit when he glanced at her. Yep, he had it bad.

"Ismene tells me you know the warrens. Is that true?" she asked. Nara set her satchel on the table and leaned back in the chair.

Wes tore his eyes from Ismene. "It's true, I suppose. I've been down there a dozen times over the last three months. I haven't found what I'm looking for, but I have been building a crude map." He leaned closer, and his glasses slid down his nose a little. He pushed them up again. "Ismene refused to tell me what it is you're after. She said you swore her to secrecy."

"I did." Nara nodded gratefully to Ismene. "I'm trying to find the site of a very powerful magical object. One with a signature strong enough that only Virkonna's will mask it."

"Let me see if I understand what you're saying. Magic

gives off a signature, like radiation, and you think Virkonna's signature is masking whatever you're hunting for." Wes adjusted his glasses and gave an excited smile. "You want to get down below Virkonna so you can search for this signature. If we're beneath her, and if that's the reason you can't find it, then it should be a simple matter to detect. You, ah, are a mage, right? Because I don't have *fire* magic. Or *dream*, for that matter."

"Do you have any magic?" Nara asked, raising an eyebrow.

"Well, kind of. Let's just say I can fight, if I have to."

Wes seemed uncomfortable with the topic, so Nara dropped it.

"Can you get us down there so we can search?" she asked. "Don't worry about divination. I can take care of that part."

"Yeah, but we're probably going to want some muscle," Wes ventured cautiously. He glanced at Ismene, and his shoulders straightened. "I mean, if you want to carry anything back. I'm assuming whatever you're looking for is heavy. Cause I wasn't talking about for fighting. I'm, like, really dangerous. So I can keep us safe."

"Thank god for that," Nara muttered sarcastically. "Whatever would I do?"

"He really is deadly." Ismene's tone was hurt. Apparently Wes wasn't the only one who had it bad.

"I'm sure he is." She wasn't, but it hardly mattered. She could keep them both hidden, and with her armor she could keep them away from anything she didn't feel confident dealing with. "So we've established that you can help me. Are you willing to? And what will it cost me?"

"That's a very good question." Wes attempted to lean casually on the stack of books next to Ismene, but the stack slid and he ended up dumping all the books on the floor. Ismene gave a horrified gasp, and Wes bent to begin picking them up. "Oh my gods, so sorry. How terribly clumsy of me."

In that moment, Nara detected a slightly different accent. She tapped her lip as she considered. There was something familiar about Wes—about the accent he was trying to affect, not the one she'd just heard him slip back into.

"Wes, have you ever heard of a holodrama called *Relic Hunter*?" It was her turn to snap her fingers. "That's it. That's where I know the hat from!"

"Oh, dear." Wes went very pale and abandoned all pretense of his manly Ternus drawl. "I am, ah, aware of that show. But why don't we keep focused on the matter at hand? You need a guide. I will guide you. In exchange, all I ask is ten percent of the profit from whatever we find. I do have to eat, after all."

"Done." Nara said instantly. Part of her felt bad for lying. Because, if they found the Spellship, he wasn't getting anything beyond a kiss on the cheek and whatever the major might be willing to spare.

Maybe she could talk Ismene into going on a real date with him. That would probably be worth more than any eldimagus.

33

UNSTABLE MUTATION

Nara slid her staff back into the void pocket, then threw the threadbare cloak over her armor. She completed the disguise by sketching a simple illusion spell, this one designed to slightly alter her features and hair color. An outside observer would see a tired woman in her fifties trudging to an early morning job.

"Wow," Wes said,

The sudden noise broke the pre-dawn stillness, and Nara flinched and glared at him.

He lowered his voice. "Sorry. That's some really impressive magic. If I'm being completely honest, most of what I know is theory. I haven't had a chance to see a lot of spells cast—I mean, spells that weren't killing people."

He leaned in closer and adjusted his spectacles as he peered at her face. "There is literally no trace. Nothing to suggest you are anything other than you appear to be. Fascinating. We have stealth tech back on Ternus that can do something similar, but the patterns it uses aren't random enough. It can be detected, if you know what you're looking for."

Nara found the idea that they could achieve through technology what she'd labored to learn to do through magic a little annoying. If that was true, it meant anyone could use it. The power could become ubiquitous, if the technology were cheap enough. That, more than anything else, was why she mistrusted technology: not what it could do, but what it could allow anyone to do.

"We should be off before the sun comes up," Nara pointed out. She pulled her cloak tighter about her. "I don't think anyone is watching this building, but it's best to assume they are." The sergeant's voice echoed through her head, reminding her that she was more likely to live if she assumed everyone was trying to kill her.

Wes adjusted his hat, which was slightly too large for his head. She wondered again why Ismene thought he was so deadly when he strongly resembled the storks in the park near the Temple of Enlightenment.

"I'll, uh, lead the way." Wes gave her a weak smile and tucked a small tablet like the one Pickus used into his belt. As he moved his duster aside, she caught a glimpse of a pair of golden pistols. She saw them only for a moment, but the power wafting from them was almost palpable. At least he had a real weapon.

Wes opened the door and hurried out into the slowly lightening darkness. A soft orange glow touched the eastern horizon, an oddity when Nara was used to a planet where the sun rose in the west.

There was already a fair amount of foot traffic as laborers trudged toward the fields outside town. It still wasn't clear what they grew, though Nara supposed it didn't really matter.

"This way," Wes prompted. He led her across the street and down a narrow alleyway. They passed between pairs of low squat buildings that looked like warehouses, possibly to store whatever the laborers grew.

They emerged outside the buildings on a steep slope covered in scraggly planets. Wes began sliding down, planting his butt in the dirt as he slid down a good sixty meters to a narrow path.

Nara glanced back they way they'd come, but there was no sign of any pursuit. None of the laborers came this way. She glanced up at the rooftops, but didn't catch sight of any Wyrms or any hatchlings. She fed a tendril of *void* magic into her suit and drifted down the hill to stand next to Wes.

"Well, that seems like a way better idea," he admitted as he shoved a hand down the back of his pants. "I'll be picking out gravel for weeks. Anyway, we're almost to the entrance." He started up the path at a fast walk. He removed his hat and rolled it up tightly, then shoved it inside his duster. "There's no natural light down there."

"I have *fire* magic," Nara offered. "I can take care of light."

"Yeah, that's a really bad idea," Wes said. He wrapped a headlamp with an elastic band over his forehead. "Listen, I don't want to make any assumptions about what you do or don't know, so how about we do like a quick two-minute strategy session? If you find that I'm, uh, techsplaining, just glare and I'll stop."

Wes watched her carefully for a moment. Nara raised an expectant eyebrow.

"Yes, well, we're heading down into the warrens," he began. "The warrens are massive. They cover the entire continent. Basically, we're looking at layers of strata. Each strata connects to a different epoch in the age of dragons. This planet has been inhabited continuously for at least a hundred thousand years, and during that time, countless wars have been fought."

"The warrens?" Nara prompted when he started to wander off topic. "Not that I don't want to know more about the history of Virkon, but first I want to understand where we're going."

"Ah, right. Well, Virkonna is down there at the center of the warrens. I mean, I know you know that, since it's her magical signature we're trying to circumvent." Wes stopped in front of a cluster of boulders. There was a shadowed gap between two of them. From a few meters back, it didn't look like anything, but as Wes approached, Nara realized it led inside a cave. "Anyway, a Catalyst as powerful as Virkonna draws primals. Do you know what a primal is?"

"Conceptually." She ducked into the cave, blinking as her eyes attempted to adjust. "I know they're drawn to Catalysts, and the magical energies of a god begin shaping them into a race that god would have found pleasing. I'm guessing all the drakes here come from primals, and they're an early stage of what will eventually become dragons."

Wes took a moment to adjust the strap to his headlamp so it fit snuggly. He immediately turned toward her, shining the light in her eyes.

"Ow." She held up a hand to block the light.

"That's all correct. I still don't know where primals come from originally. Someone probably does, but no one on Ternus." Wes turned the light away from her and began picking his way deeper into the cavern. "I've only seen one other Catalyst, but I've studied quite a few. You're right about the drakes. If this world were empty, and primals found it, eventually the drakes they became would breed true, and become real dragons."

"The magical cycle of life," Nara said. She ducked under

a low, rock ceiling, and when she stood again they'd entered a much more recognizable trail. The tunnel was perhaps a dozen meters wide, and relatively clear of debris. It was in better repair than she'd have expected, and smelled more of wet rock than the raw sewage her mind had conjured.

"And you're familiar with the unstable?" Wes asked. He fell into a fast walk, his light bobbing as he headed up the tunnel.

"The what?" Nara asked as she fell into step behind him.

"The unstable." Wes glanced back at her, but this time Nara was ready. She got a hand up in time to stop him from blinding her. The light turned away again and she removed her hand. "They're primals that absorb too much energy. A common phenomenon as we get closer to Virkonna. The unstable mutate in unpredictable ways. I saw a drake with three heads, one of which was on its tail." He shuddered.

"That sounds lovely. Let's do what we can to skirt anything like that," Nara suggested. "We don't want to get close to Virkonna, just close enough to pass here so we can get below, remember?"

"I know these tunnels fairly well, but not where we're going." The tunnel sloped downward gradually, but in a very straight line. "It's possible we can skirt Virkonna, I just want to make sure you know the kind of dangers we'll be facing."

"Trust me." Nara smiled. "We can deal with anything we run into. I'm very sneaky when I need to be."

"Ooh, sneaky I like. It's the direct confrontation thing I prefer to avoid," Wes said, rather sheepishly.

"Ismene said you're a deadly killer," Nara pointed out skeptically.

"Oh, I am. Super deadly." Wes adopted what she

assumed was meant to be a dangerous expression. Even Bord could have managed better.

She sincerely hoped they didn't run into any real threats, because if they did, she was going to be pretty much on her own.

34

KEM'HEDJ

V oria had spent the last few days expecting a Krox attack. She'd laid a fresh set of wards to her quarters, and had been vigilant in her scrying. But, nothing had come. The Krox, if they'd recognized Ikadra, hadn't reacted at all.

She knew better than to assume that meant anything. If this pair of hatchlings were intelligent, they could merely be biding their time and waiting for the right opportunity to strike. She'd do well to remember that.

Voria had a better idea of what to expect when she returned to the gathering of Wyrms. There were more in attendance this time, all in their curiously hairless attempt at human forms. As before, refreshments floated on little trays, bobbing up to groups of twos and threes that stood chatting and laughing throughout the cavernous room.

She scanned the crowd carefully, but there was no sign of the Krox hatchlings. That should have relieved her, but instead it filled her with dread. If they weren't here, there was no doubt some other mischief they were up to.

There'd still been no word of Aran's final fate, and that

terrified her. What if they'd gone to finish him off? Not that finishing him off would be easy, but even Aran could only deal with so many enemies arrayed against him. He was strongest when backed by his team.

Then there was the matter of Nara. Voria approved of the girl's initiative, but not her choice of companions. The Ternus Royal Academy had a terrible reputation among scholars, not just on Shaya, but on every world that took pride in the accumulation of knowledge.

Their so-called archeologists had almost no real requirements to join, not even the ability to cast spells. Anyone could pick up a drill and claim they belonged to the order, so long as they paid their annual fee, and they were known more for tomb robbing than anything approaching archeology. That didn't exactly fill Voria with confidence. It was possible Nara had chanced upon one of the competent ones, but she doubted it.

A familiar, and rather irritating, Wyrm threaded through the crowd in her direction. Aetherius gave her an imperious once over, and sniffed in apparent disdain. Finally, he inclined his bald head a fraction of a degree. "I see the Shayan has returned. Have you come to take your mind off the death of your friend?"

Voria's heart leapt into her mouth. "What do you know?"

"Oh, you haven't heard." Aetherius raised a hand to his mouth in mock surprise. He gave her a cruel, too-wide grin. "Why don't you come play a game of Kem'Hedj with me, and we can discuss it? I'm told you're an accomplished commander. We require our commanders to master it, as we believe it can approximate their skill in battle."

"All right," Voria allowed. She followed Aetherius toward a floating game board, one of many dotting the room. A pair of men had been moving in its direction to play, but one look at Aetherius and they headed for another.

The olive-skinned Wyrm stopped before the table. He tapped his forearm with a long-nailed finger, and a single scale floated up into the air. He waved and it landed on a square near the center. A single move didn't tell her much, beyond that he favored an offensive strategy. Instead of attempting to control a corner he was claiming position near the center, and it would allow him to better encircle her own pieces if she encroached.

"Forgive me, but I don't have scales," Voria pointed out. "Our version of this game uses stones."

"Ah, how rude of me," Aetherius replied. He was all mock embarrassment, the kind that would have felt trite on a secondary school playground. Aetherius rose to his full height and waved across the crowd. "Olyssa, would you join us?"

Olyssa threaded her way over, and stopped next to Voria. She glanced askance at Aetherius. "You're going to play a Shayan at Kem'Hedj?"

"Why not? She is our equal, or as close as tree children can get," he pointed out smugly. "But I was hoping you might aid her, as you are her host for this event. She has no scales with which to play."

"And if you best her you get to claim some of my scales, is that it?" Olyssa gave a snort that would have broken a human's neck. "Very well. I suppose that is a small price to pay to see what sort of skill a Shayan commander possesses. I will admit I am...not optimistic, Major."

"That's fair. He has several centuries more experience." Voria shrugged, though that nonchalance only masked her growing fury. She wanted to know what this bastard knew about Aran, and after she had that information, she wanted

nothing more than to publicly humiliate him for the way he
had treated her, and her crew.

Olyssa placed a hand over her arm, and there was a
bright flash of brilliant blue light. She extended the hand to
Voria, and a dozen glittering scales sat in her palm. "When
these run out, I will provide more."

Voria sketched an *air* sigil, and used a bit of wind to
carry her first scale onto the game board. She set it in opposition, a few spaces away. The instant it clicked into place, a
vision overtook her. Possibilities spun out in all directions,
each showing where a piece would land, and what possible
responses could be.

There was a moment of vertigo, then she was leaning
against the base of a nearby perch. All eyes were on
Aetherius, who still deliberated over the board. He extended
another finger, and a scale levitated to the board. It settled
adjacent to her own, the first attempt to box her piece in.

Voria waved another piece over, placing it behind his.
They exchanged turns for a while, each attempting to
capture the other's pieces. Voria lost one early, but made up
for it two turns later when she captured three of Aetherius's.

She played feverishly, driven forward by the vision. Voria
placed pieces almost instantly each turn, a stark contrast to
Aetherius and his more deliberate plays. He set down
another scale and looked up at her sadly. "I believe we are
nearing the end, Shayan. I admire your boldness, and the
speed with which you make decisions. But those decisions
are hastily made, and were they made on the battlefield
would mean the end of your troops."

He placed another piece, boxing her forces in. Her own
blue scales were surrounded by a sea of white. But Voria
had anticipated that, had seen this possibility a hundred
turns back. She placed one more piece, and schooled her

features to a passive mask as she waited for Aetherius to realize what she'd done.

"Impressive," Olyssa murmured beside her. "You've set up two eyes. He cannot take both, and so long as one is open you have a route to escape. Well done. I thought you'd lost that entire quadrant, but now it looks as if you possess a near equal part of that territory."

Olyssa referred to two gaps in Voria's territory, arrayed in just such a way that Aetherius couldn't entrap them. Placing a piece in one would allow her to use the other to capture it, thus making the move illegal. She'd lost a little ground, but only a little.

Prior to meeting Neith, Voria had been an indifferent *Go* player at best. She didn't have the patience for the complex strategies, and unlike many of her classmates never engaged in any of the play-by-missive leagues they had established.

Aetherius, unsurprisingly, continued his offense. He pressed her in another quadrant in a desperate attempt to surround her. This, too, she had anticipated many, many turns ago. Voria dropped pieces as fast as he, the pattern growing until much of that quadrant was filled.

Then Voria dropped a scale in a third quadrant. It threatened his position there. If she dropped one more piece he'd lose four, and she'd command a full third of that quadrant. He had no choice but to respond.

Their battle moved to that third quadrant, white battling blue as their pattern of pieces spread. It eventually touched the second quadrant, just as Voria had known it would. Her forces from the second joined the third, and she encircled a dozen of Aetherius's pieces. They disappeared from the board, and appeared in a stack next to her—a stack worth more than all the pay she'd ever received from the Confederacy.

Voria smiled down at the board. If she continued like this, she could take it all. And now, Aetherius knew it. "So you were going to tell me about my friend, Aran. You implied he was dead."

She hoped the opportunity to jab her with the revelation would prove irresistible, since he was losing. She wasn't disappointed.

"Ah, an amusing story, that." He peered down at the board with a deep frown as he sought a way to extricate himself from Voria's trap. "Apparently, your champion fought his way all the way to the temple. An impressive feat, for an Outrider. But then, we don't expect too much from them. Olyssa sees hers as tools. I see mine as pets. One does not expect a dog or a cat to pilot a starship. And they shouldn't be surprised when the pet defecates on their floor."

"Indeed." Voria hoped the ambiguous answer would keep him talking. Wyrms didn't seem much different from people, and enjoyed the sound of their own voices just as much. Perhaps more.

"Your pet, if you'll allow the indulgence, made it all the way to the temple. Thanks to the treacherous armor he smuggled onto the march, he even managed to kill all the forces arrayed against him." Aetherius sounded genuinely impressed. "You have no idea how rare that is. Almost all such marches end in death, usually well before the Outrider reaches the top of the Temple. Yet, after your friend found victory, my grandmother struck him down. She cast a bolt from the heavens, and incinerated his body. Nothing but a greasy stain of ash remains."

Voria raised a trembling hand to her forehead and closed her eyes. She accounted herself a good judge of character, and Aetherius had taken a little too much pleasure in the delivery to have been lying. He was recounting a memory, no doubt shown him through divination. She could perform the same spell, and verify the truth of it.

"It is your move," Aetherius pointed out. He didn't seem pleased about it, and she couldn't blame him. Three more turns and he lost another seven pieces. It would only get worse from there.

"Pass," she said.

Shocked murmurs rippled through the crowd of Wyrms that had gathered around her table. If Aetherius also passed, then the game would be over. Their respective territory on the board would be totaled, as would the number of captured pieces. If the game ended now, that total would put her ahead, by the slimmest of margins.

"Why are you doing this?" He leaned forward over the board, his slitted eyes locked on her as if trying to puzzle something out.

"Because you've badly misunderstood something, Aetherius." Voria rose and smoothed her jacket. "You and your people wonder if you're better than a Shayan at a game you'd played for millennia. You were certain you'd win, certain you'd embarrass me. But what you didn't know?" Now it was her turn to lean over the game board. She speared him with her gaze. "I don't care about games. I save my interest for war. You want to see what I'm capable of? That's the only place you'll ever see it."

Aetherius eyed her thoughtfully. "Pass," he finally said.

35

THAT'S A BIG SNAKE

Nara dearly missed the sun. Being trapped underground took her back to the Umbral Depths, back to the world in the darkness. Only this was somehow worse. In the Umbral Depths there was darkness, but there was also vast emptiness.

Here the stone pressed all around her. Some tunnels were barely wide enough to squeeze through, and twice she'd had to use a teleport spell to get past an area where her armor wouldn't fit.

Sound echoed oddly here, often magnified in strange ways. It made sleeping difficult, and she'd taken to wearing her helmet as she slept. It blocked the sound and made her feel at least a little safer.

Thankfully they hadn't seen any of the unstable Wes had mentioned. It was a phenomenon she'd never heard of, one of many things Wes had been happy to talk about as they journeyed. He was proving to be a wealth of information, and knew a surprising amount about both history and magical theory.

Nara had been hesitant after Voria's skepticism, but Wes

was proving far more capable, academically at least, than she'd hoped.

"Do you want some coffee?" Wes whispered loudly. He snapped a packet and dropped it into his cup. It began to bubble and hiss, and the water darkened into a bitter-smelling brew.

"More than anything." She removed her helmet and set it on a rock next to her. "How close to Virkonna are we? I have no sense of scale down here." Nara removed an MRE from her void pocket and snapped it open.

She waited for the meal, something called lasagna, to heat. She had no idea what it was made with, but it was passable enough. Aran loved these things. She preferred cake, or any of the other Shayan delicacies she could summon on the *Talon*.

"We'll pass below her today. We're entering a tunnel called the spiral, because it...well, it spirals." Wes sketched a descending corkscrew pattern in the air. "We'll pass the first bend inside of an hour. That's where things will start to get dangerous, I think. We're close enough to Virkonna to see some pretty scary stuff. If we do, I'll warn you with a manly yell."

"A manly yell?" Nara blinked.

He smiled cheerfully. "Fair point. It may not be manly. But it will be a yell." He offered her a sealed cup of caf, which she gratefully accepted. Caf was one of the very best things Ternus had introduced to the rest of the Confederacy.

Wes started up the tunnel, the light from his headlamp bobbing as he began to hum to himself. He did that often as he walked, and Nara often found it amusing. Today, less so.

"If we run into anything, don't yell, manly or otherwise." She drew even with him and made sure he was looking in her direction. That brought the light, of course, but she squinted at him anyway. "Our survival will depend on our ability to hide. I can teleport us. I can make us invisible. I can summon illusions to confuse pursuers. Stick close to me, and stay quiet. I will keep us safe."

"No manly yells, got it." Wes kept humming.

They travelled for a little over an hour before they reached the first bend. It wasn't anything remarkable, just a slightly steeper grade that curved sharply around and back the way they'd come. There were subtle changes, though.

More debris littered the corridor, and some of the walls had collapsed inward. Often that was caused by some sort of rockslide, but they passed several instances where it appeared something had burrowed into the tunnel.

"Nara," Wes called softly. He clicked his headlamp and the bright white light was replaced by a soft red beam. It would be much less visible from a distance, but it also turned everything around them into dim shapes. "Come take a look at this."

Nara crept over to Wes, who'd dropped into a crouch. She joined him and squinted down at the ground where he was pointing. She couldn't make out anything.

"One sec," Wes whispered. He fished his pocket tablet out and used the screen to illuminate the ground. "See this?"

A meter-thick line wove back and forth through the dirt, in the direction they were going. Nara licked her lips. "That's a big snake. Do you have any idea how old it is?"

"Nope," he admittedly cheerfully. "I'm not a tracker or anything, just observant. If I had to guess I'd say it's recent. Especially given the smell."

Nara realized she couldn't smell anything with her helmet on, and was immediately grateful. They'd encountered many incredible odors during their trip, and she wasn't eager to discover another.

"We may as well press on. If we run into it, we'll deal with it." Nara started up the corridor, and Wes followed. The further they went, the more she realized Wes didn't know the area as well as he'd claimed. He had an excellent sense of direction, and was great with maps, but it sounded like he had surprisingly little actual experience.

Nara reached into her void pocket and withdrew her staff. She carried it loosely in both hands, ready to cast if a threat presented itself. That kind of vigilance grew harder to maintain the further they went, especially as the hours passed. But she stubbornly kept her staff out. There was no telling when she'd need it.

The tunnel evened out into a long, straight line, though it continued to slope down. As they continued forward Nara could feel something above her and to the right. Something immensely powerful.

"What is it?" Wes asked. "Did you hear something?"

Nara pointed up and to the right. "Virkonna is right there. No more than three hundred meters away." Being that close to a sleeping god was more than a little terrifying. After meeting Neith, and Drakkon, she had no illusions. A god could snuff them out with a thought.

"All the more reason to keep moving." Wes started up the tunnel again.

She flew after him, then landed and started walking next to him. "That means in the next hour or two we should be far enough away from Virkonna for me to search for other signatures."

Rocks clacked off each other as something moved in the distance. Something large. Nara moved instantly and settled her hand around Wes's mouth. She pulled him gently against her armor with one arm, and hissed into his ear, "Don't cry out."

She pulled him gently into the shadows of a nearby pile of debris. Wes went limp in her grasp, his eyes wild as he raised a trembling hand and clicked his headlamp off. Nara sketched a quick *fire* sigil, and a flame appeared above that area of the tunnel.

A large scaled body reared up in the shadows, white scales glinting as an elongated head investigated the light. A forked tongue flicked out as the creature moved around the light. Its skin bulged and oozed in strange ways, and a thick, viscous fluid flowed from putrid sores all over its body.

Before she could see more, the snake's head shot forward, and it swallowed the spell. They were plunged back into sudden darkness.

"That thing *ate the spell*. Think about what it will do to us," Wes whispered fiercely. "We need to get out of here. Maybe we can creep back up the way we came. We can find another way."

"Be quiet," Nara hissed back. She thought quickly, more quickly than any normal human could manage.

The snake, whatever it was, *had* eaten the spell. That suggested it fed on magic, which matched everything she'd learned about primals. There had been similar snakes on Marid, though those were smaller, and a lot more timid. This thing was sick, whether from too much magic or something else she couldn't say. But that hadn't diminished its appetite. It wanted magic, which meant she understood how to motivate it.

She studied the cave. A forest of rocky stalagmites and stalactites broke up the room, making it difficult for something that large to move between them.

"Wes, you want me to tell Ismene that you're a hero, right?" Nara whispered sweetly.

She couldn't see his face well enough to make out his suspicion, but she heard it in his voice. "You're going to ask me to do something stupid, aren't you?"

She rested her hand on his arm. "Not that stupid. I'm going to make you glow, and all you have to do is run."

"I was going to do that anyway," he hissed back. "But I'd prefer not to paint a neon sign on my back."

Nara squeezed his arm. With her spell armor she could have made it painful, but she didn't. She made it firm, though. "Wes, I hired you to guide me down here. Are you seriously going to tell me you're going to cut and run at the first hostile encounter?"

Wes froze. He was silent for a long moment. In the end his shoulders squared, and his pride seemed to win. "Okay, go ahead and magic me. I'll hightail it back the way we came, and if the snake gets close I'll try shooting it. But I don't think my guns are going to be of much use against that thing. I doubt yours will either."

"Just trust me, please." Nara released him, and sketched a *fire* sigil. A tiny nimbus of flame surrounded the archeologist, casting wild shadows around them.

She knew he was right. Direct magic use against that creature would probably just feed the thing. If she were going to kill it, she'd have to use indirect means.

"Well?" Nara barked. "What are you waiting for? Move!" She did her very best to imitate Crewes, and apparently it worked.

The archeologist scampered away like a rabbit, darting between rocks as he picked a path back the way they'd come.

Nara spun to face the snake, its scales glittering in the

distance. A large, glowing eye fixed on Wes's retreating form. The snake slithered forward, crossing the ground with much greater speed than she'd anticipated.

She took a deep, slow breath. This would require absolute precision to pull off. She scanned the room, focusing on the stalactites dipping down from the ceiling. Several were large enough to weigh tons and all ended in sharp points. Perfect improvised weapons.

The snake slithered between them, weaving closer to Wes at an alarming rate. He began to shriek, and started scrambling up a large stalagmite. The snake exploded through several pillars as it sought Wes.

Nara slowly raised a hand as she judged the snake's path. There, that one. She sketched a level three void bolt, and flung it at the base of a stalactite, right where it met the cavern ceiling. The bolt disintegrated rock, and a three meter spike of jagged rock came down on the snake.

It punched through the creature's skull, pinning it to the ground. The snake began thrashing wildly, its tail knocking over pillars. Wes scrambled further away, barely dodging a frantic strike from the dying snake.

Finally, the thrashing ceased, and the light left its eyes.

"See," Nara yelled, her voice booming through the cavern. "I told you we'd be fine."

Wes adjusted his spectacles and studiously avoided looking at her. "I won't be fine until I change my underpants."

36

SISTERS

Frit wasn't sure what to expect when she entered the circle of redwoods. The towering trees screened the little clearing from sight, offering a certain degree of privacy from prying eyes. Several women stood in that clearing, and every one could have been a sister.

The shade of flame differed slightly on each, but they had the same hair, though different styles. The same delicate features. All were female, of course. And every last one of them stood at exactly the same height. It was as if they'd been stamped from a mold. Perhaps they had been.

"Welcome, child," Nebiat's warm voice came from behind her and she turned to see the smiling dreadlord. She wore her human form, though Frit doubted that made her any less dangerous. Nebiat waved at the others to approach. "Thank you all for coming. You represent those brave enough to seek change for your kind. I approached others, but many were too frightened to risk their lives, as you all are."

Frit tightened at that. She hadn't agreed to risk her life,

though she supposed the simple act of coming here was doing exactly that.

Nebiat gestured expansively, taking them all in. Her smile was warm and genuine. Frit mistrusted it, knowing the dreadlord could appear to be whatever she wished.

"Look at each other. For many, this is your first time seeing another Ifrit. Each of you was created by a Shayan house. You were captured as a primal essence, most likely drifting happily through the void. They dumped you off at the Heart of Krox to catalyze, then picked you up before the process completed. You were placed, in a nascent state, into a pattern inducer. An inducer that shaped you into exactly who and what they wished you to be."

Frit looked around at her sisters, who were studying her with just as much curiosity. Even their clothing was similar, with a *fire* sigil on the collar. Only one other girl had *void*. Two girls wore swords, meaning they must be war mages.

"Even your names are a joke to them." Nebiat frowned suddenly, and lowered her arms. "Please, introduce yourselves. Frit, would you begin please, child?"

Frit's eyes widened as they all looked at her. She cleared her throat, and puffed out a bit of smoke. It hurt being the focus of so much attention, even the attention of her sisters. "I'm Frit. I serve Eros, up in the palace. That might sound fun, but it isn't. It's rotting, from the inside. I see terrible things every day."

She glanced at the girl on her right, whose fiery eyes widened in alarm.

"I'm Ifra," she managed. She seemed like she might say something else, but then looked to the next girl.

"Rita," said the next girl.

"Frat."

"Iff."

Each name came like a blow, and in that moment Frit
finally understood Nebiat's goal. She was expertly guiding
them to their own realizations—in this case, that their
names were all plays on the word Ifrit. Their names were,
literally, a joke to their masters.

"We can't let them treat us this way," Frit snapped. The
other girls looked at her as if she'd suddenly sprouted
horns. "You can't tell me you enjoy living like this. Being
their playthings."

"Of course we hate it," Ifra said. Frit turned to her, and
the girl dropped her gaze immediately. Her voice fell to a
near whisper. "It's just that...what can we do?"

"That's the real question, isn't it?" Nebiat interjected
smoothly. She wrapped a comforting arm around Ifra,
seemingly untroubled by the smoldering heat. "You'll have
to decide. Together. As a group. I cannot choose for you, but
if you need my help...I give it freely, with no price or
reservation."

Nebiat held up a slender rod. The black metal glinted in
the sun, tantalizing. They all recognized it, of course. Nebiat
handed the rod to Frit, and Frit accepted it. The others all
stared at her as if seeing a promised savior.

Frit felt a fool. Nebiat was grooming her, she realized.
She knew Frit had been given more freedom, and had developed a bit of a backbone. The rest of these girls were
broken. They couldn't lead. Frit could, and Nebiat knew it.
That explained her interest.

The question was, how did Frit feel about that?

She looked to her sisters—her timid, frightened, sisters.
They'd be used by Shaya, until they were used up. One by
one, these girls would die fighting their wars. And for what?
A life of slavery? It wasn't fair. It wasn't right.

Someone needed to do something. *She* needed to do

something. Frit tightened both hands around the rod. "We can't stay here. Living like this isn't right. We're sentient beings. We have thoughts, and dreams. We aren't property."

"What can we do?" Ifra asked. She'd been the only person brave enough to speak more than her name. She seemed to gather her courage. "We have the rod. We could leave right now. Go somewhere else, and live free."

"But if we did that," Frit pointed out, "it would leave the rest of our sisters here, enslaved. If we leave, I can promise you Eros will take it badly. He'll increase security for every Ifrit, and they'll all be punished for our actions."

"What do you have in mind, child?" Nebiat folded her arms and watched Frit with intense interest.

Frit turned to Nebiat. "Nothing rash, that's for sure. You all find other sisters, and convince them to escape. We get as many as we can. Then, if Nebiat will help us, we escape this world and never look back. But I don't want to leave any sister behind who wants to go. Nebiat, will you help us?"

"Of course, child." Nebiat nodded magnanimously. "You are family. I will give anything you ask. Simply name it."

37

FETCH

Nara advanced up the corridor slowly. She crept along, her body plastered to the right wall. Wes moved a few meters ahead, slowly approaching a faint glow in the distance. It was the first light of any kind they'd seen, which made her immensely wary.

The first snake hadn't been the largest they'd seen, and the sightings were becoming more numerous as they proceeded further underground. They'd passed far enough away from Virkonna that her signature no longer blotted out everything magical around them.

That had allowed Nara to spot another signature, which lay a good distance below them. Below them and in the direction of the glow. It pulsed quietly, much less powerful than Virkonna, but rhythmic and strong.

"What do you see?" She moved to within a meter of Wes.

The bespectacled archeologist peered around a rocky corner, his face illuminated by the glow. After so long in darkness, even that much light felt a blessing.

"Best you take a look." Wes pulled back from the edge of the tunnel, and gestured for her to take his place.

Nara looked around the corner...into something at once terrifying and beautiful. Hundreds of snakes of various sizes slithered across the floor of a cavern that stretched kilometers into the distance. Fifty-meter-thick stalagmites stabbed up into the air, higher than Nara's vantage. She could see holes bored in their rocky sides, and shapes moved inside those holes.

As she watched, a draconic face crept to the edge of one, and a white drake leapt out. It glided to the ground, where it seized one of the smaller snakes and hauled it up into the air. The snake wriggled in the drake's grasp, powerless to escape.

A larger snake, this one at least a hundred meters long, reared up silently behind the drake. The snake lunged, and both the drake and the smaller snake disappeared down its gullet. The snake lowered itself silently to the ground, and slithered on as if nothing had happened.

"Do you have a plan to get through there?" Wes whispered.

He pressed against the back of her armor, and she gently pushed him back. Wes was what Pickus would call a stage-5 clinger.

"I might." She continued to study the layout of the room. "Get out all your magical gear. Anything, any gadgets that can tap into arcane energy."

"I don't have much." Wes removed his battered pack and opened the flap. He rummaged around inside and withdrew several items.

The first was a pair of well-cared-for binoculars. They had a line of sigils drawn along the top, mostly *fire* and *dream*. He added a sheathed combat knife with no visible sigils, and a canteen with *air*, *life*, and *water* sigils all along the outer edge.

"I guess you could count these, too." Wes reached into his duster and withdrew his golden pistols.

Before becoming a true mage, Nara had lived and breathed spellpistols. She'd loved hers, and knew how to handle them. Wes, sadly, did not. He fumbled with both, and nearly dropped the second one. He awkwardly dumped both into the pile.

"That's everything I've got." He looked up at her over his spectacles. "Now what?"

"Well, if you had to pick one of these objects to be expendable, which would it be?" Nara asked. She eyed each of them, and figured any would work for what she had in mind.

"Hmm. I'd get rid of the pistols, if that were possible. It isn't though." He heaved a regretful sigh. "They always come back."

"What do you mean?" She asked. An idea had begun to germinate.

"Well, I didn't choose to bond the pistols." He picked one up and handed it to her. "They're really powerful and all, but I'm not a warrior. I dress like someone in a holodrama, but that's just to scare off toughs. It works a surprising amount of the time." He cleared his throat awkwardly. "I won't tell you the whole story about how I found them, but the weapons pretty much fight for themselves. They drag me along for the ride."

Nara accepted the pistol and inspected it carefully. She'd seen a great number of magic items, ranging from simple items like the binoculars all the way to a fully developed eldimagus like Ikadra. Nara put these pistols very nearly on Ikadra's level in magical power.

The craftsmanship was unmistakable. Each pistol was a single piece of smooth golden metal, with a simple trigger guard and a curved grip. A sea of tiny runes lined the barrel, and Nara would have needed a magnifying glass and several days to catalogue them all.

"And these pistols always come back?" Nara prompted. "So, if you were to throw one into that cavern, what would happen, exactly?" She leaned around the corner again and studied the layout of the room.

"Well, they always reappear in the holsters," Wes said. He moved his duster aside and showed her the dark leather holsters. Both were etched with tiny runes, though Nara couldn't make them out. "I don't always notice, but it's generally no more than a few minutes. Never more than an hour."

"That's perfect. It means we don't have to sacrifice your binoculars."

"Wait, why are we sacrificing my stuff?" Wes bent and began scooping objects back into his pack. He left the pistols.

"Well, here's my plan. I'm going to fling your pistols into that cavern." She mentally calculated the trajectory she'd need to plant them at the best possible locations. "I'll put one next to that pile of snakes, and the other by that one. I'm betting they'll try to eat your pistols, and I'm hoping that will make a commotion. While they're fighting, we fly around the edge of the cavern, toward the signature I detected. Hopefully we can find an exit on the other side."

"I can't think of a downside. Here you go." Wes picked up both pistols and handed them to her. "I don't mind being without them for a bit. Of course, knowing them, this will be the one time they don't come back."

"Well, time to find out." Nara stepped from cover and raised her casting hand. She sketched a quick series of *void* sigils, and a purple nimbus appeared around both weapons.

She pointed into the room, and they shot out into the air, soaring hundreds of meters.

Their path carried them past many of the spires, and drakes emerged by the dozens. They launched from their little cubbies, flowing after the pistols like a swarm of bats chasing an insect. The pistols continued to fall, each landing in the muck at the bottom of the cavern. Right next to two of the largest snakes in the place.

Pandemonium broke out. Snakes lunged for the pistols, only to be attacked by larger snakes. Drakes darted in, some snatching up smaller snakes, while others battled to reach the pistols.

"Okay, time to go. Climb on," Nara instructed. Wes obediently climbed onto her back, and Nara sketched a sphere of invisibility. She lifted off and flew at maximum speed around the outer edge of the cavern. Nara angled her flight to pass by unoccupied areas, which was easier now that so many of the drakes had flown off toward the pistols.

Her breathing thundered inside the confines of the helmet as they zipped along the ceiling. Nara whipped between stalagmites, tracing the best path she could.

Several tense minutes passed, and her breathing finally eased. She began to descend toward the far side of the cavern, and glanced over her shoulder to find the chaos had begun to die down. Just in time.

They'd made it.

Nara scanned the cavern wall, slowing their descent until she found it.

"There," Wes said excitedly. He thrust a hand over her shoulder. "See that shadow there, next to the cluster of rocks? Lots of snakes have slithered along the ground there, and they must be going somewhere."

Nara dropped down in that direction and landed just

outside the shadowed area. A narrow tunnel stretched into the darkness before them, but unlike the rest of the tunnels, this one had been carved. A perfect rectangular hallway disappeared into the distance.

Faintly glowing sigils lined the walls, though more than a few had winked out, leaving gaps.

More importantly, a potent magical signature pulsed in the distance, beckoning Nara forward. They had arrived.

38

ALLIANCES

This time Voria had a better idea of what to expect when the missive summoned her to Olyssa's eyrie. Dragons, as it turned out, preferred to live a portion of their lives as humans. Olyssa's manor—it helped to think of the cavern that way—wasn't so very different from the manor houses of Shayan nobles.

She had her servants, in this case humans wearing white dresses with blue trim. Several stood in attendance around a plush, cushioned chair where Olyssa lounged. She cradled a goblet absently in one hand, and held an open book in the other.

"Welcome, Major," Olyssa called. She made no move to rise, and Voria noted there were no other chairs in the chamber. Apparently she was supposed to stand. "Thank you for coming. The entire Council is still buzzing about the way you bested Aetherius, particularly the way you spared him at the end. That kind of unexpected mercy was...highly embarrassing, given his previous treatment of you and yours."

"I can't say I'm disappointed to hear that Aetherius lost

face," Voria admitted. She folded her arms, and lamented the fact that she'd left Ikadra back on the *Hunter*. But carrying him made her too much of a target. "And I appreciate the invitation today. I must admit I'm a bit surprised by it. You've not been particularly receptive to my previous requests."

"Can I be candid, Major?" Olyssa languidly sipped from her goblet.

"Please." Voria didn't know any other way.

"I underestimated you. I believed you were some simpering mage dispatched by an ailing government." Olyssa set the goblet down in midair and rose from her chair. She waved a hand and a Kem'Hedj board appeared in the air a few feet away. "By besting a master of Aetherius's skill, you've raised some troubling questions. You've shown that, perhaps, you are as worthy of our ear as the Krox. Until that moment, my people would never have considered an alliance. But now? Now, if not an equal, then at least you are not so very far an inferior."

Voria found the back-handed compliment flattering. It was still insulting, but that was just the way of Wyrms. They were immortal killing machines with the very real potential of achieving godhood. A certain amount of hubris was to be expected.

"Does that mean you are willing to consider an alliance with the Confederacy against the Krox?" Voria asked. Bluntly, of course. She was damnably tired of the games these Wyrms seemed to enjoy.

"I am considering it, yes. Aranthar's death was...regrettable." Something like pity flitted across her features, but it was gone too quickly to be sure. "However, it removes the single largest impediment to an alliance. Before, I could not forge such an alliance, because he was a dragonslayer. But now? He is dead and his honor above reproach. I called you here to discuss working together. Would you like to play as we talk?"

Olyssa waved at a game board in the corner and it floated over. A stack of golden scales appeared in a floating pile near Voria.

Voria moved to the game board and clasped her hands behind her back. The floating pile of scales followed her. "I'd enjoy that, I think. Tell me, what do you think of the Krox? I only know them from our perspective, which is...not a pleasant one."

Olyssa flicked the first scale onto the board then smiled up at Voria. "Now that is a very complicated question. I suspect we know a great deal more about Krox than your people do, as we witnessed both his rise and fall. Krox is not viewed favorably on our world, because Krox isn't a dragon."

"I don't understand," Voria said. She levitated a scale onto the board in the opposite corner from Olyssa's piece. "Nebiat, the woman you might call my nemesis, is a Wyrm. We've fought countless hatchlings, what we call enforcers."

"I understand your confusion, Major." Olyssa dropped another scale, this one adjacent to the first, both placed on the opposite side of the board. It was a defensive strategy. A group of two or three pieces was much more difficult to capture than a single lone piece. She'd built a beachhead, of sorts. "What you know as *Krox* are the children of the earth-mother. Each dragon egg is implanted with a spirit before they are born, and that spirit inhabits the body of the creature that is born. The Krox are, in reality, the children of the earthmother herself."

"That's horrifying." Voria recoiled a half-step at the very thought of the process. The Krox were...stealing bodies?

"Please, let us return to more pleasant matters." Olyssa gestured at the game board.

Voria nodded. Her vertigo returned as possibilities rolled out of her in waves. She struggled to isolate the game, and not every possibility linked to this moment. That level of control was difficult, and a bead of sweat rolled down her temple.

She saw a hundred variations of the next ten moves. Focus. Some of those possibilities were more likely than others. She followed those paths, studying each outcome before moving on to another.

"What are you doing?" Olyssa asked.

The voice brought Voria back to the moment and she looked up guiltily. "Contemplating my next move." She schooled her features into as unreadable mask as she could manage. "Why do you ask?"

"Because I've seen that look before." Olyssa's tone had grown suspicious. "My mother read futures the way I read books. She never lost a game of Kem'Hedj, not once. Because she could see the outcome before the game even began."

Voria rocked back and forth, a habit she'd fought hard to break as a child. Particularly when she'd been caught doing something naughty. "Wasn't your mother a goddess?" she finally asked.

"Yes," Olyssa said, dubiously. She flicked another scale onto the board. "Do not mince words with me, Shayan. I know magic when I see it. What sorcery do you possess and how did you come by it?"

"All right, yes, I can see possibilities. And yes, that does make this game a bit...unfair." Voria levitated a scale adjacent to the one Olyssa had just laid. "It's early, but I'm guessing you'll last about six hundred turns."

It awed her that such a thing could be known. That she could know it. Neith had changed her in a fundamental way. A way that, she suspected, mortals were not ever meant to know.

Olyssa's face went...well, *feral*, for lack of a better term. The pretense of her being human vanished, though she didn't change physically. Her reptilian eyes widened, and her jaw worked in a way no human mouth could manage.

The anger, if that was what it was, passed quickly. Olyssa mastered herself and took several deep breaths.

"It is difficult for me to accept that one such as you"— she eyed Voria with no small amount of contempt—"could be...elevated in such a way. I do not understand how such a thing is possible. Only a god could have given you this ability, and not just any god. A god of immense age and power. How did you come by this?"

Voria opened her mouth to answer. She'd never told anyone about Neith, never spoken directly about any of it. Not with anyone, other than the people she'd gone with, after they'd returned from the Umbral Depths. And in that instant, she learned she could not. She wanted to speak, but no words came out.

"I see." Olyssa nodded knowingly. "I should expect no less. Were I a god imbuing anyone with powers that might lead inquisitive mages to come searching for my identity, I would ensure no one could speak about me."

"It is a rather potent defense," Voria said. She relaxed her shoulders and allowed a deep breath, now that she could speak. "I can't tell you who gave me the ability, but I can tell you they did it to stop Krox from rising. This god or goddess believes Krox will dominate the sector if not stopped. Your goddess will become nothing more than a plaything. I have seen enough evidence to believe it. Shaya will fall. Virkon will fall. Ternus is little more than a minor distraction. And all that before Krox's true work begins."

Olyssa's discomfort appeared to grow with every word. She sat on the edge of her chair and fluffed a cushion behind her. She hadn't added a scale to the board in some time.

"I find your words no surprise," Olyssa muttered. Her gaze was far away. "Nebiat and my brother Khalahk were mates, once. He saw in her the child of the earthmother, and he called out to that. It blinded him to the truth. The Krox part of her dangled that hope, and used it to manipulate his emotions. Krox, and his children, are ever the manipulators. Aetherius may not remember that, but I do."

"Will you ally formally with us?" Voria asked, not daring to hope.

"I cannot offer a formal alliance on behalf of my world, but I can make it known on Virkon that I consider you an ally," she offered. "The other flights respect me, though I do not command the strongest flight any longer."

"That belongs to Aetherius, doesn't it?" Voria asked. She resisted the urge to roll her eyes. Of course he had the largest flight. Who else would the Krox toady up to?

"It does." Olyssa nodded. "He has the strongest flight, and what's more, the other flights listen to him. They respect our flight, but in the past we always had Khalahk or Rolf to speak for us. Now? We have no Wyrm of their strength. I am old, and I am knowledgable, but I am no battle leader. I am a politician now, and at best a soldier when it comes to war."

"You've seen what I can do." Voria stood up straighter, and squared her shoulders. "You may not be a commander, but I am. Ally with me, Olyssa. I will lead the fight against the Krox, and I will drive them from this world."

39

BACK TO THE FUTURE

The first thing Aran became conscious of was the dripping, echoing every few seconds as if he were in some sort of enclosed space. He opened his eyes and blinked a few times as they adjusted to the near total darkness.

He was lying in something cold and sticky. It covered his right side, and had already soaked through his shirt. The stench emanating from it made his eyes water. He staggered to his feet, then paused to listen. Had something moved in the darkness?

Several seconds later, it hadn't repeated. Aran slowly tapped the bracelet around his wrist, but nothing happened. He raised it to his face for examination. A new line of white-blue sigils ran along it, probably from whatever Virkonna had done to his armor. Unfortunately, whatever magical upgrade she'd initiated didn't look like it had finished yet. He had no idea how long it would take, and it looked like he was without spellarmor until then. Lovely.

Aran reached into his void pocket and withdrew his spellblade. It thrummed eagerly in his hand, a sorrowful note, then a happy one. He'd been keeping it in a void pocket, but if it really were a living thing what must that be like? A troubling thought for another time.

He started up a corridor, holding his bracelet aloft as an improvised light source. It did little to banish the shadows, but it did glint off the oily walls, lending them definition. Whatever the terrible-smelling oil was, it seemed to cover almost anything.

Where had Virkonna sent him? Inside some sort of underground complex? There was no way to know, at least not without exploring.

"How about a little light there, bud?" Aran asked his sword. To his surprise, and relief, it responded by flaring to life. A warm orange glow came from the blade. "Thanks. Maybe it's about time I give you a name."

"The blade already has a name," a soft voice slithered through the darkness.

Aran whirled as he shifted instinctively into Drakkon stance. "Who are you?" He didn't bother to demand they show themselves. Did that ever work?

"Narlifex is legendary," the voice whispered. It came from a few meters up the corridor, but as Aran slowly advanced he saw nothing. No eyes. No movement in the shadows. Only a wall of darkness that consumed all light that touched it. "Though the version you hold is young, and untested."

A harsh rasping came from the darkness, and Aran tensed. After a moment, he realized it was coughing. That was strangely reassuring, because it meant whatever was in that darkness had at least some semblance of humanity.

"Clearly you know something about me. How about you tell me about you? A name, maybe?" Aran demanded. He advanced another meter up the hall, and now stood within striking distance of the wall of darkness.

"We must move swiftly. Please, follow me. Quickly. If we do not arrive at the ordained time, everything you care for will be scoured away." The darkness receded slowly up the corridor.

Aran hesitated for a moment. Should he follow? It was likely this thing was leading him into a trap. If so, Aran decided to spring it. He started up the corridor, stepping as carefully as possible to avoid the largest pools of rancid goo.

The darkness never changed pace. It drifted forward ahead of him, turning down corridors as it moved unerringly toward whatever destination it had in mind. Aran had plenty of time to consider the situation, and wonder where he was. It was possible this was an underground complex, but it was also possible he was inside a vessel of some kind.

If he was, he prayed this wasn't the Spellship. That seemed unlikely, as Ikadra had been quite clear he was the key. How could Virkonna get him inside a locked ship, and if she could, what was the point of a key? Also, if this was the ship, wow did it suck.

Unless he'd just happened to appear in the sewage tank, and the rest of the vessel wasn't covered in alien ass juice.

"Listen I realize you've got the whole insane cryptic wall of darkness thing going on," Aran called up the corridor. "But do you think we could talk while we go wherever it is you're leading me?"

No answer.

"Great, nice chat." Aran sighed. Maybe he'd ask his questions anyway. "So where are we exactly? Inside a ship? On a random moon? The inside of a toilet meant for gods?"

"I was an Outrider once," the shadow said. "I don't

remember how long ago. Decades? Centuries? I do not know."

That got his attention. Aran quickened his step, but stayed quiet. If this thing wanted to talk, then he was going to let it.

The shadow stopped. The darkness lightened, and a humanoid shape gained definition. It—she—turned to face Aran. He still couldn't make out her features, but he could see long, greasy hair.

"My name was Rhea, last Outrider of the last dragon-flight," she whispered. Her voice quavered, and Aran thought he spied a tear on her cheek. "I kept the faith. I waited. And then I gave in to despair. I don't know how long ago that was. But here you are."

"You were expecting me?" Aran asked. It made a kind of sense. Gods used auguries the same way mortals used missives. Maybe Virkonna had told these people he'd be coming.

"Your blade is so young. You are so young. Not at all like the statues." She leaned a bit closer, and the stench grew overpowering. He forced himself to ignore it.

"Statues?" Aran barked a laugh. "Are you serious? I'm a pariah on pretty much every world I've been on. Especially this one, if this is Virkonna."

The figure cocked her head, and leaned a little bit closer. He could see her face now. The cheeks were coated in the same oil as the walls, but under that lay a beautiful woman, one with glittering green eyes.

"What year do you think it is?" the woman asked.

Aran had to think about that. The marines from Ternus used what they called a sector standard calendar. Most people adhered to that, though apparently Shayans had their own calendar...that they didn't want to share. "It's 985 sector standard."

She began to laugh—a long, keening, freeing laugh. It echoed off the walls, up the corridors. Aran tensed again, not liking the idea that she was so openly broadcasting their position. He waited patiently, and the laughter subsided.

"The year is 7,985 galactic standard." She leaned back into the shadows, and the stench retreated. "Come. We must get you there, and we must do it quickly. We may already be too late."

40

CRUCIBLE

The temperature rose several degrees the instant Nara stepped inside the carved tunnel. That suggested an internal source of heat, magical or otherwise. And that meant this place might still be active.

Nara crept along the corridor and beckoned for Wes to follow. She didn't really need to. He'd already stumbled inside and was staring up at the sigils like an eight-year-old on winter festival morning.

"This place is older than the surrounding strata, I'd venture. Far older." He shuffled a few more steps in, peering at the walls with a gigantic grin. "I think it's miraculous that so many of the sigils are still functional."

"Agreed." Nara paused as well. "I have to admit this place is fascinating, but I'm also more than a little worried about one of those snakes wandering after us. There are tracks leading in this direction, remember?"

"That's true." Wes blinked owlishly. "All right then, I'll contain my curiosity for now. At least until we find whatever it is you're looking for down here. Which you still haven't told me, by the way. I mean, I'm going to see whatever it is soon enough. What's the risk?"

"We have no idea if we're being scryed upon at any given moment." Nara started slowly back up the corridor. She pulled her staff from her void pocket and held it defensively before her. "The safest way to ensure an enemy doesn't learn a secret is not to talk about it. Like you said, you'll see for yourself soon enough." She glanced over her shoulder at him. "I do appreciate all the help, Wes. I mean that."

"Honestly?" Wes gave her a conspiratorial smile. "I'm just doing it to impress a girl. Not you, mind. I mean you are gorgeous and all, but...I am carrying a secret flame for another."

Nara was glad the helmet hid her smile at that. Secret flame indeed. "I'd never have guessed."

The corridor ended abruptly at a solid, golden door. A sea of green sigils danced across the surface in a curtain of magical energy.

"What do you think it is?" Wes walked toward the door and extended a hand toward the sigils.

"Don't touch it!" Nara darted forward and seized him by the shoulder.

"Oh, dear." Wes yanked his hand back like he'd been burned. "I nearly wet my trousers. I hope there's a good reason. Why shouldn't I touch it?"

"Do you see any snakes?" Nara asked. She pointed at the floor.

A pile of debris had accumulated at the base of the door, and closer inspection revealed little bits of bone, and a few pieces of dry skin.

"It's a ward of some kind, and I'm guessing it uses corrosive magic." Nara kept a careful distance back as she inspected it. "There has to be some sort of magical release, or way to get past it. I'm just hoping we don't need Ikadra."

"Need who now?" Wes asked. He poked at a bit of snake skeleton with his boot.

"Ignore me," Nara muttered. She shouldn't have mentioned Ikadra. "I'll see if I can disarm it."

She considered what she knew of wards. A powerful enough mage could brute force them with a nullification spell, but if their spell wasn't correctly tuned, it could trigger a magical explosion. Nara might be willing to try a spell like that, but not against a god-forged artifact. So she had to find another way.

Neith had gifted her with a dramatically increased intellect, and had insinuated she had some special role to play. Given that the ship had been left for the major, it stood to reason that the gods intended them to find it. Theoretically, she had everything she needed to find her way past this door.

But that didn't make solving this any easier.

"Hey door," Wes said suddenly. "Can you let us inside?"

She removed her helmet, just so she could raise an eyebrow. Wes shrugged. "What? It was worth a shot."

The hum coming from the door changed briefly in pitch. Only for a moment, and not enough that someone unskilled in magical resonance would even have detected it.

Nara turned to the door. Maybe Wes was onto something. What if the password was verbal? What would this thing want or expect to hear? If she could tell it Neith had sent her, then it might let her inside. "I am a vessel of the keeper of secrets. I have come to retrieve that which was left, to be used against Krox's return."

The door didn't seem terribly impressed.

It hadn't reacted to her, not in the same way it had

reacted to Wes. Why the difference? The resonance remained steady. She considered her words. What was she doing differently? She'd told the door who she was. Wes had asked the door a question.

Did it respond to questions?

"How do we open you?" she asked.

Wes raised an eyebrow, but Nara ignored him. As she'd hoped, there was a faint change in the magical resonance, and it happened when she'd asked the question. Could the spell think? She'd heard of sentient spells, and after meeting Ikadra the concept of magical life wasn't all that odd.

"You look like you're puzzling something out," Wes ventured. He leaned closer to the door, studying it through his spectacles. "Can you disarm it somehow?"

"I doubt it." Nara placed her hand near the field, and felt the pulsing, acidic energy. "It's a nasty mix of *void* and *earth*."

"Cosmic acid. Eww." Wes folded his arms. "Well I know you're not likely to want to turn back, but I'm all out of ideas."

Nara took a deep breath, and blocked out Wes, and every other conceivable distraction. She chewed on the problem, considering the mind of the god who'd created this door. If you knew that you're going to be sending a mortal to open it, and that mortal will have to figure out how to do so, then it stood to reason that Neith had given her everything she needed to solve the problem. There's no way she'd have not done so, because she'd have seen the possibility of Nara failing. So, she had what she needed.

She needed to ask the door a question, she just needed to figure out the right one. Odds were good she was over-complicating this.

"Can you understand me?" she asked.

The resonance changed sharply, then shifted back.

"Well, you know I'm the vessel sent here to retrieve the First Spellship." Nara tapped her lip as she thought. "Will you lower the field for us?"

The ward shimmered out of existence, and the door rose slowly into the ceiling.

"Wait, was that a spell?" Wes demanded. "How did you get the door to open? I mean, how did you know what to say? I know a lot about the age of dragons, and none of what you just said comes from anything I've read. Keeper of secrets?"

"I know you've got a lot of questions," Nara allowed. "Do me one favor. Save them up until we get inside. Once we find what I'm looking for, I will answer every one of your questions. I promise."

Wes seemed to consider that for a long moment. "I can manage that."

Nara stepped through the doorway into what appeared to be a workshop. The walls were a soft blue-silver color, and exuded a faint, but incredibly powerful magical aura. The room smelled musty, as if it hadn't been opened in a very long time. Which it likely hadn't been.

Wes crinkled his nose. "Ugg, this place smells like a tomb."

A variety of tools, most unfamiliar, lined one wall. Three tables sat in a perfect triangle, and tools were still scattered across one of the tables. There was no sign of whatever they'd been working on, but the tables glowed faintly with residual magical energy.

"Something powerful was created here," Nara murmured in awe. She walked slowly through the workshop. "Many somethings, I think. The signature of this room is...layered. Like this place was used for a long time."

"By who, is the question?" Wes asked. He'd picked up

something that resembled a screwdriver, but with six tips. "And what did they create?" She glanced at him and he smiled sheepishly. "I know, I know...save them up. Just thinking aloud."

Nara realized there was a doorway on the far side of the workshop. It drew her like a magnet, and she walked quickly to it. On the other side lay a catwalk, overlooking a long, empty hangar. It had room for an enormous ship, but if the Spellship had ever been here there was no sign of it now.

She closed her eyes and forced a series of deep, calming breaths. True mages did not cry.

There was a solution here. Some gods might be cruel, but she doubted any were stupid. They'd sent her here, and they intended her to find this ship.

"What do you think they stored here?" Wes asked. He pushed past her, through the doorway and out to the railing along the catwalk. "This hangar is easily two kilometers across. And are we 'here' yet? Because I've got questions."

"We're here," Nara finally managed. There had been a moment where she wasn't sure she could keep the tears at bay, but that moment had passed. "I'll answer your questions as we explore. Somewhere in here lies the key to finding the ship that fits in that hangar."

41

SHINURA

After a little exploration, Nara found what she guessed must be the control room. It sat a level above where they'd entered, and afforded a much better look at the facility. The view from the observation deck outside the control room was breathtaking.

"Nara, what is this place?" Wes asked from behind her.

She turned and found his face filled with the same wonder that had awakened when they'd come into the tunnel. Wes loved this stuff, a love she shared. She wondered what it must be like to be able to pursue knowledge for knowledge's sake, unentangled by vast galactic auguries that determined the fate of everything.

"I don't know, but I suspect the answer is in this room." She turned from the balcony and headed back inside.

"You are correct," a frigid voice said behind her. Nara whirled, shocked to see the oddest person in the corner. Had he been there the whole time?

He looked human enough, but a pair of draconic wings jutted from his back. She also noted the tail flicking back and forth behind him in what she guessed might be agitation. He had a shock of bright white hair and piercing blue eyes with storms playing across them.

"Who are you?" Nara kept her tone neutral—if anything, friendly. She had no idea who, or what, this thing was.

"I am the Shade of Inura," he explained. Nara took a moment to study his armor. It was highly stylized, with a clear dragon motif. Pretty on the nose.

"Who is Inura, and when you say *shade* do you mean you're a ghost?" Wes got out all in a rush. If he was alarmed by the dragon-guy's sudden appearance, he didn't show it.

"By shade, I mean simulacrum. A copy, if that word is too big." The man's dark eyebrows knitted together and he glared at Wes. "I am no ghost."

"Inura? As in the Inuran Consortium?" Nara asked.

"Inura as in the Wyrm Father of *Life*." The shade folded his arms, and the tail continued to flick.

Now that knocked Nara back a step.

Wes approached the strange new arrival, which highlighted how tall the shade was. Aran would only come to this guy's shoulder.

"Wow," she said dryly, "you've really got this *answer the question in as few words as possible* thing down. What is your role here? And is there any specific information you think imparting to us would be beneficial, from our perspective?"

The man smiled, exposing a sea of very draconic fangs. "Finally, some intelligent questions. I was created to serve as an assistant to Inura and Virkonna. I oversaw construction here, for seventy-eight millennia." He puffed up a bit. "Neith has sent you, hasn't she?"

Nara opened her mouth to confirm, but no sound came out. Of course.

The man laughed. "I can see she has. I recognize the mark of my sister. Well, Inura's sister. I am 'merely a shade.'

You must be her vessel, which means you are here for the Spellship."

"That's right," Nara said. Speaking was easy, now that she was no longer trying to say that specific word she promised not to think about for the next few minutes. "Can you tell us where it is?"

"I can't. I can only guide you to the *temporal* matrix." He lent a little extra significance to the word *temporal*.

Nara's eyes widened, and a laugh bubbled up. "Can you tell me *when* it is?"

"Wow, three intelligent questions in one day. That's a record. Please, follow me." He turned and walked back inside, toward the workshop they'd originally arrived at.

"What would you like us to call you?" Wes asked. "Shade? Inura? Shinura?"

"That's...actually quite clever." Shinura seemed impressed with Wes.

He led them them to a section of golden wall and passed his hand in front of it. The wall slid up into the ceiling, exposing a small, empty room.

"It's a transport." Shinura stepped inside. "Come on." He fluffed his wings as he stepped inside.

Wes looked to her, so Nara stepped inside. She still hadn't taken off her helmet, and wasn't planning on it any time soon. She didn't know what Shinura was, but she wanted to be able to grab Wes and flee if needed.

The door slid down and the room went completely dark. The light returned and the door slid up. Instead of looking out on the workshop they now overlooked a massive magical circle. Three rings rotated above it, exactly like a ship's command matrix. The only thing missing was the stabilizing ring.

"This is the...temporal matrix?" she asked as she cautiously approached.

"Yes." Shinura moved to stand near it. He scratched behind his ear and withdrew a wriggling insect. He popped it into his mouth and she shuddered involuntarily.

"All right, Wes." Nara turned in his direction. "This is where you earn your pay."

"I'm not getting paid."

"Right. This is where you earn some more goodwill," Nara corrected. "We've got to figure out the correct questions to ask our new friend here. We need to figure out how to operate the matrix, and we need to do it well enough that we don't accidentally teleport ourselves into a star."

"Oh, there are much worse outcomes than that, I assure you." Shinura ruffled his own hair. Nara had originally assumed it to be a dark brown, but now she thought it might be auburn in the right light. "You don't want to make a mistake with this thing. You could wipe out multiple universes, or alter the fate of countless others."

Nara tapped her chin as she considered the best way to proceed. She needed more information. "If you had to use this matrix, what do you wish you knew before you made the attempt?"

"I wish I could bestow some sort of title on you," Shinura said with a toothy grin. "You are just full of excellent questions. What do I wish I knew? I'd want to fully understand that this matrix rests at a temporal flux point. Let's see if I can dumb this down for you."

"I don't need it dumbed down." Nara folded her arms and glared at him. He couldn't see her glare in the mask of course, but she glared anyway.

"I can perceive spectrums you cannot begin to imagine."

Shinura rose to his full height and his wings flared out above him. "You are limited to three dimensions. Five senses. You cannot understand the myriad realities, or how they are interconnected. How changing one seemingly irrelevant detail in your limited reality can cause vast swathes of possibility to unravel. You are toddlers trampling a divine garden."

"I didn't ask you how limited we are. I asked you what you wish you knew." Nara still wasn't sure if she liked this guy or not.

"I wish I knew that a temporal flux point connected trillions of realities, and the slightest misstep could eradicate many of them." Shinura shook his head. "Listen, mortal, you've clearly been touched by a god. You've got some magic, sure. But be damned sure you understand what you're getting yourself into if you step inside that thing."

"I get it. It's scary. Bad stuff. Universes destroyed," Nara said coldly. "There is a lot riding on this, Shinura. How do I find the First Spellship? Is there a specific series of sigils? Do I need to think happy thoughts? Tell me how to find what I need, or a whole lot of people are going to die."

"Fine, since you're determined." Shinura's tail stopped flicking. "I will teach you the basic time parameters. You will need to browse the timeline until you find the ship's signature. It's quite powerful, which is why we needed to move it to a time where no one would be searching for it. Our enemies would have found it otherwise."

"All right." Nara removed her helmet. "Show me what I need to do."

42

THE HEART OF KROX

F rit hadn't returned to the Temple of Enlightenment since Eros had brought her to the palace several weeks ago. Even when she'd lived here, she hadn't been allowed out of her quarters after curfew.

A year ago that wouldn't have been an issue, and no one would have policed it. After Nebiat, however, they were hyper-vigilant. Anything and everything that could be a security threat was scryed, and guards were everywhere, even at libraries and schools.

She hurried to the south door, and rolled her eyes as she passed the poster that had been plastered to the wall outside.

Is someone acting suspicious? Speaking up could save lives.

It wasn't that she thought vigilance a bad idea. They could and should be watchful, after what had happened. But posters like that would only create the opposite effect. The common people saw binders everywhere, and there were likely thousands of reports a day. It took an already overburdened defense force and turned them into report takers.

They were far too busy to spot a real threat, and she hoped that meant they wouldn't spot her, either.

Frit ducked through the door and exhaled a relieved puff of flame when none of the wards activated. There wasn't any reason for them to keep her from the library, but she wasn't supposed to be here at this hour. That was reserved for real students, not slaves. She pulled her hood up, but left it loose so it didn't look like she was hiding.

She wove a familiar path through the stacks, which took her along the back wall. It kept her well away from the headmaster's room, what had once been Eros's office. Back then she'd been trying to avoid his attention, though truthfully she avoided everyone but Nara—Nara, and now her new sisters.

The initial six had grown to over three dozen. She'd been amazed at how many were willing to risk their lives in pursuit of their own freedom.

Frit slowed her pace, then stopped entirely when she reached the last shelf in the row. From here, there was a chance she'd be seen. If that happened, she'd be hauled in front of Eros for punishment. She had no idea how he might react. Normally, he'd ignore the situation. But if he caught even a whiff that she'd been speaking to Nebiat, her life would come to a swift and violent end.

She took a deep breath and exhaled smoke through her nose. Then Frit walked slowly toward the restricted area, which was blocked off with a simple cordon. She lifted the cordon, and whispered the password. Eros had sent her to fetch many tomes, and didn't care that she wasn't authorized to be here...so long as she was coming on one of his errands. That was the lie she planned if she were caught.

No one stopped her, though a few people walked the restricted area. Frit moved unerringly toward the shelves, just like she'd have done if on a real errand. She moved into the back section, which contained the area on dangerous Catalysts.

She scanned the spines of nearly a dozen books before finally locating the one she sought. It had a brown spine with the title *The Heart*, and no author name. Frit flipped it open and scanned the acknowledgements. The tome was dated 672 sector standard, so over three centuries ago.

Frit flipped to the beginning and began to skim the contents. The answer she sought lay on page four of a relatively unprotected tome. The secret read like poetry, the prose delivered as an artist might, not a scientist, or true mage.

And I caught sight of a vast ball of swirling, golden energy. Not golden like a sun, which will destroy sight if observed through a naked eye. This was a clean, wholesale brilliance that drew the eye. The still-beating heart of the once mighty god Krox.

She slowly closed the book and slid it into her satchel. There were, no doubt, more secrets to be gleaned, and she should be excited to learn them. But...she just couldn't bear to. Not right now. The Heart of *Krox*. Nebiat had been telling the truth. They *were* related, in a way.

And that raised some very troubling questions. It meant that, just maybe, Nebiat was being completely truthful and honest. She might really want to free Frit's people. That didn't make her good, but it might mean she was honest. It might mean Frit could trust her to help free her sisters.

It could also mean exchanging one master for another. What if they escaped, only to be imprisoned by the Krox? Being a slave wasn't the worst fate she could think of.

Frit shook her head. She'd already been here too long. Pausing to inspect a tome to ensure it was the correct one was believable. Reading entire passages was not. Not even Eros would send her to do something like that.

She hurried from the restricted section, and breathed a puff of smoke in relief when she replaced the cordon behind her.

"What are you doing in the restricted section?" Ree asked from behind her.

Frit turned slowly to face the war mage. Ree glared suspiciously at Frit, all imperious in her golden armor.

"Well?" Ree demanded. Her right hand settled on the hilt of her spellblade. "Out with it, Frit. I have to log this. Just give me something. I don't want to have to punish you, or deal with Eros when he gets pissy about it. Why are you here?"

Frit burst into flaming tears. All the fear, and confusion, and loneliness...it was just too much. She so badly wanted to spill the truth, but knew doing it would end in her execution.

"I'm sorry," she cried. She couldn't bring herself to meet Ree's gaze.

"Hey, it's okay." Ree softened slightly. "I'll ad lib a bit. It's not your fault Eros makes you break the rules. Just...try to avoid doing it again."

Ree stepped out of her path, and Frit plunged past. Thank Shaya that Ree had a millimeter of compassion.

Then she caught herself. No, not Shaya. What had Shaya ever done for her? Thank Krox.

43

READY FOR WAR

Kaho carefully placed the golden torque around his neck, laying it flat against the scales on his chest. Then he reached for the headdress, and attached the fan to the back of his head. It made him look like a lowly saurian, but his mother was a stickler for tradition. Looking the part of the dutiful hatchling might make her a hair more willing to cooperate, and he'd take any advantage he could get.

"You look a fool, brother." Tobek sneered at Kaho as he stalked into the room. He still wore his spellarmor. He never took it off, not since running into the Outrider and his company back on Shaya. Kaho almost felt bad for them. Almost.

"Would you rather speak to her?" Kaho demanded. "Because I can remove all this, and we can let you grovel. And don't pretend you'd do anything else, because as much as you like to act the Wyrm, you are still a hatchling, too, brother."

Tobek opened his mouth to return a taunt, but hesitated. He sighed. "You look a fool, but I might do the same in your place. Be quick with your groveling, and let us be about this. I long to kill something. It's past time we show these aging Wyrms that the Krox know how to fight."

Kaho merely nodded. He'd already turned his mind to the conversation he was about to have. Unlike Tobek, he didn't have the luxury of solving his problems with violence. His problems were much more complex, and required creative solutions. Sometimes, they required a little groveling.

He raised his index finger and sketched the first *fire* sigil. He took his time, slowly drawing the perfect whirls and curves. He added a *dream* sigil, drawn with the same artistry. They swam toward each other and burst into a greater missive. The shimmering spell showed nothing for long moments, but eventually the silhouette of a human woman appeared.

It quickly gained definition, showing Nebiat's dark skin and her bone-white hair. She stared dispassionately at Kaho through the strangely round irises she wore as a human. "I am in the middle of important business, child. Why do you bother me?"

Something exploded behind her, leveling the wall of the building she was inside. She turned and sketched several elegant *void* sigils, which she linked with *fire*. A bolt of disintegration shot toward the hole in the wall at the precise moment a fifteen-meter robot crashed through. The bolt of disintegration took it in the knee, sheering off the limb and spilling the robot to the ground in front of Nebiat.

She darted forward and slammed the butt of her staff into the electronic eye. The weapon sank into the robot's stylized chrome skull, and a fan of sparks sprayed from the wound. Nebiat turned back to the missive. "Speak quickly, child."

"We have learned what Voria retrieved in the Umbral Depths." Kaho led with that, because he knew nothing else would so quickly secure her attention. She fixed that terrible gaze on him, and he plunged on. "It is a staff. An eldimagus from the final days of the godswar. We believe it is the key to the vessel we've been searching for. Your auguries were correct."

"But?" Nebiat's eyes narrowed.

Kaho rushed to explain. "But getting it will require us to launch an attack on the Confederate forces. Those forces are currently under the protection of Wyrm Mother Olyssa. For us to secure it, we'd have to risk her wrath."

Nebiat whirled and quickly ended another robot, then turned back to the missive. "Do it. Take the staff. We will reason with Aetherius, and explain that this is really done in his best interests."

"And, how should I do that, Mother?" Kaho asked. He gave her a deep bow, and held it until she spoke.

"Stand up, child." She didn't speak again until he'd straightened. "You did right to contact me. To persuade Aetherius this is in his best interests, tell him you wanted him to have plausible deniability. Now his chief rival has been embarrassed, but he can truthfully say he had no fore-knowledge of the attack. It makes him look good, and costs him nothing. Spin it just like that. Do you understand?"

"Yes, Mother, thank you. We will retrieve the staff, and once we have it, I will contact you." He bowed again, and when he straightened the missive had been terminated. He turned to his brother, who'd been careful to stand out of view. "Go and fetch your enforcers. Tell them to ready for war."

44

INCOMING

I kadra's tip clinked along the deck as Voria made her way to the battle bridge. This part of the ship was blessedly empty, and though that was tactically dangerous, at least it gave her room to think. Even the normal echoes from the hangars were absent, since Davidson had pulled his men into defensive positions along the cliffs overlooking their parking spot.

She still hadn't received a missive from Nara, which troubled her. Aran's situation was bad enough without having to also worry about the girl. Voria still believed Aran was alive, though she didn't understand what had happened to him. The gods almost certainly had a plan, and the idea that Virkonna would have casually offed him after *he won* seemed ludicrous to Voria.

"Morning, Major," Bord called cheerfully as she strode onto the bridge. He stood inside the defensive matrix, and was chatting with Kezia and Pickus.

Crewes snapped to attention in the offensive matrix and sketched a salute. Voria returned it, then Crewes relaxed. He'd been quiet since returning from his trip with Aran.

Voria worried that he blamed himself for his possible death, which wasn't fair. But she also knew someone couldn't merely tell you that. You needed to come to the conclusion on your own, or it meant nothing.

"Good morning, Specialist," Voria called back. She moved to the command matrix and slipped inside the stabilizing ring. "Sergeant, I don't suppose Nara has sent word?"

"Nope," Crewes looked up from his matrix. His eyes were, if possible, harder than usual. "I expect she will when she can."

"How did your game of Kim Jabber or whatever go?" Bord asked. "Did you beat her? Was she pissed?"

"We didn't finish the game," Voria replied absently as she tapped a *void* sigil and linked with the *Hunter*. The ship responded so much more sluggishly than the *Talon*, but she was also much more familiar. Voria had fought countless battles on the *Hunter*. Both she and her vessel had outlived the odds, thus far. "I did lay the groundwork for a formal alliance, but it's only verbal at this stage. I believe Olyssa will be an ally, albeit one who sees us all as inferior species."

The scry-screen's edge flashed red to indicate an incoming missive. Finally. Voria tapped *fire* to accept it, but was surprised when it wasn't Nara's face that filled the screen.

"What is it, Major?" Voria asked as Davidson's bearded face filled the monitor. Since both he and Aran had adopted one, the fashion had already begun spreading among the men.

"Sir, we've got incoming. Five Krox trooper carriers on the horizon. They're coming in low, but making no attempt to hide. They want us to see them." He glanced over his shoulder at a squad of men erecting a gauss cannon emplacement. "We're getting repositioned as quickly as we can, and we'll be dug in by the time they get here. ETA four minutes."

"Five troop carriers, even if they were entirely empty, is enough to overwhelm our position," Voria pointed out. "If they are full, as is likely, we have precisely zero chance of survival."

"What do you recommend, Major?" Davidson eyed her soberly.

"I'm going to run." Voria tapped a *void* sigil, and fed magical energy into the spelldrive. The ship gave a deep shudder as it rumbled to life. "We'll stick to the mountains to the south, and use the peaks to screen ourselves. Krox carriers aren't known for their speed."

"We don't have time to get everyone loaded, sir"—the cannon behind Davidson fired, drowning out some of what he said—"should stand and fight, sir."

"And that is exactly what you will do, and why I am planning on running." The *Hunter* lifted into the air, and began rising from the ravine where they'd taken shelter. "I seriously doubt the Krox are intending to wipe us out to a man, Major. They want the *Hunter*. They want me. I strongly suspect that if I flee...they will pursue and leave you in peace. But if I am wrong, die well."

She killed the connection and tapped a *fire* sigil to trigger another missive. This one she sent to Olyssa, who she assumed was at another one of the Council's endless parties. The spell didn't connect. Voria pursed her lips, considering. Was Olyssa refusing the spell for some reason? Or...was it being blocked somehow?

"Crewes, get your people suited up," Voria barked. "Now. I think we're about to have company." It was merely intuition, but something was off about this entire situation. An assault where the Krox let them see their approach? That made no sense, unless it was to hide another move.

"You heard the lady. *Move!*" Crewes sprinted from his matrix. "Down to the *Talon*. Now. Armor up, people."

Voria adjusted the scry-screen to show a bird's-eye view of the ship. Her heart sank as a midnight blue cruiser shimmered into view and attached to their hull with a *thunk*. It came from directly above the battle bridge.

"They know what they're about," Pickus said, staring up. "If they can cut through the hull, they're going to drop right down into this room."

"Sir, we ain't got time to get our armor." Crewes slid to a halt near the door. "If they're coming through, they'll gun down whoever stays on the bridge, and chase down the rest of us."

"Specialist Bord, prepare a ward," Voria ordered. "Pickus, I want you in the command matrix. You're flying the *Hunter*."

Ikadra's emerald began flashing wildly.

"What is it, Ikadra?" Voria asked.

"Umm, these guys are here for me. Well, they're here for the Spellship, and I think they realize they need me to get it." Ikadra's voice showed an emotion she hadn't yet seen the sarcastic staff demonstrate: fear. "We should get out of here."

"That's not a bad idea, sir," Crewes said. "We can fall back to the *Talon* and escape."

Voria reached for the ability Neith had given her. She spun out possibilities, letting events unfold in a thousand thousand different ways.

She followed Crewes to the *Talon*, but they were ambushed inside. She stayed with Pickus on the bridge, and they killed her, and took Ikadra. She teleported off the *Hunter*, and watched as the ship slammed into a mountain, killing everyone aboard. Every path ended in some sort of tragedy.

The ceiling gave a tremendous pop as a three-meter section was disintegrated from above. Two Krox enforcers leapt into the room, already firing acid bolts from their spellrifles before they'd even landed. The first bolt sailed toward Pickus, but Voria sketched a quick counterspell and intercepted it.

The second bolt hit the sergeant. He grunted and staggered back a step. Then his face twisted into rage, and his eyes were replaced by pools of burning orange flame. "You want to trade some spells? Yeah, let's do that." Crewes inhaled deeply, then exhaled a cloud of white flames. They clung to the Krox, who screeched in agony.

That distracted his opponent for a fraction of a second, and Voria used the time to cast a level three void bolt. It caught the enforcer in the face, killing it instantly.

Four more enforcers rained through the ceiling, and a quick glance up verified that another group was waiting. After that would come the big guns. Probably the war mage Aran had tangled with, and possibly a true mage backing him up.

That made this fight unwinnable, unless she could produce a miracle. Voria activated her ability again. She scanned countless timelines, searching for any solution. She watched as the four enforcers landed. Kezia died in the first volley, her blond curls suddenly slick with blood as her tiny body crashed to the floor. Bord rushed to her side, but died in a hail of acid bolts.

The sergeant enjoyed more success, but then a war mage in black spellarmor rushed through the breach. He seized Crewes's head in his hands, and twisted. She and Pickus died immediately after.

A thousand different paths. A thousand different deaths. Yet there had to be a solution. There was a possibility, there had to be. But for her to see it, she had to understand it. What could she do that might save them?

Why were the Krox here? What did they want. She already knew.

"They want you," she whispered aloud, looking up at Ikadra. Voria moved to Bord's side. "Give me a ward. Now."

Bord raised his gloved hands and a dome of pure white interlocking sigils sprang up around her. Voria stepped directly under the hole. "Krox Commander, can you hear me?"

"I hear you," a deep voice rumbled back cautiously from the shadows above. "I have come for the staff, Shayan. Give it to me and we will let you live."

"No, you won't," Voria called back. "If I give it to you, you'll kill us all."

"I suppose you're right," the Krox allowed. "I will kill you either way."

"But not if time is an issue," Voria taunted. "Do you have a true mage up there?"

"He does," called back a second voice. A figure moved to the edge of the hole. He wore a golden ceremonial head-dress, and ritual face paint.

"I'm going to teleport my staff outside the ship and let it fall," Voria called. "You'll have two choices. You can assault our position with the small force you've brought, and waste time and effort killing us, or you can go after the staff. You can try to reach it before my ground forces, an entire armor reinforced battalion."

"You're bluffing. You'd never willingly abandon the staff," the Krox called back.

"He's right, right?" Ikadra whispered, his voice rising a

full octave as his emerald flashed wildly. "You aren't going to just drop me? It's scary out there, and I don't want to go with them. They'll use me, Voria. They'll take the Spellship."

"We don't have any other choice," she shot back. "I'm sorry, Ikadra, but if we resist, then we all die. I'm using Neith's ability to verify that. This is, literally, the only way anyone in this room survives."

Voria raised a hand and sketched the first *void* sigil as she prepared to blink Ikadra outside the ship. A counter-spell sailed down from above, but it rebounded off Bord's ward. Voria completed the spell, and Ikadra vanished.

45

DAVIDSON

Davidson hadn't been inside his tank often enough of late, but this was hardly how he'd hoped to remedy that situation. He placed his hand against the console, and a wave of icy blue energy flowed into the tank, linking them fully. Magic, though he preferred to think of it as energy.

He could feel the tank around him, the Inuran alloys welded together into something that, after Marid, could be called alive. She, he was positive she was a she, hadn't learned words or anything, but she wasn't so different from the dog he'd had growing up back home on Ternus.

"All right, blue. Let's see what we can do here." He tapped the console and the HUD rippled to life, complete with scrolling tactical data. It overlaid the map of the ridges where they'd taken shelter, and he couldn't help but give a proud smile.

The Marines had fortified their positions behind thick slabs of a rock that resembled granite. Not only were they physically isolated, but their position was also screened from view. Gunners on the approaching Krox carriers would have a devil of a time finding targets, while they had clear lines of fire.

"Captain Gunnersen," Davidson said into the comm, "Direct all fire toward the closest Krox carrier. Focus primarily on her engines."

"Not her guns, sir?" Gunnersen's confused drawl crackled back. "Won't that leave us vulnerable?"

"Temporarily, yes." Davidson tapped several more buttons, and the hovertank rumbled to life. He guided her from under an outcrop, and noted that the other hovertanks were moving smoothly to follow him. "If we can disable their engines, they can't chase the *Hunter*."

"The *Hunter* is going to abandon us?" Gunnersen sounded horrified.

"Quite the opposite. She's making a run for it, so they'll ignore us." Davidson tapped the HUD and it zoomed in on the fat, ugly Krox carrier. "We're going to even the odds a little. If we can cripple one or, if we're lucky, two Krox carriers, then Voria might have a chance."

"We'll get on it, sir." Gunnersen's voice sounded more confident, making Davidson glad he'd taken a moment to explain. He'd done it over an open channel for a reason. Having come up from the ranks, he knew what it was like to be given crap orders without explanation, and had vowed not to be that kind of officer.

Davidson watched with pride as the batteries began to fire. They'd set up gauss cannon emplacements in several fortified positions, for exactly the kind of assault they were about to face. White streaks shot up into the purplish sky, converging on the enormous black engines at the rear of the massive Krox carriers.

The damage, if there was any, was undetectable.

"Keep firing," he barked into the comm. More white

streaks shot into the carrier, which ignored them. It joined its brothers as they changed course. "They're breaking for *Hunter*. We can't stop 'em all, but we make sure the rear carrier stays put."

His heart went cold. The Krox weren't even firing at them. They didn't consider the Marines a threat. Well, their mistake.

Davidson settled his hands over the stick. It connected to the tank's main cannon, which he hadn't yet fired in combat. He'd run some combat drills, but blowing up targets didn't give him a real idea of what it could do. Time to find out.

He lined up the crosshairs over the engine, aiming for the area where the last volley of gauss rounds had just impacted. Davidson took a deep breath, and drew from the strange ball of icy blue energy in his chest. It answered both quickly and easily, and that power roared through him, into Blue. It gathered in the barrel, and a moment later a spear of brilliant blue streaked into the Krox vessel. The entire tank kicked back three meters from the force of the magical blast, and he went light headed in the wake of the spell.

The entire housing along the aft side of the burner exploded in a brilliant shower of flaming debris. Cheers went up from his lines. The damage was superficial, but that was enough. "We can hurt them, people, if we try hard enough. Take. Her. Down."

The tanks beside him began to fire, and the engine sputtered and went out. His men began to cheer.

Voria still had four carriers to face, but the last one would be too slow to catch her, at the very least.

46

YOUR END OF THE BARGAIN

A flurry of acid bolts rained down on Voria's position from above. They rippled off Bord's ward, which faded in color as more shots fell. Voria smiled grimly.

She sketched one of the most complex third-level spells she knew, a spell she'd last used back in orbit over Marid. A crackling ball of black and purple energy appeared above the hole.

"Get clear!" One of the Krox roared. The acid bolts stopped as they dove for cover.

Two of the enforcers were too slow, and were sucked into the ball of energy by the immense gravity.

"Oh, man, that is just too tempting a target." Crewes sucked in another breath, and a river of flame washed over the enforcers. Their screams were thankfully brief. The smell of their charred bodies, on the other hand, lingered.

There was a frigid rush of wind as the Krox shuttle disengaged from the hull. Voria wove drunkenly across the deck, and just barely caught the stabilizing ring to the defensive matrix.

"Pickus, take us southwest and keep low. Use the mountains to screen us," she ordered. Voria tapped a *fire* sigil as she began the missive to Olyssa. "Crewes, can you use *water* magic to seal that breech? I can't hear myself think over that wind."

"Sure thing, sir." Crewes stepped under the hole again. He raised his spellcannon and lobbed a fist-sized blue crystal at the hole. As it reached the gap, it expanded outward into a ball of super dense ice. It thunked into place, swelling around the hole the Krox had made. The howling finally stopped.

The scry-screen went red as the missive connected. The screen showed Olyssa's hairless face set against the backdrop of another Council party, as expected.

"What is it, Major?" Olyssa asked mildly.

"We're under attack by Krox forces," Voria explained. "They've taken Ikadra, and are now pursuing us into the mountains south of our landing site. We're severely outnumbered. You said we had your protection. Well, I'm invoking that protection. If we don't get help, you're going to be down an ally. There's no way we can survive this kind of offensive."

Olyssa's slitted eyes widened. Her jaw worked as she struggled for words. Voria suppressed a surge of annoyance. This was a mighty Wyrm Mother of the last dragonflight? No wonder they were dying out.

"I will speak to Aetherius right now. I will call him out for his duplicity." Olyssa regained more composure with each word. "Survive but a little while, and I will do what I can to get Aetherius to call off his hounds."

"So, your protection is asking Aetherius to ask the Krox to please not kill the people you said you'd protect?" Voria's tone lacked any veneer at all. She couldn't hide her feelings any longer, not in the face of incompetence. "Olyssa, five troop carriers are encircling us. Five. Your people are obsessed with honor, are they not? Does that seem an honorable fight? Five against one?"

"I said I would get Aetherius to stop his hounds," Olyssa snarled. "Know your place, Shayan. Speak to me that way again, and—"

Voria terminated the missive. Her secondary mission had been to secure an alliance, but the primary one was still the Spellship. She could do neither if she were dead, and that meant going into triage mode.

Somehow, she needed to salvage something from all this. They still had the *Talon*. They'd stand a much better chance of escaping aboard her. But that meant sacrificing the *Hunter*. Again.

"Uh, sir?" Pickus said. He tapped a *fire* sigil and the scry-screen shifted to show Davidson's position. One of the Krox vessels was bombarding them. Spirit bolts rained down on their position, and Voria knew their armor would do nothing to protect them.

But Davidson wasn't helpless. His tanks kicked back, one after another, belching white streaks that shot into the Krox vessel. They exploded on impact, and little streamers of smoke rose from the impact points. A streak of blue shot up from the hovertanks, punching through the carrier's engine. That engine detonated spectacularly, and the carrier began to list drunkenly.

"You have your orders, Pickus. We can't help them." Voria seized control of the scry-screen, and shifted it toward the quartet of ships descending on their position. "Davidson will hold against that carrier, if we can keep the other four busy chasing us."

47

MERGE

Nara stood inside the temporal matrix. She took shallow breaths, the weight of what she was about to do crashing down on her.

"Well?" Shinura demanded. He crossed the room to stand next to the matrix's slowly spinning rings. The multi-colored sigils lent his strange, not quite human visage a hellish cast.

"In a minute. I want to be damned sure I know what I'm doing," she snapped. "Besides, if I get this wrong, there are no more choices. So I need to make sure I take care of anything important, first. At the very least, I need to check in with Major Voria. She needs to know what we've found, and we should see what she wants us to do. She might want to be here for this."

Nara hoped she did. She hoped Voria would say, *Don't do anything until I arrive*. But she knew that wouldn't be the case. Neith had given Voria a different gift, and a different purpose. Like it or not, this was Nara's.

She raised a hand and sketched a quick missive. It was accepted almost immediately, and an illusion of the major's face appeared next to Nara. She'd worked for some time to blend a missive with an illusion, and was pleased with the outcome.

"Nara." Voria gave her a distracted look, then focused on whatever she'd been doing. "Now isn't the best time, though I'm pleased to hear from you. Report."

"I've located something called the Crucible," Nara began. She kept her report as brief as possible. "The ship was built here, but it has been moved to another time. There is a temporal matrix that will allow me to search the time-line for the ship. I don't know if it will move me in time to wherever the ship is, or move the ship back to our time. But that's what it will take to reach the ship."

"Noted. We have a severe complication," Voria explained in her brusque monotone. She had such a Shayan way of understating problems. "The Krox have assaulted our position. We are fleeing from four carriers, and I don't like our odds of getting away, even with the *Talon*. Worse, the enemy has recovered Ikadra."

"Then they'll be on their way here." Nara's heart sank.

"Almost certainly. It's too much to ask to assume they don't know about that place. If anything, they likely knew about it before we did." Voria's image staggered, possibly from a blow to the *Hunter*.

"What do you want me to do?" Nara asked. She'd rarely felt this small.

"Use your discretion, true mage. We have to assume this spell is being scryed, and your enemies could arrive in minutes. They must not recover the Spellship. Do whatever it takes to ensure they do not, am I clear?" Voria demanded.

"Crystal, sir," Nara said. She didn't much like the whole military discipline thing, but it was really nice not having to always be the person making the final decision.

Unfortunately, this wasn't one of those times. She had a difficult choice to make, one that influenced not just her, but Wes. She turned to the archeologist. "You heard that conversation. I need to stop them, Wes. I can't do it alone. I suspect Shinura won't be any help, and that leaves you."

"She's right," Shinura said. "I can't really help you, not unless either Inura or Virkonna remove that particular geas."

Wes took a deep breath and adjusted his glasses. His face had gone pale, but his gaze was steady. "I have to be honest. I'm a bit of a coward, and when I say *a bit* I mean *mostly*. But here's the thing: these pistols are pretty nasty. I might not be able to help, but they can."

"You want to give me your guns?" Nara asked.

"If only." Wes gave a bitter laugh. "They'd never allow that. I think they're with me until I die. Maybe this is how that happens. Tell me what to do, and I'll do it."

"All right." Nara took a deep breath and marshaled her confidence. "First, we get to the Spellship. Then we find a way to set an ambush. Shinura, I need a couple answers. Will I be transported to the ship, or will the ship be transported here?"

"You will be transported to the ship," Shinura said. He stood on his tiptoes and stretched, then offered a cavernous yawn, like a cat.

"And how will I get it back here, assuming I can get control of it?" she demanded.

"The ship itself can travel through possibilities, if it's at a temporal flux point. Which, as I said before, this is." Shinura began picking between two fangs with a clawed nail.

Nara considered that. Her enemies would need to find this place, puzzle out how to use the matrix, and arrive at the ship. That would take time. If she could get there first, she could hunt for some sort of advantage or weapon...a way to hurt them. Even if they found nothing, at least she and Wes could arrange an ambush.

"Will anyone inside the matrix be sent to the Spellship if I'm able to locate it?" Nara asked. That was the last critical question she could think of. Her understanding of magical theory covered just about every other eventuality.

"Yes." Shinura lowered his hand and gave another bored yawn.

"Wes, climb inside. We're ready to make the attempt." Nara began a series of deep, even breaths. This was a new experience, but it wasn't difficult to understand what she needed to do. She'd see the timeline, in some way, and she'd need to look for a magical signature. Once she located it, she needed to guide them in that direction.

The skinny archeologist climbed awkwardly inside, and took great care not to touch her. "Well, I wanted to see more spell use. There's that, I suppose. Still kind of a little terrified, though."

Nara closed her eyes, took one final deep breath, and opened them. She began tapping sigils, almost instinctively. All three rings whirred to life, and a wave of mixed magical energy rolled out from the matrix in a multicolored pulse. The edge of the room lit, showing the galaxy around them.

Something thudded against the door. Once, twice, a third time. A spellblade punched through the golden metal, the metal around the blade melted away, and the hole grew until it was large enough for the Krox wielding it to climb through.

Nara recognized the draconic armor instantly. This was the Krox who'd nearly killed Ree. The one Aran hadn't been able to take. And he was coming for her.

She caught Wes's gaze. "I don't want to alarm you, but if you can't slow him down, then we're about to die."

"No pressure, right?" he smiled weakly at her. "Okay, I'll see what I can do."

Wes slowly withdrew his pistols, and stepped around her so he could get a clear shot at the Krox. Nara pivoted so she could see the combat while still manipulating the matrix. "Shinura, I don't suppose you can offer us any additional help?"

"Work quickly?" he offered unhelpfully.

A nimbus of brilliant white appeared around both pistols, and they began to buck wildly. The weapons discharged a stream of golden pulses, which converged on the Krox in the spellarmor. The flurry knocked him back through the hole, and into the chamber beyond.

"Just keep doing whatever you're doing. I'll keep knocking him back," Wes said over his shoulder.

Nara was impressed. She turned her attention back to the matrix, and the galaxy around them. She reached out with her mind, tapping sigils to maneuver through possibilities. She scanned slowly in all directions as she hunted for something, anything, that might be the Spellship.

There were a number of powerful magical beacons, and she examined each in turn. Most were Catalysts, the various corpses of dead gods littering the cosmos. A few were weapons of war. A space station orbiting a dying star. A living planet ready to devour anything that approached.

She searched, on and on, aware of the whine of Wes's pistols in the background. She focused on the task at hand, tuning out the possibility of her own death. The only way out was through this.

A bright green light twinkled in the distance. Nara tapped several more sigils, moving her perspective toward it.

The light grew closer and stronger. She pushed onward, until she entered this system, or a version of it.

The planet was a smoking ruin, devoid of life. That didn't mean it was empty. Shapes prowled the darkness below, around the base of the pyramid where Virkonna was supposed to sleep. Twisted shapes. Demonic shapes.

Nara's perspective fell through the pyramid, through the stone, and earth. Through the tunnels below. It fell and fell until it emerged into the empty hangar they'd seen on their arrival.

That hangar was no longer empty. A ghostly version of a ship sat there.

Nara tapped a final set of sigils, and merged her timeline with the one containing the ship.

Somewhere in the distance, Wesley screeched, "I've been shot!"

48

DENSITY

Aran tapped his bracelet again. Nothing. Every time the darkness felt especially unbearable, or the stench grew particularly bad, he tapped it again. Wherever they were, it seemed endless. They'd been walking for what felt like hours, crossing dozens of corridors, and climbing several sets of slick stairs.

The warmth and humidity made breathing difficult, and he was thankful for all the cardio Erika had put him through over the last few months. All that pain made this possible.

"There is still time. Let there be time," his guide murmured as she climbed another set of stairs. Aran had studied her carefully, and it was clear her mind was deteriorating. She'd only experienced a few moments of lucidity, but hadn't explained much beyond giving a date seven thousand years in the future.

He understood conceptually that time magic was possible, but the idea that he could be that far in the future was... well, a little terrifying. Everyone he knew, and everything he'd ever known was gone now.

Well, not everyone. Nebiat would still be there, and the hatchlings he'd battled would now be full Wyrms.

So his enemies would be dramatically stronger, and all his friends were dead.

It was difficult wrenching his brain away from that thought. How was he going to get back? He had to trust that Virkonna had some sort of plan—and that her plan cared enough to ensure his own survival.

A dollop of oily goo dripped from the ceiling, and landed on his cheek. He sighed. Being a hero sucked.

Aran hurried up to catch up with his guide, who'd given her name as Rhea. His arm ached from holding his spell-blade aloft for light, and he switched hands for the millionth time. If this kept on much longer, he'd have to use *air* magic to keep it aloft. "You said you were an Outrider?"

Most attempts at conversation had failed, and Aran was surprised when she looked directly at him.

"Am," she said. "I *am* an Outrider, even with all that has happened. I kept the faith. I waited. And you came. I watched them all die, you know. One by one, the Blood of Nefarius took them. It changed them, like it's changing me."

"Is that what this stuff is?" Aran held up his oily fingers.

She nodded soberly, then turned back to the stairs and climbed more quickly. He followed slowly, considering what she'd told him. The oily substance, the Blood of Nefarius apparently, was everywhere. He tore a strip from his shirt and wiped furiously at his cheek. "What was it like before the...Blood?"

"War. Endless war," she muttered as she crested the last stair. She stopped at the top, panting for breath. Several moments later she straightened, and her breathing gradually returned to normal. "First Krox. Then each other. And finally Nefarius. We won every war, but each time there were fewer Wyrms to guide us. When they finally came for this world, they took the Wyrms. They didn't kill them. Every last one was captured. We don't know where they were taken."

She shuffled forward again, up a corridor that was narrower than the others had been.

"At first, we wondered why Nefarius hadn't completed the destruction of this world. We didn't realize he'd left the Blood behind."

"How far does it go?" Aran risked interrupting.

"Our whole world has been taken." She paused, and her shoulders hunched. After a moment Aran realized she was crying. "Every day it spread. Those it took dragged others into the Blood."

Aran couldn't recall ever being so horrified. He couldn't think of a worse fate. To have this muck slowly cover everything, slowly take people you loved.

He put a comforting hand on the Outrider's shoulder, and pulled her into a fierce hug. She sobbed into his chest, and Aran held her. He let her cry for as long as she wanted. The feel of her slick hair made his skin crawl, but she hadn't had human contact in years from the sound of it.

"I don't know everything you've sacrificed. I'm sorry." He stroked her hair, and his hand came away greasy. "You said we have to hurry."

"Yes." She disengaged instantly, and hurried up the corridor.

"Can you tell me where we're going?" Aran asked as he hurried after.

"To the door. You must be at the door when it opens," she explained distractedly.

She followed the narrow corridor to another set of stairs, and slowly climbed them. She was forced to pause again at the top, her chest heaving as she struggled to recover her breath.

"One by one, it took them, until I was the last," she explained again. Her emerald eyes fixed on him, staring out from a slick, oily face. "At first, I hid. But then I began to age. I didn't know how long it would be until your return. I had to make a choice."

What did she mean? His hand rose to his mouth when he understood. She'd intentionally used the Blood to delay aging somehow.

Something roared in the distance, loud enough to rattle the walls.

"What was that?" He turned in that direction and dropped into a guard position.

"That is Kheross. We must go." She hobbled away from the stairs, up a wider hallway that sloped gradually upward. Every other floor had been level, which was promising. Hopefully this was taking them to whatever the door was.

"Should we be worried about that thing?" Aran asked as he glanced over his shoulder at the darkness.

"He was a friend, once." She shook her head sadly. "I have done what I must. I kept the faith. I waited." She sat down heavily and planted her back against the wall. She raised a trembling hand and pointed up the corridor. "Follow it up. You will come to a door. When that door opens, do what you must. Fulfill your destiny."

49

ESCAPE

Frit spent the next week dreading sudden word that Ree had reported her misdeed and it had somehow gotten back to Eros. Thankfully, that moment never came. Eros was as distracted as ever—if anything, more so.

The political situation worsened, and as it worsened, so too did his temper.

"Master," Frit said. She bobbed a curtsy when he finally lent her an irritated eye. "I know you'll be in session all day with the Caretakers. Everyone else has left for the festival—"

"And you were hoping you could go, too?" Eros snapped. He rose and began pacing. "That's what you're concerned with now? Frivolous dancing? Buttered pastries?" He rounded on her suddenly, and his face twisted in a snarl. Somewhere in those eyes lurked the fury of a god, the hint that he was the true Guardian of Shaya.

"Master, I was hoping to go to the Temple of Enlightenment," she got out in a rush. "To work on my split fireball." It was a spell she'd already mastered, but that way if she were forced to return for any reason she could show her "progress."

Eros froze. His frown lessened slightly. "Yes, you are more focused than most of the others. You may go to the library to study, but when you return I want to see this spell. Understood?"

"Of course, Master." She bobbed another curtsy, but he'd already forgotten about her.

Before she turned, for a fraction of a moment, she experienced the oddest swell of pity. Eros was slowly going mad, of that she was sure. He wasn't adjusting at all to the sudden new stresses of his office. As the new Tender, on one side, he had a god intruding into his mind. On the other, a pack of backstabbing Caretakers who were more interested in his job than in rooting out dreadlords.

They sabotaged his inquisition as much as helped it, and that only served to make him more paranoid. She didn't want to be around when he finally cracked.

Frit turned and hurried from the chamber for the last time. She stopped briefly by her quarters to snatch up a single pack, only half-full. It was all she owned, this handful of possessions. That was all her decade on Shaya added up to.

Frit slung the pack over her shoulder and threaded back through the palace. Thankfully, since the Shayans couldn't abide admitting they had servants, they kept servants out of sight. She took a series of servant stairwells all the way to the base of the palace, where she hailed a transport.

Thankfully, transports were automated and couldn't discriminate against slaves. She stepped aboard the skiff and seized the railing. She visualized her destination, and the skiff excitedly lurched into motion, zipping down toward the seventh branch.

She had several minutes to consider her choices as the skiff descended. Technically, she still wasn't committed. She hadn't committed any crime that couldn't be forgiven, and it was unlikely Eros would even know anything had happened. Frit glanced longingly up at the palace.

No. That was the old her. That was slave Frit, reaching for normalcy, for safety—even if that safety lay inside a collar. She would make her own fate, and help her sisters do the same. If that cost her life, well, then the Shayans would find out exactly what kind of weapon they'd created.

And besides, dozens of her sisters were depending on her now.

The skiff finally reached the seventh branch, and deposited her on a mossy forest floor. Gorgeous redwoods towered up around her, and she grinned in wonder as she spun in a slow circle. This was only the second time she'd ever come to a park, but that created certain logistical problems.

The ground began to smoke under her boots, and Frit hurried along the soft forest floor. As long as she didn't stand in one place for very long, it was unlikely she'd start a fire. The ground was still wet, whether from dew or from rain, she couldn't say.

Frit made her way toward a large stand of trees in the distance, the same place she'd last met her sisters. She hurried through the gap, relaxing slightly when she counted nearly three dozen of her sisters. Everyone had made it safely. That seemed a near impossibility.

"Is everyone ready to go? Has Ifra removed your collars?" Frit asked.

A chorus of nods answered, but no one spoke.

"Do you have the Fissure scale?" Ifra asked quietly.

Frit glanced down to reach into her pocket, and her eye

fell on a gap between the trees. Booted feet flashed around the trunk. Then a second set. And a third.

"Ambush!" She seized the Fissure scale and snapped it in half, tossing the fragments on the ground near the center of the clearing. "Defend the portal until it stabilizes."

"What do you mean?" Ifra choked out.

"If we want freedom, we're going to have to fight for it." Frit made a fist and glared around at her sisters. "We make a stand."

"I don't believe it," called a familiar voice from outside the circle. "Frit, I know you're in there." Frit's eyes widened. It was Ree. "You know what I'm about to do. You're working with binders. Surrender, now. Get your friends to surrender. We'll take you to Eros. The Tender can work this out. He'll smooth it over. We have control rods. Don't make us slaughter you."

Frit blinked. Ree didn't realize they were free, that they could actually fight. She thought she'd be slaughtering rabid pets, not battling trained mages.

"You sound more like you're convincing yourself than me," Frit yelled back. She was shocked by her own ferocity, at the fury swelling inside her—a fury that would soon burst. "I don't want to hurt you, Ree, but if you come in here I *will* kill you, and your friends. And this whole depths-damned tree if I have to. All we want to do is leave. We're not working with any binder. We're just tired of being enslaved. Walk away, Ree. Let us do the same."

"You know I can't do that," Ree called back. "Last chance, Ifrit. Don't think I'll spare you because we've fought together."

Frit's hands began to shake. After all they'd shared, after fighting together, Ree still wouldn't let her go. So be it.

The Fissure was slowly gaining definition, a tiny crack

veining across the space. Cold seeped out of it, and hellish purple light peeked through the edges. But it wasn't wide enough to step through, and wouldn't be for many precious seconds.

"Sisters," Frit called in a low voice. She took them all in with her gaze. "We were trained to fight. To kill. We use that training here and now, on them. Fight, like you were trained to fight."

All around her, hands tightened on weapons, and faces grew more determined. They were with her. Frit turned back to the gap in the trees, just in time to intercept Ree's charge.

50

CROSSING THE LINE

F rit forced herself to stand her ground as the tall, beautiful war mage burst into the clearing. She wore her spellarmor, of course, which flashed as it passed through a stray beam of sunlight filtering through the redwoods.

For all Frit's bravery, she'd have died in that instant, if not for her sister. Ifra leapt in front of her, her blade crashing into Ree's with a tremendous clang. Ifra extended a hand and a rush of superheated flame boiled over the spellarmor. Ree stepped back with a cry, but quickly recovered.

She advanced on Ifra and launched a series of vicious attacks. Each of Ifra's desperate parries came a bit later, and Frit knew the fight could only have one outcome. She looked around at her other sisters, each struggling desperately to survive as golden-armored war mages rushed through the gaps in the trees.

"No!" Frit's hands came up, and she began sketching two sigils at the same time. A *fire*, and a *void*, each drawn with a separate finger. The sigils grew toward each other with shocking speed, and when they connected the spell completed with a flash.

A ball of purplish flame rolled into Ree. Those flames clung to her armor, flowing over the surface until every bit of the golden surface blazed. At first Ree didn't even seem to notice. She launched a kick that hurled Ifra into a redwood. Before Ifra could recover, Ree lunged with her spellblade, and the weapon pinned Ifra's chest to the tree.

Ifra's agonized scream burned itself into Frit's memory. Ree's fist sailed forward, smashing Ifra's face and ending her voice forever. Frit's fury swelled until it blotted out the edges of her vision. The only thing she could see was Ree.

She thrust both arms toward the war mage and poured more magic into the flames still clinging to Ree's spellarmor. The flames strengthened, growing out around Ree to lick at the trees. They set the grass ablaze instantly, but it took several more moments to show a visible effect on the armor.

Gold cracked, and blackened. It happened in pockets, but those pockets spread. The armor began to warp and buckle, and Ree shrieked. The inside must be a hellish inferno, by now.

Frit's eyes narrowed and her mouth twisted into a sneer. She willed more *fire* and *void* into the spell. Ree's shrieks grew more frantic, and she sprinted from the clearing. Frit took a step after her, then caught herself.

She wasn't here for vengeance. She was here to save her sisters.

Frit moved swiftly to Ifra, but a cursory examination confirmed her fears. Ifra was dead. Frit took a moment to close her sister's eyes. Then she turned back to the combat to find the Shayans falling back. Nearly a dozen of their war mages were down, but their true mage still lurked outside the circle. Frit briefly considered pressing the assault. They could wipe them all out, could get a tiny piece of the vengeance they all craved.

She found the need for that vengeance in every face around her. But at what cost?

"The Fissure is wide enough," Frit growled. "Go. Go, now! We've already lost too many." She shoved Rita toward the portal, and one by one her sisters dove through.

Frit turned toward Ifra one last time. Ree's sword still pinned her corpse there. Frit sketched a split fireball, and flung three fireballs at three separate redwoods. The thick trunks went up like kindling, and the flames spread quickly. She hoped the blaze took this whole damned forest.

She leapt through the Fissure, bracing herself. This part terrified her in ways she couldn't even express. Nebiat had claimed Ifrit could survive in the void, but Frit hadn't been able to verify that. She'd found a bit about the Heart of Krox, but nothing about Ifrit physiology.

The cold drew a gasp as it broke over her skin. She winced and scrunched her eyes shut, but the feeling didn't worsen. Frit cautiously opened an eye. Her other eye came open, and so did her jaw. The space they'd entered was beautiful.

A vast, purple nebula colored the sky before them, the swirls and eddies twinkling with an endless array of stars. It was, without exaggeration, the most beautiful thing she'd ever seen. The mood was spoiled when she realized Ifra hadn't lived to see it.

She turned back to the Fissure, which stood open behind her. It had reached its apex at about three meters, and showed the blaze she'd created. There was no sign of Ree.

"Come." A puff of smoke left Frit's mouth as she spoke. Her voice shouldn't have traveled in the vacuum, but her sisters all turned toward her. "We have a long journey ahead of us. But when we reach its end we will finally be home, and no one will *ever* use us again."

She prayed that was true. Nebiat had freed them, and though she might not be the demon that the Shayans had taught, that didn't make her some magnanimous guardian. There'd be a price for her aid, and Frit hoped the price wasn't too high.

For now, at least, she was happy to pay it. Her sisters were safe.

51

UNWINNABLE

Voria slipped back into the command matrix as Pickus slipped out the far side. She hurriedly tapped the *void* sigil and bonded to the spelldrive. "Sergeant, take over offense. Bord, I want you on defense. Pickus, Kezia, get down to the *Talon* and get her prepped for launch. If we have to fall back, that will be our only hope."

"Aww, come on, Major. Can't I go with Kez? That freckled gigolo is going to make a move on my lady." Bord whined.

"*Your* lady?" Kez demanded. "Get to work, Bord. Make me proud. Then, joost maybe, we'll talk afterwards about a proper date."

"You heard the lady. Move people. Move!" Crewes roared, so loudly a vein throbbed on his neck. Kez and Pickus both sprinted from the room, while Bord took up the defensive matrix.

Voria turned her attention back to the *Hunter*. She closed her eyes, allowing its senses to overlay her own. They were above five hundred meters above the deck, moving between a pair of slender peaks.

Behind them, all four carriers were advancing, and one was very nearly within firing range. "Specialist Bord, be ready to erect a ward, please." Voria already missed being on the *Talon*, where she could tap into any matrix at will. She should be the one counterspelling this.

The carrier flashed, and a white spell shot in their direction. "Now, Specialist."

Bord growled low in his throat and tapped the *life* sigil on each ring. Brilliant white energy rolled off him in waves, and sank into the bottom of the matrix. The scry-screen showed a quickly appearing sea of sigils snaking around the ship. They drew together to complete the ward just before the spirit bolt hit.

Voria's hands shot to her ears as the screams of the damned ripped through the ship. Thankfully, that was the only effect. "Well done, Specialist."

Bord released the ward and leaned against the stabilizing ring, panting. Voria eyed the approaching carrier. The initial exchange hadn't gone terribly, but they'd used resources. Bord could only cast so many wards before he was too exhausted to continue. She needed to minimize their losses.

And there was a way to do that. A way that had been given to her, she suspected, precisely for this battle and others like it. Voria tapped into her new senses, and examined the possibilities springing forth from this one. She followed the tide, watching as the *Hunter* died a hundred different deaths. A thousand. Each time, they were caught out in the open by two or more carriers and killed.

She wiped the back of her wrist across her forehead, and it came away slick with sweat. She pushed harder. There had to be a possibility where they lived. All they needed was one.

"Major," Crewes said, "looks like they're firing again, sir."

"Bord. Ward us." She continued to search, processing tens of thousands of options. Pain shot through her temples, and for a just a moment she lost vision in her right eye. She blinked, and it returned.

"Sir?" Crewes called from a long way away. She shook her head, and released the possibilities she'd been examining.

"I'm all right, Sergeant." She bonded with the *Hunter* once more, and dropped a hundred meters to hug the side of the mountain below. The move screened them from the enemy, as it had in the many possibilities she'd examined.

She dropped into a steep ravine, as she had a thousand times. Two carriers crested the mountain behind her.

"Ward us, Specialist."

The ward went up, and the spirit bolts were deflected. They passed low around the mountain, out of range of all four carriers. Voria pressed a *void* sigil, then an *earth*, then a *void*.

"Major?" Crewes asked.

"Trust me, Sergeant." A crackling ball of black energy shot skyward, seemingly aimed at nothing. The first Krox carrier appeared over the horizon, just in time for the black ball to impact. Voria jerked her hand down hard, and the Krox carrier slammed into the mountain. "Finish them, Crewes!"

"With pleasure, sir." The sergeant's fingers flew across all three rings, tapping every *fire* sigil. He roared as waves of *fire* magic rolled into the matrix. The *Hunter*'s spellcannon filled with a brilliant orange glow, and a river of flame blasted into the carrier.

Turrets melted to slag instantly, and within a few moments the hull itself melted down the hillside like wax.

The carrier detonated spectacularly, at the precise moment the second carrier was coming over the same hill. The explosion knocked it backward, out of sight.

Voria used the opportunity to dive down another ravine. Every attempt she'd made to press her advantage here resulted in their deaths. They had to run.

She snaked along the ravine, wincing as the *Hunter*'s hull screeched when they brushed the side of a mountain. Stones pinged off as they squeezed through the pass.

"Sir." Crewes said in a high pitched voice. "I don't want to backseat fly, but can you try to avoid the walls? You're making me nervous."

"Noted, Sergeant. Bord, get another ward around the ship. Give it everything you have, quickly," she ordered as she guided the ship lower.

A Krox carrier came over the hill, and launched a very un-Krox-like weapon. Dozens of fat missiles streaked from two ports on the aft side of the ship. They flew unerringly toward the *Hunter* in a mass, far too quick to dodge. Voria had already seen a thousand times just how destructive they could be.

"Specialist?" Voria called. She seized the stabilizing ring with both hands, praying. If he failed to get that ward up in time...

A sea of white sigils burst around the hull, then sealed just in time. A blinding glow covered the scry-screen for long moments, leaving them blind. Voria waited tensely, and counted a precise seven seconds before guiding the ship into the air.

"Sergeant, fire at that outcrop there, on the left side." Voria pointed at the scry-screen, indicating a long slab of granite easily a kilometer across.

"Yes, sir." Crewes didn't ask questions. He fired the same

spell, and the river of flame melted granite into lava, all along the base of the outcrop. It leaned drunkenly, then began to tumble free...just as a Krox carrier pulled into view underneath it.

The enormous weight of the mountain slammed into the carrier, and knocked it down into the ravine. It tumbled, flipping end-over-end before hitting the bottom and detonating spectacularly. Voria gave a grim smile, though her heart also began to beat more swiftly. This was as far as she'd made it in the visions.

Every path past this point ended in death.

52

POORLY PLANNED AMBUSH

Nara's ears rang terribly as she staggered free of the matrix. Wes stumbled in a slightly different direction, where he promptly fell to his knees and puked. She nearly join him. The nausea abated slightly, but it returned when the wave of stench hit her.

She rose slowly. Her legs shook badly, and if she weren't wearing spellarmor it was likely she would have fallen. She fed a bit of *void* into her armor and rose off the floor, then slowly lowered her helmet back over her head. She went limp, breathing slowly while she let the sickness pass.

By the time she felt comfortable moving, a thick sheen of sweat had broken out, and she started shivering. Apparently traveling through time came with a physical cost.

Nara drifted from the matrix toward the doorway at the far side of the room. It led into the same control room set above the same hangar, though time had not been kind to this place. The walls were corroded, but she'd expected that. What appalled her was the refuse, and the filth smeared on everything. It was as if someone had intentionally set about ruining this place in an attempt to make it as foul as possible. An oily black substance coated every surface, even the ceiling.

She paused to remove her staff from the void pocket, then turned back to Wes. "Come on. I know this place is disgusting, but we're going to have company sooner than we'd like."

"Right, right," Wes muttered, then pulled himself to his feet with a groan. "I've been shot in the leg, but it's superficial. Sadly, I've been through worse. Shall we explore a bit?" He tied a handkerchief around his pant leg, which was dark with blood.

"You seem a little cavalier about having been shot." Nara was genuinely surprised.

"I said I was a coward, but I'm actually rather good with pain." He delivered a weak smile. "I know time is very limited. Shall we get started?"

"Let's." Nara drifted to the edge of the control room. The wide window overlooking the hangar had long since been shattered, and fragments of glass crunched underfoot as she approached.

Almost all the sigils on the walls had gone dark, and those that remained failed to banish the shadows. Nara peered through the space where the window had been, down at the long, dark shape dominating the hangar. The ship's exterior was covered in filth, though here and there blue-white circuitry showed through. That circuitry pulsed with magical power, and she suspected if she got closer she'd find every bit of it imprinted with sigils.

"Wow." Wes adjusted his glasses. "That thing is massive. Easily three kilometers long. Possibly bigger. I take it this is what you were searching for?"

"That's it." Nara stepped through the gap where the window was, then turned to Wes. "Hop on."

"You know," he said as he climbed onto her back, "it's a real pity we can't just take control of that thing and use it to blast the Krox following us."

"There's a staff that serves as the key, and we can't get in without it," Nara explained. She realized she'd never taken the time to tell Wes much of anything. "The Krox stole that key. They're going to use it to get inside the ship. Our only chance, as I can see it, is to set up an ambush."

"As long as that ambush doesn't require me to be terribly mobile." Wes's words were delivered through gritted teeth. "Sorry about all the blood on your armor. I'm sure it will wash off."

"I wish we had Bord with us." Nara wished she had everyone else, too. "Hang in there, Wes. We'll get you into a covered position, and I can hide you with an illusion until they get close." She only had one healing potion left, and as cold-blooded as it sounded, she needed to save that for herself.

"So we're going to attack them and hope we can over-whelm them?" Wes asked.

Nara glided over a pile of crates covered in a vile black goop that seemed to be the source for the worst of the smell. She sketched a trio of *fire* sigils and cast a fire bolt into a spot behind the crates. The oily substance sizzled away, and it emitted a high pitched scream as it dissolved.

"Is this stuff...alive?" Wes asked, his voice rising nearly an octave. "Why don't we stay airborne?"

"Because they'll pick us off if we're not in cover," Nara countered. She landed in a relatively clean spot, then cast a second fire bolt to clear a spot for Wes. She set him gently on the ground, then used her armor's enhanced strength to maneuver a stack of crates.

She strained, and eventually it budged with a disgusting pop. She only moved it about fifty centimeters, just enough to give Wes a line of fire at the control room she assumed their enemies would come through, while still affording near-total cover.

"Where are you going to be?" Wes asked.

"I'll be moving around," Nara explained. She rose into the air and scanned the hangar. The safest place to start would be the last place they'd expect. She sketched an invisibility sphere, then zipped to the area over the control room they'd entered the hangar through. She hovered directly above the warped ceiling.

They'd have to come through below her. Wes would open up when they came through, and she'd find a target of opportunity. This was exactly the kind of killing Eros had suggested she learn to master. She wished she had a bit more practice, but hopefully surprise would be enough to down their opponents.

If it wasn't, if she couldn't stop them here, then there was nothing to prevent them from getting inside the Spellship. Nothing preventing them from using that Spellship to return to their own time, where they could deliver the hammer blow that would end the Confederacy forever.

But she'd seen the Krox war mage at work, the one who'd called himself Tobek. Whoever he was, he was better than anyone else they'd ever faced. She wasn't positive she could take him even if she had Aran. Without Aran? Things were looking pretty damned grim.

Was this the right move? She fought the urge to second guess herself. She might be able to find a way inside the ship, and maybe she and Wes could hide there. They could sneak out after the Krox returned to their own time, and maybe find a way to take the ship back.

No. That wasn't an option. She must stop them here, or they would lose this war.

53

NO

Nara catalogued her remaining potions. She had two counterspells and one healing. Eros would chide her for still wearing spellarmor, but she found the idea that true mages should deprive themselves of powerful advantages absolutely idiotic. You used every tool at your disposal, especially the ones that allowed you to fly and protected you from spells or bullets.

Of course, Eros never left Shaya. He was literally as far from the front lines as you could get. Exactly the type of person you did not want training your mages. People like Frit were criminally underutilized. What if an Ifrit were assigned to every ship in the—

Nara snapped back to reality when something crunched underneath her. Then something else. She heard voices, and strained to pick up the words.

"I see no sign of them. Are you certain she survived? There would be footprints in this muck," a harsh Krox voice asked.

Another voice answered, "She was wearing spellarmor,

brother. And even if she were not, there are any number of spells that could be masking her presence. It's possible she died trying to find this place, but I think it foolish to assume so. I remind you, Mother will punish failure harshly. Do not assume we have won. Such hubris was Major Voria's mistake."

Nara bit her lip. She heard two other figures moving below, and she hoped they were simply garden-variety enforcers. Those could be knocked out with a simple paralyze spell. But the true mage and the war mage? Both were far more likely to resist, especially the war mage.

She caught Wes eyeing her through the crack in the crates she'd created. She slowly shook her head. Not yet.

The first Krox, the one in the spellarmor, glided from the window down to the ramp extending across the bay under the Spellship. He landed at the edge, and slowly aimed a massive spellcannon at the door.

"It is safe enough, brother. Or appears so," the Krox war mage rumbled.

Nara sketched a missive with a single word. *Now*.

Balls of golden light streaked out of the darkness between the crates. They weren't aimed at the war mage, but instead at a target directly beneath Nara. The true mage. She smiled. Wes wasn't as naive as he appeared.

She crept to the edge of the roof, and sketched a paralyze spell. She flung it at the war mage, who'd turned to face Wes's position. The spell slammed into his back, exploding in a shower of pink mana shards. Damn. His armor must have been enchanted with some sort of magic resistance. It had been worth the attempt, at least.

Nara dropped prone and glanced over the lip of the roof. The true mage had erected a ward, which deflected Wes's fire. He stood confidently behind it, seemingly content to allow the war mage to deal with the threat. They hadn't even noticed her failed paralyze. Perfect.

She considered her target carefully. If she cast on the true mage, and he resisted, then both enforcers would be free to attack her, plus he could do the same. He was far more likely to resist than they were, so starting with them seemed like the smart way to go.

Nara sketched another paralyze, and threw it at the enforcer to the right of the true mage. Both the true mage and the other enforcer turned toward their suddenly paralyzed companion. Nara threw a second one at the other enforcer, who fell just as readily.

The true mage looked up, and his slitted eyes fell on her. He stepped closer and aimed his staff in her direction. Not just any staff, Nara realized. He held Ikadra. She braced herself for the spell, knowing there was no way to escape it at this range.

"Disintegrate her," the Krox rumbled in an emotionless voice.

"Uh, I'm not really comfortable doing that," Ikadra protested, his sapphire pulsing. "She's kind of a friend of mine. Like a really good friend. If I had legs, and a penis, we'd probably be *that* kind of friends, if you know what I'm saying."

"Kill her!" the Krox ordered.

Nara hit him with a paralyze spell. He staggered backward, then threw up his arms with a roar. The spell exploded into mana fragments, and his gaze fell hatefully on her. He began sketching a spell of his own.

"Later." Nara blinked.

She appeared on the far side of the ship, in the shadows beneath one of the thrusters near the stern. The hatchling spun around, trying to find her—with no luck, of course.

She was nearly impossible to detect. He gave a frustrated roar, then leapt from the control room. Nara lost sight of him for a moment, and crept along the engine until she could see him.

He'd landed on the rusted bridge that connected to the Spellship's docking port. She expected him to head immediately for the doors, but instead he stopped and began sketching a spell. Nara considered countering it, but that meant giving away her position. She waited to see what he was casting.

"Nar-*a*!" Wes screeched as he came shooting out from the crates. His long legs pumped as he sprinted away from the war mage, who zoomed above him in spellarmor. Apparently he was more mobile than he'd thought. "Help *meee*!"

Damn it. If she didn't do something, Wes was dead, but if she dealt with this, it would give the true mage time to use Ikadra. A cold, distant part of her mind whispered that she should let Wes die. What was he to her? His death was easy enough to justify.

"No," she whispered to herself. "That's the woman I used to be, and I am not you anymore. Wes is a friend. I got him into this. I'm going to save him."

Nara thought furiously. She couldn't hit the war mage with a direct spell, or rather, if she did she had to assume it would fail. There was still a chance it might work, but that chance was slim. She needed a better option.

What if she hit Wes with a spell? Nara grinned as her hand came up and began sketching. Half a dozen copies of Wes burst out from the original, all running in different directions. She'd even tended to the little flourishes, like a trail of blood for each illusion.

Tobek skidded to an angry halt, the barrel of his spellrifle twitching between targets. He gave a frustrated roar, then slammed a gauntleted fist into a crate. The crate crumpled, and sent up a spray of oily goo that splattered Tobek's armor.

The hatchling leapt into the air and used his wings to guide him toward the true mage. He landed just as a shimmering blue ward rippled outward to protect both of them. It enclosed them fully, and blocked all access to the Spellship's docking doors.

"No," she breathed. Now they were protected by that ward. Any spell she cast would be deflected. The Krox had won.

54

WHY DON'T YOU LET ME HOLD THAT?

A ran reached the end of the corridor, which simply dead-ended into a blood-drenched wall. He assumed that wall probably contained some sort of door like the others he'd seen, but he had no idea how to locate it.

"Huh." He lowered his spellblade. It quivered disappointedly. "I guess we just hang out and wait. I have no idea how precise the gods are with—"

A crack appeared in the wall and the door slid up. Apparently, the gods were pretty damned precise. The door disappeared entirely into the ceiling, and left Aran nose-to-snout with a very surprised Krox.

It was the true mage he'd battled on Shaya. The towering reptile wore an elaborate headdress, and his face had been painted with gold, black, and white makeup. He held a staff in his right hand—a familiar staff.

Aran's hand shot up and he seized Ikadra. "Why don't you let me hang on to that?" He brought Narlifex down with so much force the blade hummed. The metal heated of its own accord, and the sword's eagerness burst through their link. It sliced cleanly through the Krox's wrist, severing the hand even as it cauterized the wound.

The Krox stumbled backward with a draconic screech. It seized the charred stump with its free hand, flapping its wings as it leapt toward a shimmering ward. From its position Aran guessed that ward had been shielding the doorway from the room outside. The ward winked out of existence, and the Krox glided away with impressive speed.

Aran scanned the area outside the door, and realized a few things at once.

First, he'd been trapped inside an absolutely massive starship. And second, the other Krox he'd faced back on Shaya, Tobek the war mage, was trying desperately to kill a screaming human with glasses and...was that the hat from *Relic Hunter*?

Six versions of the space archeologist, if that was what this guy was, ran screaming in six different directions. Aran had seen that spell enough times to guess who the caster might be.

"Nara?" he yelled. His voice echoed through the hangar, and the Krox chasing the archeologist halted instantly. Tobek turned slowly until his gaze settled on Aran, then those cruel eyes widened.

"You!" he roared. Tobek broke off pursuit for the archeologist, instead gliding in Aran's direction. He banked in the air and his wings flared above him as he closed the gap.

Aran shot a glance at the now-handless true mage, who was hightailing it toward a shattered control room on the far side of the hangar. He couldn't deal with the mage without first handling Tobek, so he pivoted to face him.

"Yes, me," Aran yelled back. He smiled up at the rapidly approaching Krox. "And this time I'm ready. You're not the only one with spellarmor." The gods had already proven how precise they were. Aran confidently tapped his bracelet, and waited for the armor to flow over him. Hopefully Virkonna had added something to give him an edge here.

Nothing happened.

A two-handed spellblade materialized in the Krox's grasp, and he brought it down on Aran with the force of a falling star. Time seemed to slow, and Aran took in the magnitude of the creature falling toward him. Now that Tobek was close enough he could see the agonized faces emblazoned on the midnight armor. Each was locked in a silent scream, perhaps the very moment they'd died.

He wasn't going to end up another face.

Aran flipped backward, and used *air* to enhance the leap. He landed on the far side of the rusted bridge, which gave him more room to maneuver. Unfortunately, the ground was coated with the same dark blood as the interior of the ship. He slid wildly, and slammed into the railing, barely catching himself.

He stared over the edge into an abyss, the deep bay where the ship was stored. A lake of black, shimmering liquid filled the bay to within a few meters of the top. The stench was a living thing, so foul his eyes teared up instantly.

Aran struggled to maintain his balance, and tapped desperately at the bracelet. Nothing. "Come on, come on. This isn't funny, Neith. Or Virkonna. Or whichever one of you is responsible for this."

"I do not know which god you are praying to, human," Tobek roared. His wingbeats sounded behind Aran. "It will not save you."

Aran dove to the right, and slid hand-first through the blood. He gathered a handful, then rolled to his feet in the relatively clean spot his impact had made. The war mage dove from above, his sword held before him like a lance.

Aran summoned *air* and formed a bubble around the fistful of blood. "You know I get you don't need to breathe in space, but if you're going to wear spellarmor you really ought to consider going with a full helmet." He flung the blood into Tobek's face, and it splattered all over the Krox's eyes.

The move only bought him a moment, and Aran was determined to use it. He leapt into the air, and used *void* to enhance his mass. He summoned a massive ball of ice around his left foot, and swung it in a wide roundhouse designed to capitalize on his momentum.

The ice slammed into Tobek's face, knocking him from the air. He slid through the blood, rolling a good twenty meters before slamming into a rusted console on the other side of the bridge. Aran doubted it had done any real damage, but it gave him a few seconds to breathe.

"Nara?" Aran roared, now that he had a split second to think.

"Here." She winked into existence a few meters away.

Her armor was also covered in blood, but he couldn't see any obvious damage. Relief washed through him, a knot of tension he'd been carrying ever since the two of them had been separated. He kept one eye on Tobek, who was already climbing to his feet.

"Oh, thank Virkonna. It is so good to see you." And it was. He hadn't realized how much he'd missed her. Aran tapped his bracelet again. Nothing. "We need to keep Ikadra out of the Krox's hands. And, ideally, we need to figure out how to use him to control the ship. Think you can handle it?" Aran tossed Ikadra to her. The staff, he realized, had been utterly silent during his battle with Tobek.

The sapphire flashed as Nara caught the weapon, but the staff's ever-present wit was curiously absent.

She pointed down at Tobek. "Aran, I've been watching the fight. You're not doing very well against this guy. Let's get inside the ship, and get the depths out of here."

Tobek leapt to his feet, and flared his wings for balance. "I will kill you, human! You cannot run forever."

"Get in the ship and go," Aran snapped. "We can't leave this to chance. There's too much riding on it."

Nara was silent, but only for a moment. "What should I expect inside?" Nara asked quickly. She was looking at the Krox, who was struggling to maintain his balance on the slick floor. "And are you sure you don't want help? This guy kicked the crap out of Ree. We could take him together."

"We can't risk losing and them getting Ikadra. Take the ship back to the present. I'll make sure they stay here, or die trying." Aran tensed as Tobek leapt into the air and flapped in their direction. "The ship's interior is coated with blood, and there's at least one possible hostile. Right inside the door you'll see an unconscious woman. She's an Outrider, and not a threat, at least not that I can see."

"Aran—" Her voice softened, and he wished he could comfort her.

"Go!" he roared. His attention was already focused on Tobek again.

"Be careful." Nara winked out of view.

Aran turned back to the Krox just as the hatchling came down on him from above. A cloud of pallid white fog billowed from Tobek's mouth, and Aran desperately dove to the side. He used *air* to leap twenty meters, and rolled behind a stack of blood-covered crates.

His heart leapt into his throat when he realized he was face-to-barrel. A golden pistol was pressed against his nose.

The man holding it wore the *Relic Hunter* hat and a pair of grease-covered spectacles. He peered over them at Aran, as if trying to identify him.

"I'm hoping you're not with the Krox. It would be a terrible shame to melt your face. Not that I have much choice in the matter. That's all on the pistol," the archeologist said. He gave a little wave with his other hand, and a sheepish smile. After an eternal moment the pistol lowered from Aran's face. "Well, it seems they've decided you're not a threat. I'm Wes."

"I don't suppose you know how to use those?" Aran asked. Any help would be welcome, and the pistols looked decidedly lethal.

"Of course I know how to use them. Why would you think otherwise?" Wes gave an indignant sniff, one Ree would have highly approved of.

"Because you're hiding behind a stack of crates?" Aran offered.

"Ah, well, you make an excellent point. There's no arguing with that." The archeologist's eyes widened at something over Aran's shoulder.

A clawed foot crashed into Aran's shoulder and flung him into the crates with a hollow boom. Blood exploded everywhere, and it probably saved Aran's life. Tobek's gauntleted hands tried to seize him, but he slipped right through his clawed fingers.

"I think I just wet myself," the archeologist shrieked. His pistols snapped up and aimed at the hatchling. The weapons began to buck, each firing a steady stream of golden pulses. The energy detonated against Tobek's spellarmor, and redirected its momentum. The Krox was knocked to the side, and Aran took the opportunity to roll to his feet.

The archeologist continued to fire, and the Krox turned in his direction. Aran reached deep into his chest, and blended three aspects of magic. He fed it all into his blade, as he'd done before. This time Narlifex answered that call, and added magic of its own.

Fire burst from the weapon, and a moment later lightning began to crackle around the flame. Both shifted to purple as *void* flowed up the blade.

We. Kill. Now. The words reverberated through his mind. They'd come from Narlifex.

Aran feinted toward Tobek, and the Krox lunged with his claymore. Aran hopped back in a fadeaway, and flung his spellblade at the Krox. He used *air* to guide the weapon's flight, slipping around Tobek's parry and punching into the thick armor between the neck and shoulder.

The blade sank deep, and discharged the spell. Lightning and fire flowed down the weapon, disappearing inside Tobek's spellarmor. He seemed unimpressed, though his eyes narrowed dangerously.

Tobek's neck elongated and his chest swelled, then he breathed another cloud of *spirit*.

Aran rolled out of the way, but Tobek followed up immediately. The Krox hurled his blade at Aran, in a parody of the move Aran had just used. The tip punched through Aran's side, and pinned him to the wall behind him.

Aran gritted his teeth, both eyes tearing up. The blade had punched through his midsection, above the kidney, he hoped. "It sure would be nice to have spellarmor, too."

He seized the hilt with *air*, and wrenched Tobek's much larger sword free with a roar. The pain was immense, especially as the tip left his body, but he compartmentalized it. The adrenaline helped, though there'd be depths to pay when the dust settled.

The Krox wrapped his hands around the hilt of Aran's spellblade, which was still lodged in his shoulder. He tugged it free of his armor, and began a cautious advance. "What will you do, little Outrider? You have no blade. You have no armor. You. Have. Nothing!" Spittle flew from the creature's maw.

"Aren't you taking this a little personally?" Aran knew it was a weak retort, but he didn't have much else to offer. He was badly wounded, and Tobek was right. He had nothing.

Then Tobek roared in surprise, and dropped Narlifex. His gauntlet smoked, and Aran realized the palm had burned all the way down to the bone, right through the armor.

"Good sword. No more void pockets after this fight, I promise." Assuming he survived, that was. Aran desperately tapped his bracelet, though this time he wasn't expecting much. Apparently the gods had misjudged a variable. "Why give it to me, if I can't use it?"

Remember my words, mortal. Virkonna's voice reverberated through his mind. *Your technology will not save you. I have not enhanced it. I have disabled the wretched thing. It has been corrupted by Nefarius.*

"So not only are you not helping," Aran thrust his hand out, and seized Narlifex with a tendril of *air*, "but you're actively sabotaging my chances of success?"

Remember my words.

He yanked Narlifex back into his grip at nearly the same instant Tobek seized his own weapon. He rose and began to advance cautiously toward Aran. "This is the end, little human. You have done surprisingly well, enough that I would consider binding you, if you hadn't maimed my brother."

The creature's face was twisted by hatred, his cold eyes

narrow and focused. He stalked closer, and Aran stepped into a guard position.

What had Virkonna meant? Remember my words. She'd told him something when she'd flooded him with magic. Become *air*.

Tobek's blade flicked out with blinding speed, and Aran barely brought Narlifex up in time to parry. The blades rang off each other, and Tobek's gave a dark, angry scream.

Narlifex pulsed in eager rage, straining to reach the other blade. Aran restrained it and backpedaled to gain room to think. Tobek refused to allow him that space, and glided forward into another strike.

Blow after blow rained down, and Aran had no choice but to parry desperately. Tobek's spell armor, and his own natural strength and size, made this a very one-sided fight.

Become *air*.

Tobek's blade finally clipped Aran's forearm, adding another source of pain, and slowing him further. He growled low in his throat, and pounced on the larger war mage.

Narlifex thrust into Tobek's gut, the tip melting a red circle as it disappeared inside the Krox. Tobek roared, and dropped his blade. He seized Aran's wrists, wrenching them into the air until Aran hung, pinned in place.

His shoulders strained, and he could feel the tendons stretching painfully. Aran's hand went numb, and Narlifex tumbled from his grasp to clatter onto the bridge.

"As I said, human," Tobek rumbled in a smug voice. His snout moved closer until he was eye to eye with Aran, "this is the end." Tobek sucked in a breath.

Aran closed his eyes. Become *air*. He touched the well of energy in his chest, and focused on the most familiar of all elements, the very first he'd ever been granted. It lay there, pulsing with more power than it ever had.

Become *air*.

Aran had channeled magic many times, and each time that energy had passed through his body. But what if he kept it? What if he let it flow into his limbs, but didn't discharge it? What would happen?

"Nothing to lose," he muttered through gritted teeth.

Tobek breathed.

Aran poured *air* through his limbs, the potent magic infusing every part of his body until even his eyes crackled with white-blue power. The breath washed over him, but Aran felt nothing. No pain, or numbness, as he had before.

"What spell is this?" Tobek asked suspiciously, his grip on Aran's wrists never slackening.

"This is a present from Virkonna." Aran poured more *air* into his body, until it became painful. He burst into pure electricity, freeing himself from Tobek's grasp.

Aran considered his next move for a fraction of a moment as Tobek's eyes widened in surprise. Then he decided. He couldn't hurt Tobek because of the spellarmor.

But what if he attacked from the inside?

Aran flowed inside of Tobek's mouth, pouring into the Krox in a torrent of crackling white energy. He pooled in the creature's stomach, and willed pain and death on his foe. The energy crackled through the Krox's body, and Tobek shrieked desperately.

His body smoked and twitched as Aran cooked every part of the creature's body. He let it seize up one more time, and then he stopped Tobek's heart.

In that moment Aran became aware of two beings, a tiny, malnourished soul made of *earth*, and a much stronger being made of pure *spirit*. The *earth* soul pulsed gratitude, and then dissipated. The *spirit* soul shrieked, and then did the same.

Aran flowed out of Tobek's scorched armor, and coalesced into human form. He kicked Tobek's smoking skull. "Told you. Head protection, man."

55

OUT OF TIME

Nara cautiously stepped through the doorway into the ship's dim interior. The first thing she noticed was the stench. She'd thought it smelled bad outside the ship, but the interior was a whole other level. Without her spellarmor she'd probably have vomited, and even with it she badly wanted to take a bath.

She sketched a *fire* sigil, and a flame bloomed above her head. It illuminated the corridor, a little at least. The walls were coated in a slick substance. She bent closer, noting the faint magical signature. Was this stuff...alive?

"K-kept the faith," a voice muttered from down the corridor.

Nara hurried forward, drifting through the air so as not to touch the ground. That wasn't just an aversion to the blood. Being invisible was pointless if she left a trail of footprints anyone could follow.

Nara stopped above the figure, puzzled by what she saw. Or didn't see. The figure was enshrouded in shadow. She lay in a puddle of dark blood, which slowly congealed around her legs.

She took a deep breath and considered her options. She could attempt to burn the blood away, but risked hurting the woman. A nullification spell, perhaps? Nara sketched several sigils, then flung the spell into the blood.

The blood lunged suddenly, bubbling up around the magic. The spell disappeared instantly, absorbed if it had never been. The blood responded by boiling outward, and now covered the woman's legs entirely.

"Wait a sec," Nara realized aloud. She glanced up at Ikadra. "You were created for this moment. I'm betting you've got a solution."

Ikadra's sapphire flashed like a six-year-old who needed to pee. "Oh, that's right. You need permission to speak. Ikadra, I give you permission to speak however and whenever you like, until told otherwise." Voria would hate that, but it irked Nara that Ikadra wasn't allowed to talk whenever he wanted.

That kind of servitude reminded her uncomfortably of Frit. Ikadra might not be a person, but he was as alive as any of them, and deserved the same respect. Even if he did like poop jokes.

"You're even hotter when you're freeing me," Ikadra burst out as his sapphire flashed. "Oh, thank Neith. I can speak! That Krox had *no* sense of humor. Like, at all."

"I'd love to catch up, but I get the sense we're short on time," Nara pressed. She pointed at the blood-covered woman. "We need to help her, then we need to get to the bridge as quickly as possible."

"Oh, right. Sorry." Ikadra's emerald pulsed thoughtfully. "You have void flame right?"

"Yes." Nara could cast void flame, though she rarely used it. Frit was the true master there.

"That woman is an Outrider," Ikadra explained happily.

"She has innate magical resistance. I can further enhance her resistance. She might not like it, but if you hit her with a burst of void flame it should boil away that icky crap."

"Worth a shot, I guess. Ward her," Nara ordered.

A warm white glow built around Ikadra's tip. That glow was answered by the Outrider. Her skin slowly became luminescent. "Okay, that's the best I can do. If this goes wrong...totally not my fault."

"What do you mean, not your fault? It's your idea," Nara shot back. She took a deep breath. She must be stressed if she was arguing with a staff. She raised a hand, and sketched a delicate set of *fire* and *void* sigils.

A hot rush of purple flame burst from her hand. It billowed outward and covered the Outrider, obscuring her from view. Her body went rigid and she screamed. Nara's heart wrenched, but she kept the flow of void flame up. The flames ate greedily at the blood. As before, it tried to absorb the spell. But this time the fire won, slowly burning away the blood.

Nara kept it up for several more seconds. She forced herself to ignore the woman's frantic cries, and only ended the spell when she was positive the blood had been burned away. So had the woman's clothing. She huddled there naked, her skin pink and scalded.

She stared wildly up at Nara, a few patches of black still on her cheek and forehead. It streaked what might be blond hair, though that was difficult to tell in this lighting. She was pretty—though nothing on Ree's level, thankfully.

"Can you stand up?" Nara asked. She knew this woman couldn't see her face under the armor, and that would make trusting her hard. But there was no way she was removing her helmet, not in this place. There was still plenty of blood on the walls, and she'd watched enough holovids to expect some blood zombies to come lunging out of the darkness at some point.

"Yes," the Outrider muttered. She rose shakily to her feet. "I haven't felt this...whole in a while. Did he reach the door in time? Is that why you are here?"

Nara didn't need Neith's gifts to connect the dots. This woman led Aran to the door, and for her to do that, a god had somehow arranged the possibility.

"Yes, he reached the door. Come on." She offered the woman her free hand, and the woman accepted it gratefully. "Do you have a name?"

"Rhea," she muttered.

"Ikadra, can you lead us to the bridge?" Nara asked. She lifted off into the air and clutched Rhea tightly to her side. Thankfully the ceiling was high enough they could hover off the ground without brushing either it or the floor.

"Sure. Hey, do you want me to deal with this stuff?" Ikadra pulsed.

"If you can, sure." Nara flew slowly down the corridor, since it seemed the only way to go.

"Can you feed me a little *void* and some *fire*?" Ikadra asked excitedly.

"Sure." Nara mixed *void* and *fire* and fed the energy into the staff.

"Pew. Pew. Pewpewpewpewpew." Ikadra's sapphire pulsed in time with the words as he flung balls of void fire all up and down the corridor.

A new and even more terrible stanch billowed out around them, and Rhea promptly vomited all over Nara's armor. Eww.

Ikadra kept flinging spells as they flew down the corridor, long after he should have run out of magic. "How are you still casting?"

"One of my many fabulous talents is serving as an amplifier," Ikadra explained. "Hold on a sec. Pew. Pewpewpew. Anyway, if you cast a spell into me, I can replicate it using my own internal reserves. Basically, you can cast any spells you want me be able to use into me, and then I can do this. Pewpew."

The blood burned away ahead of them, leaving relatively clean walls in their wake as they soared through the vessel. Nara had no idea when Rhea had passed out, but her head lolled against her spellarmor, and her hair dangled low enough to almost brush the ground as they flew.

"We're almost there." Ikadra blasted away the blood in a final corridor, then they arrived in a long, narrow control room. Four spell matrices identical to those on the *Talon* faced a wall-sized scry-screen. Every bit of it was coated in blood.

"Ikadra?" Nara asked.

"Pewpewpewpew." Balls of void flame shot all over the battle bridge, and when the volley ceased, most of the blood had been scorched away.

"Now, how do we get back to our own time?" Nara gently set the unconscious Outrider against the far wall. Her breathing was deep and even, though she was probably cold. Nara reached into her void pocket and withdrew her blanket. She covered the Outrider, and tucked in the edges.

"Well, it looks like we have about eighteen seconds to make the transition, and the spell will take a minimum of six to cast," Ikadra pulsed happily.

Nara sprinted for the closest matrix and dove inside. She tapped frantically at the *void* sigil on the silver ring, then the gold, and finally the bronze. The vessel shuddered to life as she linked to it. A hundred senses overwhelmed her, from the state of the spelldrive, to each individual spellcannon.

The experience was overwhelming, and she fought vertigo as she tried to make sense of it all.

"Ikadra?" she asked as calmly as she could. "What is the spell sequence?"

"Void, void, fire, void, water, void, air."

Nara quickly tapped the sequence. Her hands shook as more and more magical energy was ripped from her dwindling reserves. Her finger hovered over the final sigil. What if Aran hadn't made it back aboard?

"We're out of time," Ikadra screeched. "Go, go, go!"

Nara stabbed the final sigil, and prayed.

56

BEST SPELL EVER

Voria circled the mountain peak as the last three Krox ships moved to flank them. That included the one that had broken off from Davidson, which was slower than the others and trailing smoke from the grievous wounds the marines had inflicted.

But despite their heroics, this was the end. In every possibility, this was as far as she'd made it. If she focused on the ship coming over the peak, then the ones on her flanks gutted them.

If she focused on a flank she lasted a little longer, but the ship coming over the top softened them up while the final ships got into position to fire. There was simply no solution. She knew, because she had tried them all.

The closest they came to survival was running, so that was what she did. Voria dropped low, no more than fifty meters above the deck. She poured a torrent of *void* and *fire* into the spelldrive and the *Hunter* reluctantly accelerated.

The Krox carrier cresting the mountain loosed another torrent of missiles. "Bord, another ward. Quickly. They've launched more...what did you call them, Pickus?"

"Nukes, sir. Or more properly nuclear missiles," the tech mage explained. He stood behind Crewes, ready to relieve him if needed.

Bord's hand shook as he tapped the final *life* sigil, and he grunted when the ship tore more magical energy from his chest. He sank to a knee, and barely caught himself against the stabilizing ring.

The ship lurched suddenly, flinging Voria into the side of the matrix. Her wrist bent painfully as she caught herself against the stabilizing ring.

"Sir, we took significant damage from that blast," Crewes said. He tapped a *fire* sigil and the scry-screen adjusted to show the lower decks. Much of the cargo bay had been cooked, and parts were still ablaze. "I don't think we're going to survive another hit, even with one of Bord's wards."

"Not sure I can do another one," Bord said weakly. He rose, trembling, and leaned against the stabilizing ring.

Kezia moved to stand outside it, and rested a hand on Bord's. "You did good. We'd be dead if you hadn't joost saved us."

"Well done, Specialist." Voria was doubly glad she'd ordered Davidson to secure his position. If they'd been down there in the hold, every last surviving marine would have radiation sickness. Bord could treat the symptoms for a few people, but not for an entire battalion. And anti-radiation meds only did so much.

"Sir," Crewes called. The scry-screen shifted back to show the other two Krox carriers pulling into view. The closest one hadn't fired again, though she knew it would in a few more seconds. It always did. In every possibility.

"It has been a privilege and an honor serving with all of you." Voria kept her tone even, but she couldn't stop the tears. "We've done more, survived longer, than anyone could have ever expected of us. I am immensely proud of all we accomplished."

The sergeant was the first to understand the import of her words. His shoulder's squared. "It's okay, sir. You did more than anyone could have, or should have asked. I'm proud to serve with you, Major."

"I'm sorry," she said, her voice cracking. "I did try, Sergeant. But I cannot find a way out of this."

A cloud of nukes launched from the first ship. A heartbeat later, answering clouds came from both other vessels. How ironic that the Krox were killing them with a weapon developed on Ternus. A magical war, settled by technological means.

"Sir, maybe we can make it to the *Talon*," Kezia called desperately. She seized Bord, and her voice fell to a whisper. "There has to be something we can do."

The space between the *Hunter* and the missiles rippled and twisted. Voria's brain fought to make sense of what she was seeing. Two separate realities stretched before her. In one, the missiles streaked toward them, impacting. In the other, something materialized in that space.

The second reality overpowered the first, and a truly massive vessel appeared. The ship was long and menacing, like the barrel of a weapon designed by the gods themselves. Blue circuitry glinted from the hull, but only in small patches. Most of the vessel was covered in a thick, viscous fluid. At first, anyway.

All three clouds of Ternus missiles slammed into the vessel.

"Bord, give me anything you can," Voria called with the kind of confidence she knew he needed to hear. "Kezia is depending on you. We all are."

Bord disengaged from the drifter and his face set in a

mask of grim determination. He raised a trembling hand and tapped the first sigil. Energy rolled off him, but weakly this time. He tapped the next sigil, and grunted as more white energy rolled into the hull. Finally, he raised that trembling hand and tapped the third sigil.

A wall of white sigils burst around the ship once more. It obscured the scry-screen, cutting them off from the distant explosion. Voria tapped *fire* and shifted the scry-screen to a bird's-eye view. A wave of brilliant death burst over the gargantuan ship. Most of that flame was shunted away, stopped by a shimmering blue shield only a few meters from the hull.

The ship—the First Spellship, she was sure of it—served as a bulwark. It broke the flow of death, and all the *Hunter* had to deal with was a lazy wall of nuclear flame. Bord's ward held, and after several seconds the flames abated.

The specialist collapsed to the stabilizing ring, and Kezia helped him to lay down. She stroked his cheek. "You were amazing." Kezia bent and kissed Bord on the forehead.

When she rose, he wore the largest, most wicked grin Voria had ever seen. "Totally worth it," he murmured. "First. Base!" He gave a little fist pump, then laid back down.

A potent ringing began in Voria's ears. She recognized the resonance, but it built too quickly for her to react. *Void* energy flowed all around her body, encasing her in its frigid embrace. The teleport completed, and she was ripped from the bridge of the *Hunter*.

She staggered when she arrived, lurching into a wall a meter or so from her landing point. Her hand slid in something greasy, and she tumbled onto her butt with a grunt.

"Oh, no," Ikadra's familiar voice shrieked. Voria winced as it drove into her brain. "She's going to make me be quiet again."

"Sir?" Nara's muffled voice came from far away. She was being helped to her feet.

Voria blinked, and her attention focused on Nara. She remembered who she was...and where she was. "We're in the middle of combat." She looked around desperately.

There were four matrices, and in front of them, the entire wall was covered by a massive scry-screen. That screen showed the three advancing carriers, the wounded one lagging a considerable distance behind the others.

"Do we have the means of dealing with those before they can attack again?" Voria stabbed a finger at her enemy.

"Can I do it?" Ikadra begged. "Pleaaaaase. Just say the word, and I'll take care of them. I promise."

Nara offered her the staff, and Voria accepted it gratefully. Ikadra's warmth was more reassuring than she'd like to admit. "All right. If you can remove those ships, then do it. I don't care how juvenile your solution is."

"We've got missiles, too." Ikadra's sapphire pulsed wickedly, and he laughed in time.

A trio of glowing azure balls shot from the Spellship, each streaking toward one of the Krox vessels. They didn't come from the spellcannon, but rather from the hull of the ship itself. That raised a good many questions, but she could find answers later.

For now, Voria watched the balls of energy to see what they would do. The spells slammed into the ungainly Krox carriers...and disappeared. There was no immediate effect that she could see.

"That seems a good deal less flashy than I'd have expected," Voria said. She glanced suspiciously at the staff. "What did you cast?"

"I call it *so fat*." Ikadra giggled wildly. "Your starship so fat, it's got its own area code. And heavy stuff tends to fall down."

Voria had no idea what an area code was, and she didn't much care. She was fixed by the Krox carriers, which were slowly plummeting from the sky. Each gained momentum as they approached the earth, and by the time they impacted, they had enough momentum to create explosions to rival those of the missiles they'd fired.

The mushroom clouds died away, and there was no sign of any carriers, just a blasted and barren field. That field was lifeless now, utterly. If anyone had lived there, and Voria believed they had, then they were gone now. Would the Wyrms even notice?

"Did we miss anything?" Aran asked from the doorway. Voria turned to see him standing with the greasy archeologist Nara had been working with. And this time he really *was* greasy. He looked like he'd been rolling in whatever that oil was.

"Not much," Ikadra called back to Aran. "Only the best. Spell. Ever!"

57

PARIAH TO HERO

V oria rarely enjoyed parties. She hated all the posturing and the subtle manipulation. That was especially true of parties with dragons, who took all the petty games to an unenviable level.

Yet, today, she was delighted to attend.

Perhaps it was the Spellship hovering in the sky above the party. It hovered there, its imposing bulk dominating much of the skyline. The long sleek hull was positively menacing.

"That wasn't particularly subtle," Olyssa said as she sidled up to Voria. She offered a goblet and Voria accepted it.

"You mean the ship?" Voria smiled up at the vessel. "Too petty, do you think?"

"Not at all." Olyssa burst into a sudden, inhuman laugh. It, and the hairless face, were reminders of her draconic nature. "I particularly like how you dropped the shadow over Aetherius's area, but nowhere else."

Voria's gaze rose toward the far side of the amphitheater, where Aetherius stood with a group of his sycophants. The ancient Wyrm glared hatefully at her with those fierce eyes. His hand tightened around a goblet until it crunched.

"He doesn't seem amused." Voria nodded respectfully to Aetherius. The gesture wasn't returned. "I figured since an alliance is impossible at this point, I had very little to lose, and I have to admit to a certain...satisfaction in seeing that expression on his face after what he pulled."

"You've done incalculable damage to his cause." Olyssa's smile vanished and was replaced by the calculating mask. "He dishonorably allowed you to be attacked. He can claim he had no knowledge, but we all know the truth. He allowed his pet Krox to attack you, and even if he did not order it, his was the hand ultimately delivering the blow. You stopped that blow, and you exposed him. You've bested him on every level, even in Kem'Hedj. Yet you've been nothing but gracious the entire time."

Voria smiled, though only slightly. This wasn't a perfect victory. "I've made an enemy in the process. An enemy who will outlive me by centuries, or even millennia. One with the resources of an entire dragonflight at his disposal."

"He hates you, but his people hate the Krox," Olyssa pointed out. "You may have personally gained an enemy, but you have also ensured that the Krox will never be welcome here. Instead, we will stay neutral in your war."

"That's not the worst possible outcome," Voria allowed. "But we need allies, Olyssa. We are playing for the highest stakes. Higher than I think any of us yet realize."

"I believe you're right, there, but unfortunately we have other concerns." Olyssa walked to the edge of the balcony, which overlooked the vast plain where the battle had taken place. "I don't know what the dark substance coating the ship was, but I do know how it made me feel. Terrified."

"Presumably it was boiled away in the nuclear blast."

Voria frowned slightly. "We're still cleaning the ship, but I don't think you should have anything to worry about."

"And if you are wrong?" Olyssa challenged. "That muck rained over many kilometers, and it did so well before the detonation. If the wind carried any of it beyond the explosion it could still be out there. I don't pretend to know what it is, and I know you don't yet either. Perhaps it is nothing. Perhaps none survived. But so long as there is a chance, my focus is on eradicating any trace of it that survived."

Voria nodded gratefully. "I'm sorry, Olyssa. That it happened. All of it. And I'm sorry for all you've lost recently."

"Thank you." Olyssa licked her lips with a forked tongue. "I have never said this before—not to anyone but a Wyrm or a god—but I consider you an equal, Major. The way you commanded that battle, even before the Spellship arrived...well I've never seen anything like it. Or rather, I have only seen it from my mother. You took those Krox forces apart, and turned certain death into victory. I do not envy the Krox their war against you. I suspect they have no idea what they are dealing with."

"Let's hope it's enough." Voria squinted up at the Spellship. It was powerful, of that she was sure. But it was also tainted somehow. Olyssa was right. She didn't know what the oily substance was, or what threat it posed. And she strongly doubted getting rid of it would be as simple as wiping down the ship.

"What will happen to Aranthar?" Olyssa asked after a long moment of silence.

Voria stared out at the field, noting the small settlements spread out every twenty kilometers or so. How many of those had been in the path of the explosions when the Krox had fired their missiles?

"Hmm?" She turned back to Olyssa. "It's so odd hearing you call him that. I believe Aran will remain aboard his ship, and that it will remain attached to mine. We have a war to fight, Wyrm Mother."

"I see." Olyssa cocked her head in a wholly unnatural way no human could have duplicated. "I had hoped that perhaps his sister could persuade him to stay. She's up there now, talking with him."

"She might, but I doubt it." Voria smiled. He'd make the right choice. "He knows he isn't welcome here."

"Isn't welcome?" Olyssa blinked her reptilian eyes. "He is a hero now. There is no Outrider with higher standing. He was chosen by Virkonna. She elevated him, and used him as her instrument to return her great work to the world."

"So, just like that, he goes from pariah to hero?" Voria snorted. "He's going to love that."

58

GOODBYES

Aran stared out the scry-screen set into his quarters. It currently acted as a window, showing the hangar outside. The Blood of Nefarius was gone, save for black streaks on some of the walls. Those hadn't been there a few hours ago, which underscored just how quickly this stuff grew.

It also raised a great many troubling questions. He hadn't yet told anyone else what the substance was, because he'd needed time to consider. Virkonna had disabled his armor, because she'd said it was tainted by Nefarius. That meant it might be related to the blood, and that carried some damned scary implications.

Apparently Krox wasn't their only enemy.

"Little brother?" Astria's hesitant voice came from the doorway. She dropped her gaze when Aran looked at her, and raised a hand to brush dark hair back over her ear. She still wore her suit, but the mask was clutched in one of her hands.

Why was she suddenly so timid? He wasn't really sure what to do. What would a brother do?

"Listen, I know this is awkward. I really don't know how to...be around you." Aran crossed the space between them and offered a hug. Astria seemed surprised, but she relaxed into his grip. For a few moments at least. Then she disengaged. Aran took a step back to give her space. He smiled at her. "I've got a friend named Kazon that likes hugs. I'm still not sure how I feel about them."

"I find the ritual odd." Astria cocked her head. "But I am glad you are alive, little brother."

Aran adjusted Narlifex on his belt and the blade vibrated contentedly. He struggled to break the silence, finally settling on an inane question. "So how did you get up here? Dragon?"

"Nara brought me back with her when she returned from the *Hunter*," Astria explained. Her face turned down into a disapproving frown. Whatever she'd been about to say vanished. Her eyes blazed but she said nothing.

Aran followed her gaze...to his bed. Rhea rested there. The corrupted Outrider still hadn't woken, and Aran wasn't sure when she would. Or even if she should. She'd been absorbing that stuff, intentionally from the sound of it, for years.

"Her name is Rhea," Aran explained. He couldn't help but be amused. After all they'd been through, his sister was angry he might be sleeping with someone? It seemed so trivial in the face of the events around them. "She's an Outrider, Astria. From a theoretical future. A place only the gods could have reached. She watched the death of her entire world. Her entire people. She was the very last survivor."

"Virkonna's Blessing," Astria whispered. She moved to the bed, and adjusted the blankets to cover the girl more fully. "I'm...sorry I leapt to conclusions. So she was on the ship when you found it?"

"She was the last survivor." Aran moved to join Astria. "We don't know much yet beyond her name, but that will come in time. She was in that blood for a long time, and it... changes you."

"I think it does more than that," Nara said from the doorway.

Aran whirled, then crossed his quarters in three steps. He picked Nara up and spun her in a circle. She squealed, but she was smiling. He set her down. "Gods, but it is good to see you."

"You were saying?" Astria asked Nara, though she was eyeing Aran curiously.

"The blood. Pickus and I have done a little theory crafting." Nara smiled up at Aran, and he'd never wanted to be alone with anyone so badly. She took a step away from him, but shot him a wink he hoped his sister didn't see. "We'll know more soon." Her smile faded. "We're pretty sure it comes from the Umbral Depths."

Those two words did more than a cold shower ever could to bring Aran back to the moment. "It corrupts people, though the process seems to take a long time. And we rained it all over the countryside below." He considered adding that Rhea had called it the Blood of Nefarius, but held back for some reason.

"We'll deal with it," Astria said. She folded her arms. "We're aware of it, at least. Olyssa has already dispatched anyone with void flame to help dispose of it, and we have flame readers to locate outbreaks. The situation is in hand."

"I'm glad. That means I can leave with a clean conscience, at least." Aran shook his head sadly. "Definitely not the homecoming I was hoping for."

"Are you certain you won't stay?" Astria asked suddenly. "There's a place for you here, little brother. You've proven yourself—not simply to me, but to our entire world. Even Aetherius respects you. We could help Olyssa solidify control of the flights, and we could be there to help the Confederacy when the time comes."

That last got his attention. So did the prospect of actually having a family, and a past to ground himself in. He'd been running from crisis to crisis for literally the entirety of his memory. This was a chance to claim a place for himself. To be with someone who loved him, and shared the same blood flowing through his veins. And there was still so much to learn about Virkon, and his people. Not just his past, but his history and legacy.

"It means the sector to me that you'd make a place for me here. I still don't understand why I'm suddenly a hero instead of a dragonslayer, but it's nice knowing I can go to sleep without worrying about you sticking a knife in my kidney." He stuck his tongue out.

Astria looked outraged, but Nara laughed. After a moment Astria smiled, then began to laugh as well. "I'm proud of you, little brother. If you cannot stay, I know the reason must be of great import. I wish you well in the war against the Krox."

"And I wish you luck in helping Olyssa gain control here. I'm definitely rooting for you." Aran meant it, too. If Aetherius regained control, he had a feeling he could expect a lot more assassins. "I do have a final favor to ask."

"What is it?" she asked.

"We're at war, all the time. That's no place for a recovering patient." He nodded at Rhea. "I was hoping, since she's an Outrider, you'd allow her to stay."

Astria stared sadly at Rhea. She refused to meet Aran's

gaze when she spoke. "I can't, Aran. There's a chance she's contaminated, and if she is...Olyssa would have her put to death without a second thought. She isn't safe here."

Nara shuddered. "That's horrifyingly pragmatic."

"The Wyrm Mother so often is." Astria sighed. "I'm going to miss you, brother. I feel like I still don't know the man you've become."

"I have a feeling you'll be seeing me again." Aran smiled affectionately at her. "The Krox haven't found a way to kill me yet."

"And I pray they never do." She smiled faintly and vanished.

"I hate it when she does that," Nara whispered as she moved to stand with Aran. She wrapped an arm around his waist, and his strong arm slid over her shoulder.

"Seriously?" Aran chuckled. "Invisibility is one of your favorite spells."

"Yeah, but I don't like it when other people do it." She laughed and delivered him another wink. "So I can't help but notice that your bed is occupied. I'm pretty beat. I was going to go lay down for a nap." She walked to the doorway and slowly grinned over her shoulder. "Do you want to join me?"

59

NIGHTMARE

Nara recognized immediately that she was dreaming. The high-ceilinged corridors, with their glittering magical circuitry, had the sort of ephemeral quality one only found in a dream. Yet there was a clarity most dreams lacked. A magical clarity. This was no normal dream.

She wasn't in control of the body she inhabited, whoever it was. He or she wore spellarmor, and crept along the ceiling of the corridor, passing silently over many sentries. Having recently seen the Spellship for the first time, Nara was fairly certain that's where she was.

But this version was different. The dark streaks on the wall were entirely gone, and now glowed with pristine power. The empty halls were filled with olive-uniformed men and women going about the urgent business of war. That suggested Ternus was in charge of the vessel. She didn't see a confederate uniform anywhere.

She moved deliberately, sticking to the ceiling as she maneuvered up and down long hallways. Not a single person looked up, though she suspected if they had they'd still not have seen anything. The body she was riding along in pulsed with familiar magic. An invisibility sphere and several other, more powerful spells. Those were unfamiliar, and stronger than she could currently cast. Some sort of third level illusion spell, or spells.

The body finally reached a narrow corridor that led into the officer's quarters, a row of narrow doorways stretching into the distance. Almost all the doorways on this level were dark, save for one. A warm, orange glow came from that room, and Nara's body made for it.

Inside, Voria sat at a desk, brushing her hair with long, even strokes. She wore a simple nightgown, and appeared to be readying herself for bed. Nara's body paused outside the room, and raised a single armored hand.

That armor had an oily sheen to it, and after a moment Nara recognized it. It was the same metal that Aran's new armor used. Nara's hand began to deftly sketch sigils, and she realized that she was unraveling an incredibly complex ward set just outside Voria's quarters.

The speed and skill she used were...impressive. The ward was powerful, one of Voria's best. At her current skill level Nara didn't think she could duplicate the feat, though she was curious enough that she'd have been willing to give it a try.

Only then did the implications pour down her spine like icy rain. This person, whoever they were, had come to kill the major. Voria was at her most vulnerable, relaxed and unaware in the heart of her stronghold. This assassin—it couldn't be anything else—had slowly and steadily carved through every layer of her defenses, in order to catch her like this.

Voria believed herself safe, as evidenced by the soft humming while she brushed her hair. Nara longed to warn her, but as is the case with dreams she found herself unable to utter a word.

The assassin finished the work on the ward, and it puffed out of existence. Voria glanced up suddenly, the brush frozen mid-stroke. She peered up at the space the ward had occupied, and after a moment rose to her feet and wrapped a hand around Ikadra.

There was a moment of vertigo, and then Nara's perspective shifted. The assassin had blinked across the room, made possible now that the ward was gone. She was behind Voria, attached to the shadowy corner of the ceiling.

The assassin's feet stuck to the wall there, and her hands came together, fingers interlocking. She aimed both fists at Voria's unprotected back, and a torrent of void magic rolled through her. The disintegrate shot from her hands, lancing into Voria's back, right where the heart would be.

The spell cored an awful hole through the major's chest, and the woman slumped to her knees. Only her grip on Ikadra kept her up.

"W-who are you?" the major somehow managed.

"You know who I am," a cold voice answered from Nara's throat. She dropped to the ground and willed the armor to show her face. The metal flowed down her neck, pooling around her shoulders.

"Nara?" Voria's eyes widened. She gasped once, and then collapsed to the floor.

Nara reached for Ikadra, wrenching the staff from Voria's grip, without a care for the major's final moments. She turned to face the mirror where Voria had been sitting, and to her horror, saw her own face staring back at her.

She'd just killed the major, and taken Ikadra. Why would she do that? There's no way she would do that. Horror burst up in her, a frantic need to be anywhere else. This was a dream, and she needed to wake up.

60

COMPROMISED

Nara's eyes snapped open. Her heart thundered in her chest, and she was coated in sweat. She drank in deep, frantic breaths, trying to banish the dream. It had been so real. Too real.

She disentangled herself from Aran's sleeping form, and took a moment to appreciate the curve of his shoulders as he settled back into the blankets. Was this some sort of post-combat issue? Maybe she couldn't relax because she was so used to being threatened.

"No," rumbled a deep voice from the shadowed corner of the room, "in this you are right to trust your instincts."

Whatever it was sat on her hovercouch. She had the impression of thick legs, bigger even than the sergeant's. Everything else was lost in shadow.

"Do not rise," the voice said, "or attempt to cast. My work will be swift."

His hand came up, and he began to sketch. The light from the sigils illuminated his face, giving her the first glimpse of whoever—or whatever—had invaded her quarters. She caught the impression of a broad forehead and thick, recessed eyes. His skin was a mottled grey, of a species Nara didn't recognize. Then the spell completed, and his face was shrouded in darkness once more.

There had been an entire flood of them, of every color. All eight aspects had mingled, and they'd done so with impossible alacrity. No mortal caster could do something like that. She wasn't even certain all gods could.

Nara raised her hand instinctively to cast, and was amazed when nothing happened. She sketched in the air, but she might as well have been a child playing. No magic responded to her call. No sigils appeared.

The creature in the corner had no such difficulty. It sketched a second spell, and again the complexity baffled Nara. It all happened so fast, layer after layer of sigils. Nara had no idea what level the spell was, but it was higher than the major could cast. Maybe even higher than Nebiat could cast.

It ended abruptly, and a ray of dark pink energy lanced into her eyes so quickly Nara didn't have time to blink. The energy hit her like a silent thunderclap, and she collapsed against the bed. Why couldn't Aran hear that? Why wasn't he waking up?

"His slumber is magical, but it will end momentarily." The bulky figure rose and moved to stand next to the bed.

"What did you do to me?" she whispered in a small voice. She could feel something prowling at the edges of her mind. It stirred like a limb returning to life after having been asleep for a long time. A million itchy pinpricks plucked at her consciousness.

"What many would tell you is impossible." The figure gave a grim smile, the shadows exposing large, flat teeth. "I have returned your memories to you. The process will take time, but soon, you will remember everything."

"Who are you?" she asked.

He was already gone.

She sat there, terrified, until a trio of words popped into a previously dormant part of her mind. She whispered them aloud, the horror blooming inside her: "Guardian of Nefarius."

"Hmm?" Aran asked with a yawn. He sat up in bed, and wrapped her in strong arms. It felt good, banishing a bit of the horror.

"Nothing." She shivered against him. Had the Guardian been lying? Could her memories be coming back, and if so, what would it mean? Why now? And what was that awful dream? It had to be connected.

The door to her quarters slid up and Bord's head popped in. "These things really need to lock. A lucky fellow might accidentally walk in on..." Bord trailed off, then gave Aran a wide grin. "You lucky fooker. Looks like you beat me to the punch."

"I'll beat you," Kezia snapped as she entered the doorway next to Bord. She gave Nara a wink. "Major's asked us all to come to the mess. Why don't you two get decent and then join us? I think she wants to talk about what we're gonna do next."

Kezia dragged Bord from the room, and the door slid shut.

Aran scooted from bed first and pulled on his uniform. "So, uh, do you want to talk about last night?"

"There's nothing to talk about," she said. Her tone might have been a little too flat, because Aran shot her a hurt look. "I mean, what we did is normal. But it doesn't have to mean anything beyond two people enjoying some R&R." She wasn't ready to discuss emotions, not after that terrible nightmare, and waking up to...that thing.

Part of her recognized that she was putting up a wall, but she seemed unable to stop herself. She rose and pulled on her shirt, then her slacks, and avoided looking at Aran as she tugged on her jacket.

Aran exhaled a long, slow breath. "Okay, I can deal with that." He gave her a half-smile. "Whatever it was, I had fun. Shall we go see what the major wants?"

She nodded and followed him into the mess. Crewes, Pickus, and Voria had already taken seats and were enjoying different dishes. Nara moved to the food thingie—the official name, of course—and requested a slice of chocolate cake. It was the very least she'd earned after the last couple weeks. And the normalcy helped her push away the nightmare, and whatever had happened after. A bit, at least.

Aran didn't grab any food, just slid into the seat next to Crewes. Crewes punched him hard in the arm and gave him a congratulatory smile. Then he turned that exact smile on Nara, and gave her a thumbs-up. It was almost enough to banish the memory of Nefarius's Guardian, if that was who the visitor had been. She smiled back weakly.

She could almost pretend it hadn't happened, except the inside of her skull tingled...like a long-sleeping limb finally waking back up, a million little painful pinpricks. It hardly seemed possible that she could kill the major, but if the old her was suddenly coming back...who knew what she was capable of?

"Damn, must have been one depths of a night. What the hell did you do to her, LT?" Crewes asked. He slid his cup of caf over to Nara. "Here, you need this more than I do."

Nara seized the cup, clinging to it like salvation. "You have no idea."

"Ladies and gentlemen, let's get the business out of the way first," Voria interrupted. The crow's feet around her eyes had stretched another millimeter, and she looked more tired, but other than that, the major had returned full force. "I want to talk about what happened, and what happens now. We retrieved the First Spellship, which is excellent, but this business with the goo is troubling. Aran, or Nara, can one of you sum up what you think happened? Can you tell me anything more about it?"

"Mind if I field this one?" Aran asked.

"Not at all." Nara waved absently. He'd seen more of the ship's interior than she had, after all. And she needed time to think. *Nefarius...*

"When I arrived," Aran began, "Rhea was waiting for me. She'd been here a long time, and claims she was the last Outrider. I believe her. I think something—a god, or something worse—came to this world and left the...goo. Their goal wasn't necessarily to corrupt the ship, though maybe that's a side benefit. I think they wanted to stop me from being at that door when the Krox true mage opened it."

"An interesting theory," Voria allowed. "If they could stop you from reaching the door, then the Krox could have taken Ikadra to the bridge."

"That would have sucked," Ikadra said. His sapphire pulsed forlornly. "I would have had to do what he said, and the guy with the bad makeup would have had control of the ship. His brother was a real dick, too. I'm glad you ended him, Aran. You did end him, right?"

"He won't be bothering anyone ever again," Aran confirmed with a nod. "Anyway, I think whoever planted the goo wanted to stop me from getting there. If Rhea had succumbed, then there would have been no one to guide me." The way he'd said goo, both times, was slightly off. He knew something about it. Something he wasn't telling them.

That chilled her as much as the nightmare had. What was he hiding, and why?

"I have my suspicions as to who I think might be responsible, but I'm not ready to share them just yet." Voria sipped a cup of caf. "Not until I know more."

Nara had her suspicions, too. She cleared her throat, but before she could say anything, a sudden impulse overcame her and she changed what she'd been about to say. "What will we do now?"

"We'll head back to Shaya," Voria explained. "We need to make sure the ship is completely cleansed, and the Caretakers can ensure nothing is missed. Then we can learn exactly what this vessel is, and how we can use it to stop the Krox."

"I don't like putting this thing in Confederate hands," Aran said. "Once they get hold of it, they're going to try to keep it."

"A feat they cannot achieve without the most powerful staff in the sector," Ikadra crowed. His voice dropped with each repetition of the final syllable: "-tor -tor -tor."

"Ikadra has a point. If we deliver the ship, but hide the staff, then we retain control," Nara pointed out.

"Couldn't we go to the Inurans?" the sergeant asked. "The way you was winning at that game of theirs I bet you could afford to have the Consortium clean this ship."

"It's an option," Voria allowed. "But doing so would burn all bridges with the Confederacy, and with Shaya. I'm not quite ready to do that yet. We need to play the game a little longer."

"I'm not certain working closely with the Inurans is a good idea," Nara offered suddenly. "While hunting for the ship we met Shinura, short for the Shade of Inura. He told us a little about the missing Wyrm Father, Inura. Apparently he was consort to Virkonna, and he went to great lengths to expunge his name from history..."

She trailed off, suddenly lightheaded. Nara closed her eyes. A memory burst to brilliant life in the back of her skull. The memory of a bald mage, with an enchanted ruby where his right eye should have been. She was positive the memory was new, and that it had just appeared.

This was a game she had no interest in playing. Why had this Guardian restored her memories? What did he hope to gain?

A cold, rational voice answered—her voice.

He'd awakened her memories because he believed that whoever she was becoming would work for him. He believed that she was going to kill Voria, and deliver him the Spellship.

Her friends weren't safe around her. And that meant she had to run.

EPILOGUE

The being known as Talifax stalked the corridors of the First Spellship, amused by the need for the simple locomotion humans called walking. Normally Talifax appeared wherever he wished to be, as distance did not exist for one of his immense age.

Yet such magics were powerful, and powerful magic attracted attention. For the first time in two centuries Talifax was uncertain enough to choose caution over expediency. The First Spellship had been created by Virkonna and Inura, and though they were only Wyrms, they were also powerful gods in their own right.

Virkonna lay slumbering on the world they orbited. He could feel her mind, huddling in on itself as it sought respite from the pain his mistress had inflicted. But Inura was still out there, somewhere. He'd always been the craftiest of the Wyrm Fathers, which is why he'd lived when the rest had been killed, one by one.

Talifax would likely win in a direct confrontation, but he knew that Inura would only allow such a confrontation if he'd found a way to secure victory. If Talifax revealed himself here, he created the possibility of his own death.

And so he walked.

It didn't take so long as he'd feared, this walking. He passed down one long corridor, then ducked into a narrower one. Both bore pockets of rich, dark blood. Those pockets were slowly spreading, engulfing everything around him as they drank its magic. The blood of his mother, his mistress, his world. The Blood of Nefarius.

It was with this that he would conquer, slowly gathering enough magical power to awaken her. That day approached, but before it could be secured he had many tasks to fulfill. Chief among them was stopping Krox, for only Krox would be able to oppose Nefarius.

Talifax paused at an intersection, cocking his head as he took in his quarry. A humanoid figure squatted in darkness, his long hair slick with blood. The figure reached down and picked up a handful, smearing it into his eyes, then offering a contented sigh.

"Kheross," Talifax rumbled. "Attend me, little Wyrm."

Kheross's narrow face snapped up, and he blinked rapidly in an attempt to clear the blood from his eyes. "Who are you? Why have you come to this place? You'll find nothing but death here."

"Ah, you have fallen far, I see. Much further than I'd ever have guessed." Talifax bent to inspect the wretch's aura. The Blood had done its work well. Kheross had gone over fully. He was a tool of Nefarius now, whether he knew it or not. "I have come to offer you redemption."

"Redemption?" Kheross looked up and sneered. "It is not my own redemption I seek. Save Rhea. I am beyond salvation."

"Very well." Talifax folded his massive arms, and

suppressed the urge to crush the Wyrm's head between his hands. "I will give you the means to save your daughter. All you need do is administer it."

Kheross stiffened at that.

"You thought your ruse had worked?" Talifax gave a chuckle, a rare treat. "I knew of your little plot, to disguise yourselves as Outriders. To make that disguise so convincing that you, yourselves believe it, even. Rhea has no idea of her true nature. Yet you failed. You've weakened her, and gained nothing for it."

Kheross glared hatefully up at him. Good. He'd need that hatred.

Talifax spun possibilities, scanning quickly until he found the one he sought. Yes, that would do nicely. Kheross would attempt to 'save' Rhea. The vessel, Aran, would attempt to stop him. That would begin the exact chain of events needed to secure his mistress's return.

Talifax smiled grimly. "Here is what you will do."

Want to know when the next **Magitech Chronicles** book
goes live?

Sign up to the mailing list!

Check out MagitechChronicles.com for book releases,
lore, artwork, and more!

72319424R00193

Made in the USA
San Bernardino, CA
24 March 2018